THREE SEEKING STARS

THREE SEEKING STARS

Three Seeking Stars is a work of fiction. The characters, places, events, and dialogue portrayed in this book are drawn from the author's imagination. Any resemblance to actual events or persons, living or dead, is purely coincidental.

Published by Molewhale Press
www.molewhalepress.com

First Edition

Print edition ISBN: 978-1-7752427-4-1

Cover art and interior illustrations by Haley Rose Szereszewski
haleyroseportfolio.com

Map and book design by Sienna Tristen

The author gratefully acknowledges the creators of the following typefaces, which were used in designing the text of the book: 'Gentium Basic', 'Garamond Pro', 'Sqwoze', 'Century Gothic'

For everyone who does not yet know
what family means to them.

You are welcome in my hmun.

To Kongkempei, Hosaisi...
Qiao Sidh?
NONA FAHANG
ÃOTUL RIVER
ATENG

Prologue

IT WAS ONE OF THEIR LAST DAYS APART, when the summer storms rolled in. The morning air had been sluggish with water before it relented, opening into the kind of downpour that nipped at the skin. All around, young warriors whooped and hollered, running along the beach. Wrestling, shouting, kicking up the pink sand in glittering waves. It was rare that Kørno Wan's masters gave them a day off from training, and rarer still that the weather be so generous this time of year.

Beneath the flowing skirts of their lilac tent, Ahn was lazily stretched out on a heap of plump pillows. Beside him, Schenn was watching their classmates' roughhousing devolve into an impromptu sparring match. His mouth was twisted up a little on the right side, the way it went when he thought something was funny.

"Share the joke, would you?" Ahn prodded at his side with a foot, reaching for a cluster of grapes.

He laughed, shoving at Ahn's calf. "Only if you keep

your dirty toes off of me—"

"You say like I haven't had to deal with your stink every day for the past five years—"

"Lucky I'm so good looking, then." Schenn grinned, showing off his crooked front teeth. "Got that commoner's touch."

"Is that what they call it?"

A shout came from the beach—first blood. The fighters backed off, shaking hands while the next pair bounced in place, eager for their turn. Ahn reached his hand outside the tent, letting the rain prickle at his fingers.

"It's just . . . " Schenn hesitated, scrunching his nose and leaning back against the pillows. "They really can't take a day off, can they?"

Two more young warriors stalked each other, their classmates crouched around them in a makeshift arena. The winner of the previous round sat beside his defeated opponent, a fond hand rested on the boy's shoulder. As their Six-ing came closer, these fights began to take a repetitive shape; no more swapping out opponents or settling childish grudges, no more fake warrior rankings or playful bets or complaining about the thick smell of the resin the masters burned during communal meals. All that remained of their class was the matches between paired warriors, and the many eyes that followed. Learning, studying. Taking whatever they could get.

Ahn's gaze fell on Schenn: his shoulders speckled from a childhood outdoors, his short dark hair, his careless smile. He thought of the way the boy kicked off all the blankets while he slept. The way he had given up speaking to Ahn formally within a month of their training. The way he breathed so slowly when he gripped the spear.

"What if we didn't do it?" Ahn asked, something plucking a low note in his chest.

"What?" Schenn frowned.

"Our Six-ing. What if we just . . . didn't do it?" He pushed back his hair, trying to act casual as he reached for more grapes. "Tried something else."

Schenn snorted. "There's an idea. I saunter back to the Haojost farmlands, let my family know that five ranks up the path of Conquest I decided hm, no, better brush up on my numbers and start fresh in Discernment. Run errands for the local spice shack for two years. Didn't want to be a general anyway, Dad! Did you hear about today's deal on capsicum?"

Ahn laughed along half-heartedly, searching for his place in the joke. He could never find it quite like Schenn. "Probably better to pursue Health. You're a task away from the third rank already. It wouldn't take that long to reach, maybe a month or two."

"Unfortunately, I'll need that time to forge a new identity to bury my shame at running from a fight with the heir to the Empire."

"I have ten older siblings, Schenn," Ahn said, searching their basket for the bottle of elderflower wine they'd smuggled from the kitchens, "and I lack the ambition to kill any of them. So I don't know if it's really fair to call me the heir of anything."

"Fair enough. I mean, just look at the *hair*—" Before Ahn could jump away, Schenn had his hands in Ahn's hair, running his fingers through the places where Imperial silver had been spoiled by stripes of black.

Ahn groaned, pushing at his hand, embarrassed. "Schenn—"

"Where's the good breeding?" Schenn wailed, tugging at it triumphantly. "Where's the pure lineage of Qiao Sidh?!"

"Let go!" Ahn laughed, grabbing hold of the wine and pretending to use it as a club. Schenn wrestled it out of his hands, knocking Ahn back onto the pillows and leaping upon him with a theatrically scandalized look.

"Oh deviant monarch! You'll have the people thinking the Qiao Sidhur citizens are in fact a complex blending of peoples, not a collection of fancy, mean dolls in upwards of three very big houses—"

Ahn made a weak lunge for the bottle, laughing too hard to make any real headway. Down on the beach, their classmates were shouting encouragements to their favoured fighter, but he didn't bother looking to see who was winning. Instead, he watched Schenn uncork the wine with his teeth, taking a gulp before passing it over.

"I mean it, though," Ahn said, grasping the bottle's rough jute wrapping.

"Mm?"

"You'd climb the Healer's path well." He squirmed beneath Schenn, trying to prop himself up. "You have the discipline, and the temperament. Your hands are steady, and if you had a good master you could even become a surgeon—"

"Fine," Schenn said abruptly. "I survive our Six-ing, and I'll be a master Healer before the year's out. Deal?"

On the beaches, one warrior slammed her partner to the ground with a shout of effort. The sound hit Ahn like a punch to the sternum, vibrating violently into his lungs until air was a painful thing to hold. The crowd gasped, murmuring among themselves in satisfaction as the winner fell to her knees beside her partner, trying to catch her own breath.

He wished very suddenly that he hadn't brought up the Paths, their Six-ing. Any of it. It wasn't much longer now. The days were getting shorter.

"Ahn?" Schenn's voice popped in the air, jarring Ahn out of his unexpected queasiness.

"Before the *season's* out," Ahn amended, a smile stretched awkwardly on his lips, "or I'll never forgive you." He could hear the strain in his voice, and was painfully aware of how unwieldy his humour was. But Schenn quirked his brow, playing along. Indulging him. Ahn took a swig of the wine and passed it over, thankful.

"The season, then. It should be no trouble, with you chattering away in my ear." He slipped off Ahn, flopping down beside him on the pillows. "Demanding I learn the harp. Or how to dance. Ugh."

"Make your life miserable," Ahn said, rolling to face his companion.

"Not so miserable. Prince Schenahn doesn't sound

so bad." Schenn made it look so easy, navigating the topic which should not have been so tender, but was. He wore a cautious vulnerability on his face, the kind of look he got in the quiet hours of the early morning, when he and Ahn were the first or last ones awake. The secret-telling hours. "Better than you having to travel down from Hvallánzhou to visit my family for the local harvest festivals."

"I wouldn't mind."

"You say that now."

"I wouldn't mind," Ahn insisted. "Really, it would be—it would be interesting. Different."

"Real different," Schenn echoed.

Silence filled the space between them. There was more to say, but Ahn's tongue tangled on itself; his heart felt twisted and thorned as an acacia tree. Was it inside or outside of the tent that was warping around them? The crescent of students—no, warriors—was so small, but the sounds of fighting began to fill the space with unsettling force.

When they entered Kørno Wan for their training, fighting had felt to Ahn like a dance, and Schenn was the perfect partner—aligned, in sync. Constantly challenging him. Making him better, leading and following with equal grace as they grew together and matched each others' steps.

Who would it be, Ahn wondered, that would step out of line first, when the time came for blood to spill in their sacred arena?

Schenn reached forward with a peculiar look, and Ahn thought perhaps he was going to tease him about his hair again. But instead he touched Ahn's right ear, pinching gently at the lobe where the bone would pierce through. Schenn's bone. His first knuckle, if, if—Ahn reached up, grasping his wrist, but did not dare move him away. It was an ominous sort of introduction, too intimate to interrupt.

After a moment, Schenn let go, resting his hand on Ahn's shoulder with a fond squeeze. Was it his hand or Ahn's body that was trembling? "Ahnschen doesn't sound so bad either, you know."

"I could live with it," Ahn said quietly. It nearly felt true.

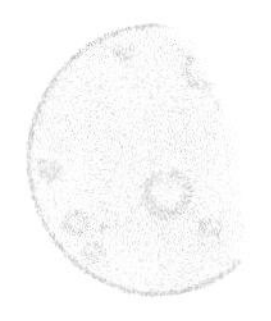

Part One: Eiji, Northward

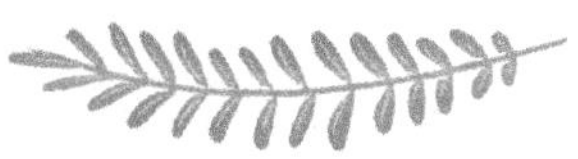

One

HOPELESSLY LOST IN a jungle and hundreds of miles from home, Ahnschen was once again longing for his harp. He yearned for the feel of the spruce warming in his palms, the friendly thrum of the strings—wanted it badly enough that he would consider even trading it for his sword. Which probably didn't bode well for his chances of survival, even if it would make Master Hvu proud.

Nearly five months without practice had undoubtedly set him back; he had only just begun getting comfortable with the instrument when he'd been called to the campaign in the lower continent. Ahn could only imagine the lecture he would get when he finally returned to his lessons. He adjusted his posture, imagining he was at a concert hall, breathing slowly as he readied himself for a performance.

It was easy to reenact the stage fright, thanks to the dozens of enormous eyes currently sizing him up. What an audience.

A week in the company of the sãoni had done little to build trust in either party. For the most part, Sohmeng had forced everyone into a reluctant stalemate. Reluctance on the side of the sãoni, that is—Ahn would have been happy never to fight another one of the beasts as long as he lived. It was one thing to face an armed human opponent, and another to hold his own against a creature the size of a carriage. No amount of training at Kørno Wan had prepared him for that.

The creatures' eyes were following Ahn's hands as he polished his armour. The gilded silver was as bright as it could get, but he had already done the rest of the tasks that had been asked of him.

"Easy," he murmured in Qiao Sidhur. "Easy, now."

One of the smaller sãoni crawled toward him slowly, circling him from a distance. It was about as large as one of his family's hunting dogs, but quicker by far. It clicked at him, unblinking.

"Sohmeng?" he called quietly, not wanting to startle the animal. The colony's ceaseless snarling had finally settled into this new staring habit—he still wasn't sure what to make of it. Half the time he was sure he was about to be eaten, the other he felt like they were waiting for him to perform a party trick.

A low growl came from behind the little lizard, and Ahn tensed up as he recognized the vivid green stripes of the sãoni that had first attacked him. The smaller one squawked loudly, pressing its body to the ground and narrowing its eyes. Ahn went very still. Was the larger one egging it on?

"Sohmeng?" he tried again.

The sãoni slunk closer, ready to pounce.

"Hei?" he attempted, however doubtful. The two of them had only been gone for a few minutes, how far could they have possibly—

"Hey Ahn!"

Old instinct sent him out of his skin, a hand on the hilt of his sword. All fantasies of the harp flew from his mind as he spun around to face the danger that—that obviously wasn't any danger at all, it was Sohmeng. Sohmeng carrying an armful of eggs with Hei in tow, squinting at him suspiciously.

"Sohmeng," he said, releasing his weapon. "I am sorry, I did not mean—"

"I know, I know. I'm sure it wasn't you." She yanked him in for another cheek rub, giving the large, aggressive sãoni a look. "Do you think I was born yesterday, Green Bites?" Its reply sounded smug.

Sohmeng's displays of affection were supposed to reassure the colony that Ahn was friendly, but between the issue of his hair colour and the poor circumstances of their first meeting, it didn't seem to be terribly effective. Even now the little sãoni that had been stalking him continued to hiss, hopping around in the dirt.

"I was—" He didn't know the word for 'polishing', so he simply gestured to the armour. "Then the small one became . . ."

"A doofus, yeah." Ahn didn't know this word either. Sohmeng passed the bundle of eggs to Hei and crouched down by the creature. It arched up to her, and she tapped it on the nose. "You should know better, dummy."

Ahn rubbed his forearm. It was still bruised from his first encounter with this colony of sãoni, but bruises weren't much of a price to pay, having come out alive. His fingers tightened, the pain a reminder of his failure: he should have been able to keep Lilin alive, as well. Over three years, they'd ridden together—he'd even been there when she first hatched in the stables of the summer palace. Training with her had been a good way to keep up his martial work after his Six-ing was complete.

He tugged at his earlobe, tried not to be frustrated when he was met with silence. Schenn could afford to say a little more, especially seeing as the only real guidance the boy had ever offered had gotten him into this mess in the first place: *Run, Ahn. Get out of here.*

Of course he had listened. He was still listening, stuck awaiting further instruction and trying not to be afraid. Fear would not serve him right now; he had to stay alert, stay focused on the situation at hand, keep himself alive.

Beside him, Sohmeng was stroking the little sãoni's head like he would a rabbit's. "I finished the tasks," he said after a moment. "Gathering stones, preparing for the camp's fire. Collecting wood." He gestured to the tidy ring he had set up, hoping it was adequate. Back in the battalion, this sort of work had been done for him while he planned with his sister in the command tent. Having reached the sixth rank in the path of Conquest before he was seventeen, Ahn had never experienced the duties of a foot soldier.

"Whoa, really?" Sohmeng sat down beside him, pulling something from her pocket. It was a pair of dice, which she tossed between her hands. "That was fast."

Ahn wasn't sure why she sounded surprised. "I can do more?"

"No, no, it's okay," she said. "I just didn't expect you to be done already. Usually Hei and I kind of take our time, unless we're really hungry. Then we rush through it and argue the whole time. It's a thing."

Ahn frowned, not sure he was understanding her completely. "Why would I take time . . . ?"

"To enjoy it? To be lazy? No point in chasing bugs off the jungle floor, y'know." She grinned at him, and he returned a tentative smile of his own. "Besides, the sãoni set the pace."

Between his musical and martial education—not to mention his ongoing work on the Philosophy path—it was hard to imagine a world where idleness was not viewed as a personal shortcoming. Even poets were hard at work using their heads, no matter if they appeared to be doing very little. Life in Qiao Sidh centered around merit, the constant pressure to achieve fostered by a healthy sense of competition. Ahn was unsure how to engage with a culture that did not keep its people in a state of perpetual motion.

It seemed to be going well enough for Hei and Sohmeng. Though apparently Sohmeng was only a recent arrival to the jungle. *Eiji*, she called it: the ground below. Different from the Empire's current name for this land: the Untilled.

Hei said something to Sohmeng in Atengpa that he couldn't follow. Though he'd been actively working on the trade tongue since landing on the lower continent five months ago, he'd never bothered learning any individual dialect. There hadn't seemed like much need for it, at the time. The plan had been to move through multiple hmun over the course of the year, establishing Qiao Sidhur presence.

Ahn was fortunate that a few words of Atenpga overlapped with Dulpongpa, but Sohmeng and Hei usually spoke too fast for him to have a chance of keeping up. All he could do was rely on Sohmeng to translate.

Wait, that was a word he knew—*fire.* An instinct bad enough to be Schenn's tugged at him, and he reached for his bag of firestarter, offering it hopefully. "Fire? Working fast." His sister would probably clobber him for the waste of resources, but it would only be a few grains. A show of goodwill. "Good help starting."

Hei stared at him, unblinking as the sãoni and twice as cold.

Ahn stared back, suddenly feeling quite foolish.

"Oh, Ahn, that's—that's really nice of you." Sohmeng pocketed her dice, giving Hei the kind of look usually worn by parents of squabbling children. "But I think Hei's got it. Wouldn't want to waste your stuff."

"Not a waste," he replied, but put it away nonetheless. After the way they'd met, he couldn't blame them for being wary of the stuff.

"So," Sohmeng said after a beat, "have you had crested

crane eggs before?" She passed one to him; it was about twice the size of the duck eggs he ate back home, its shell cream speckled in blue. "They're big wading birds, hang out around rivers. The sãoni have a real taste for the meat so there's hardly ever any left for us to hunt. But once the mothers are gone, it's easier to dig up the eggs they hide in their nests. Hei taught me that trick."

"Clever," Ahn said, turning the egg over in his hand.

"Sure easier than going for yellowbills," she muttered. Hei made a sãoni noise, and without missing a beat, Sohmeng tossed a stick into their waiting palm. "Eiji has a lot to offer. You just need to know where to look for it."

"I am still learning," Ahn said, passing the egg back. Their fingers brushed, and he felt the smoothness of her silver ring, inscribed with Qiao Sidhur patterning. Sohmeng had told him how she'd found it on a mountainside, just before she fell. She had told him a lot of things this past week, testing and expanding both of their capacity with Dulpongpa. Ahn was not much of a believer in luck, but stumbling across a piece of home when he was more lost than he'd ever been felt nearly fated.

"Speeeaking of learning," Sohmeng said with a mischievous look. "Can I try again? I think I might get it this time."

"Oh," Ahn blinked, feeling his cheeks go hot. This again. "I, I mean, I suppose, if—"

"Okay let's do it." She sat up, rubbing her hands together. This time, the string of syllables that came out of her mouth very nearly sounded like his name.

Almost. Well, no, not much actually. The pronunciation was horrendous and the pitch was all over the place, but she certainly was enthusiastic, and Ahn didn't want to take that away from her. "How's that?"

Beside her, Hei was smirking, using one of their sãoni claws to peel the wet bark from a stick. Though they hadn't participated in *Try to Pronounce Ahn's Name, Isn't it Silly, We Only Have Two!*, they seemed to take pleasure in the game.

"Wait, wait, no. Let me, um, the middle bit went Chongem . . . jir?" She struggled for a minute and then groaned in defeat. "Burning godseye, the *vowels.* I think that was worse than my first try."

"No, it was, it was much closer!" Being who he was, Ahn had never known anyone who couldn't pronounce his name. Most people knew it before even meeting him.

"Say it again," she insisted. "I can do it this time."

"You can just call me Ahn, it's not a—"

"*Say it, Yongrir.*" She paused. "That was closer, right?"

"Éongrir Ahnschen-Eløndham, Qøngemzhir, Sølshendasá, Siengunghvøs."

Hei snorted. Considering they preferred to answer to the calls of animals, Ahn found that to be a bit unfair.

". . . I might need a little more practice," Sohmeng conceded with a pout. "That's *so* many names though, Ahn. There's no reason for anyone to have that many names."

"It helps to know who we are," Ahn explained. "Like your, ah . . . the phase names? Does your hmun use those?"

The people of Kongkempei, the hmun his campaign had first landed in, all had a lunar phase attached to their names, along with an indicator of their roles in the community. He had hoped to learn more about it, before—well. Before they had left. Before the relationship ceased to be diplomatic. "You had not given me one, so I did not know."

Something strange flashed on Sohmeng's face. Hei paused their work preparing the kindling, giving Ahn a look that could have been a warning.

"Minhal," she said, chin lifted. "I'm Sohmeng Minhal. Hei doesn't use a phase name."

"I see," Ahn said. *Minhal.* He practiced the shape of the name on his tongue—he would feel foolish if he couldn't say it properly when Sohmeng was putting so much effort into his full title. "It's very pretty."

"Pretty?" Sohmeng laughed, but he could see the way her ears flushed. "You're weird, Ahn. Or Ahnschen, right? You just called yourself Ahn when we met, is the 'schen' part less important?"

"No—" The world suddenly felt tight on Ahn's shoulders, a persistent pressure that extended down his spine. His hand was at his chest before he could stop himself, fingers drawn to the great scar there. He swallowed, pretending to adjust his shirt. "No, it . . ."

Hei and Sohmeng were looking at him, expecting something he did not know how to give. Ahnschen. Ahn Schenn. Sworn by the sword to guide each other between the worlds. This was not something he had ever needed to explain—the merging of their names was a symbol of their union, its meaning obvious as the bone that pierced Ahn's ear. Everyone in Qiao Sidh could see it, and so he would never have to say it. Never have to explain himself.

Maybe that was why he had left Schenn out of his mouth on first introduction. Maybe that's why he'd been such a coward.

"I am sorry," he said, offering a smile he hoped distracted from the sound of his heart. "Difficult to explain in a new language."

"That's alright!" Sohmeng replied, patting him on the shoulder. "It'll be a few phases before the colony gets closer to your hmun. We'll have plenty of time to practice."

"Of course—good to, good to practice." Ahn nodded, trying to shake himself out of the fuzziness. He had to stay focused. The past was done, the roles were set; now all he could do was try to honour Schenn. Prove himself as the general the two of them were meant to embody together. For now that meant laying low, being as pleasant as he could in the company of these strangers and their sãoni until he could get back to the campaign.

Hei crouched beside the fire, their breath bringing its flames roiling to life. His belly rumbled alongside the sound, an easy distraction. All he had to do was survive the journey home. And despite his lack of skills in the wilderness and poor sense of direction, Ahn had always been terribly good at surviving.

Two

PARAGON OF PATIENCE and reason that she was, Sohmeng couldn't see why Hei was being so uncooperative. She stepped over the leg of a snoozing sãoni, attempting to keep up with Hei as they wove through the trees in the dark. The bioluminescent moss wasn't prime lighting, but it was easier to forage when the curious creatures had conked out. With Ahn asleep and the majority of the day's distractions out of the way, Sohmeng figured now might be a good time to attempt this conversation. Again.

"I'm just saying," she said, "things would be a lot easier if you bit him!"

"Absolutely not," they snapped, punctuating it with a Sãonipa growl.

"Why not? You bit me, and that turned out just fine." She hopped in front of them, offering a winning grin. They couldn't argue with that.

Hei flapped their hands at her, flustered. "That's—that's *completely* different."

"Different how?" she asked.

"I like you!"

"You didn't like me when you first bit me—"

"I'm not biting this man, Sohmeng." Hei looked over to Ahn's sleeping form, letting out a series of low, displeased clicks. Their jaw was set stubborn, their expression downright sullen. They were impossible to negotiate with when they got this way, but Sohmeng had beat worse odds before, and she didn't feel like relenting. "*You* bite him, if it matters to you so much."

What with those biceps, Sohmeng could not deny that she had considered it. Thoroughly. Even still, she was a woman of sense. "It wouldn't work, Hei. The colony's accepted me, sure, but you're Mama's *baby*." She chirped their sãoni name for emphasis. "I'm just Mama's baby's girlfriend. They'd still eat me if you asked really nicely."

"I wouldn't—" Hei cut themself off, presumably catching on that Sohmeng didn't mean it literally. With a loud, aggravated sigh, they dropped to their knees and began working at a wild yam vine. "That's not true. And even if it was, they hardly ever follow my instructions. I'm not anyone's alpha."

"You're *my* alpha," she teased, but Hei waved her off with another grumble.

It was going to be like that, then. Sohmeng took a deep breath, trying to re-evaluate her strategy.

Things hadn't been easy since Ahn joined them. Sohmeng had barely had time to process what she and Hei had found in Sodão Dangde before they had to adjust to the complication of bringing a stranger into their family. For a member of the massive hmun that had thrown all of Eiji out of balance and destroyed life as she knew it, Ahn seemed like a nice guy. He was patient with Sohmeng's questions, and didn't run screaming every time the sãoni antagonized him. At the very least, he seemed like their best opportunity to fix all that was broken in Eiji; if they could bring him up to his hmun and explain the impact their arrival had had on Ateng, everything could get back to normal. Maybe the surrounding hmun might even help Ahn's people find a new place to settle, where the sãoni migration route wouldn't be thrown so dramatically out of balance. That thought alone had been worth the living nightmare that was persuading Singing Violet, the most even-tempered of the sãoni, to allow Ahn on her back with Sohmeng, on the condition that his hair was covered.

But Hei had been against him travelling alongside the colony since day one. They hardly spoke a word to him, and when they did, Sohmeng was thankful for the relative language barrier. She'd thought Hei was standoffish when the two of them first met, but that was nothing compared to the brazen hostility they were slinging Ahn's way. Their distrust made sense, especially given the impact Ahn's people had had on the ecosystem, but Sohmeng wasn't just going to leave him to die.

Or allow the sãoni to eat him. That was another issue she still needed to work out with Hei.

She watched them work through the soil with their sãoni claws until it was loosened enough to retrieve the tubers beneath. For a moment she chewed her lip, admiring their grace. Trying to figure out how to make her words clever enough to match Hei's hands.

A rumble came from Mama, who was dozing off against a nearby tree. The sãoni cracked an eye open, huffing as she watched them work. Sohmeng walked over to her, snuggling up between her fore- and mid-legs. Oddly enough, Ahn's fear of the colony helped her recognize her own comfort with them.

"Don't worry, Mama," she said, stroking the sãoni's nose. "We won't be up too late. Promise."

Once the yams were packed away in their bag, Hei joined her. They thudded their head back against Mama, looking up at the stars with a deep frown. Sohmeng had seen them look worried before—honestly, it was one of their default expressions—but this was different. Bone-deep.

She ran a hand through their hair, scratching until their shoulders lowered slightly, until their breaths looked more full. She knew she had done okay when they stole a kiss, shy despite everything. It made Sohmeng want to poke them with her elbow, to tease them about how silly they were, looking at her like that. But she didn't want them to stop it either. It was nice, to have Hei be so open with their affection, their infatuation—nicer still because they never expected her to behave the same way in return.

"How are her eggs doing?" Sohmeng asked, moving her hand to Mama's bumpy cheek. The stripes on her neck were glowing deep purple in the dark, as though she too were a moss-speckled tree.

Hei, who had never been one for subtlety, leaned over Sohmeng to pop their arm straight into Mama's cheek pouch. Sohmeng wrinkled her nose, but the sãoni didn't seem bothered. "They're getting close to hatching. That might be why we've been slowing down, especially after covering so much distance in the past few days." They pulled out their hand, shaking off the excess slime. "I would like to see us move further before mating season begins. The mature sãoni are getting restless. They'll need some space so they don't get aggressive."

Sohmeng wondered if that was one reason they'd been so touchy lately; maybe it didn't all have to do with Ahn. A thought suddenly struck her. "Wait, does Mama have a mate? I've never seen anyone get clingy with her."

Hei chirped, nodding. "She's chosen different ones for the past couple of cycles. Her mate from the last is still with the colony. Younger than her, scar on the back leg."

Sohmeng whistled, giving the sleepy sãoni's head another pat. "Get it, Mama. So he played damwei for these eggs?"

"This clutch isn't hers, actually. They were laid by another sãoni outside of mating season. Rare, but it happens. She was killed by a trap left out by a hmun, and Mama scooped the eggs up for herself."

"Kind of has an adoption habit, huh?"

Hei clicked an affirmative with a tender smile, leaning their head against Mama's side and listening to her breathe. Sohmeng found herself appreciating the thoughtful silence.

Especially in the wake of all the recent chaos. "I don't expect her to mate this year. She's getting older, I think the hatchlings might have been her last clutch."

Given they were now big enough for a child to ride, Sohmeng wasn't sure they could really be called hatchlings at all anymore. "I can't imagine how she held all of those little brats in her mouth. With the energy they've got, they must have been rocking against her freaking molars."

"Only two of them are hers. The other four are from other members of the colony. The young just tend to stick together, and they follow the alpha. Same as the rest of us."

"Only two?" Sohmeng frowned, considering. The colony was made up of a bit over a lunar cycle's worth of adult sãoni—nearly thirty, by her count. Then there were the six hatchlings, or rather, adolescents, that tormented her on a daily basis. Mama had lost several eggs in her fight with Blacktooth, but she still had at least five in her cheeks. With clutches that size, there were comparatively few hatchlings in the colony. "But the number of eggs . . ."

Hei nodded, following her train of thought. They wore that same sort of sad, inevitable look as they had back in the caves of Sodão Dangde. "Many of them don't make it much past hatching. Some eggs don't hatch at all. Sãoni are sturdy once they're grown, but the early stages of their life are precarious. With all of the changes to their ecosystem, there's a lot more stress on the colonies than there used to be. It's hit their population hard." They looked at Sohmeng then, their expression pointed enough that she pretty much knew what was coming before they even spoke. "All the more reason to make sure they're safe right now."

"Ahn isn't going to hurt them, Hei," she said, exasperated.

"You can't know that."

"Uh, yeah, I can?" Sometimes she wished Hei could get a look at the colony from the outside. Their knowledge of the natural world was invaluable, but they didn't always know what to do when confronted by more human perspectives. "He doesn't stand a chance against a whole pack of sãoni, and if he moves against one, they'll all attack. Honestly, if he *blinks* wrong they'll attack. If he forgets to bury his—"

"He took one down before. You saw it, back in the clearing. Him and his fire-sand," they sneered, shaking their head.

Sohmeng rubbed her face. She could *feel* the pressure of the moons here; typical of the Sol phase to offer no assistance while begging her to deescalate. "Yes, Hei, I saw it, but if you could just—"

Mama's tail swung around, thwacking at their feet in warning. Ever the mediator, that one. Sohmeng sighed, rubbing cheeks with Hei, offering a few caring chirps that they slowly returned. This didn't have to be a fight. "I see why you're worried. But I still think we're better off befriending Ahn than we are isolating him. I'm not saying we need to marry him and declare him lord of the freaking lizards, but how you act right now matters. If you treat him as a threat, so will the sãoni."

"And if he is a threat?" Hei asked sharply.

"I don't know, Hei, then the sãoni eat him! They eat

him and I'm traumatized forever and it's all fine!" The words made Sohmeng queasy, but they seemed to reach Hei. "But right now, I'd really appreciate it if we could act like we're not on track for the worst-case scenario."

Hei tucked their knees to their chest, growling quietly. Even still, Sohmeng could see the way their expression softened.

"Travelling together is a chance to learn more about Qiao Sidh," she continued, "to plan for what comes next. Figuring out how to get the sãoni back on the migration route, repairing the Sky Bridge. There's a lot to work out before we make it that far north."

"We don't have a plan," Hei said simply.

Sohmeng's stomach clenched. She couldn't deny that it all sounded pretty half-baked; so much could go wrong between here and returning Ahn. But if she gave up now, failure was a guarantee rather than a possibility, and that was unacceptable.

All around them, the sãoni were snoozing, somehow content despite the existential threat at their doorstep. Sohmeng couldn't tell if it was comforting or frightening to watch. For all she had always longed to be taken seriously, it was intimidating to know that her choices here could impact so many other living creatures. Responsibility felt heavy instead of freeing; no wonder it had made such a nightmare of her brother.

Viunwei. If she ever wanted to lord her *look I'm alive you jerk* over him, she had to find a way to make this work.

"It's messy," Sohmeng admitted. "But it's a start. And

that start requires Ahn. When he sees that we aren't planning on turning him into sãoni food, he'll be a lot more likely to advocate for us when we get to his hmun. So . . . can you help me? Please? I just need you to be decent to him, show a little welcome."

After a long moment, Hei clicked in assent. "But I'm not biting him."

Sohmeng exhaled slowly. "Okay. That's—I understand."

"And he needs to behave." They took her hand, squeezing. "If he hurts the sãoni, or threatens you, or *bothers* me—"

"Then we'll work it out."

"We'll work it out," Hei repeated, pulling Sohmeng close. She let herself melt into the sensation of their strong body against the soft flesh on her sides. Hei was stubborn, sure, but they were also grounding. A mountain in their own right.

"Sorry for pushing you before. About the biting thing. I should have backed off."

"Pushy, pushy," Hei muttered, but Sohmeng could feel their smile as they rubbed their cheek against hers.

On the other side of camp, she could see Ahn curled against a tree. Maybe she was just being idealistic, but he looked less threatening under the light of the moons. With a little patience and communication, there was no reason that everyone couldn't be decent to each other. As she drifted off to sleep, she allowed herself to indulge in the pleasure of optimism.

Three

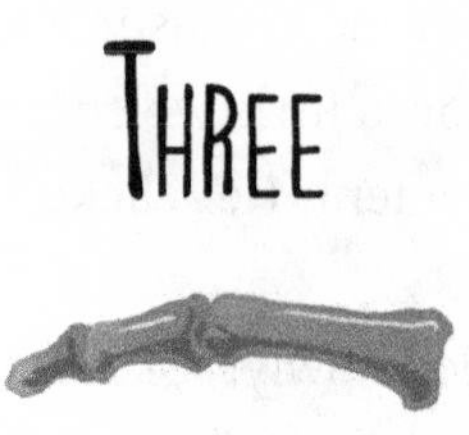

AHN WOKE EARLY, the memory of the arena heavy on the backs of his eyelids. It had been so long since he dreamed of Kørno Wan, of the packed sand and the white linen curtains, the heady scent of resin burning in the air. The eyes of his masters watching from the raised platform; the priests and priestesses singing the songs of the bilateral realms. Schenn, still apart from Ahn, wielding the blade with mastery. Ahn, still apart from Schenn, struggling to keep him back.

The scream of a bird broke through the memory, piercing enough to shake him from the moment. This was not Qiao Sidh, this was not Kørno Wan. Ahn covered his face with his hands. The air was so humid here, so thick in his throat. It made it hard to breathe on mornings like this, when he woke restless.

He had been still for too long. He had to move.

Daylight had not yet fully broken through the canopy, and the ethereal glow of the bioluminescent moss was still visible. Cautiously, he lifted himself up, glancing at the still-sleeping forms of his captors, his rescuers. Sohmeng and Hei lay curled together against the colony's alpha, surrounded by the rest of the sãoni. The image of peace, even in a place such as this.

Ahn took up his sword. Quietly, he slipped from the camp and sought out a private copse of trees to still his mind in. Once he was sure he was alone—as alone as anything could be in a rainforest—he began.

He started with the postures, an old routine from his school days, designed to bring bodily awareness before beginning more complex practice. The blade was light in Ahn's hand, his feet sturdy on the ground. He stretched his body into the shape of the Mountain, the Bear, the Midwife. *Breathe*, he commanded himself, working through the Eagle, the Hunter, the Sun.

His older sister Ólawen, just Óla back then, had put a wooden sword in his hand when he was three years old. He'd taken to it like it had been passed to him from the other realm. Perhaps it had, when he'd reincarnated last.

The motions felt all wrong. He was unfocused, nearly *bored*—what right did he have to feel bored of what had soothed him for so many years? He sped up the choreography until it felt more like a dance, sharpened his footwork as though there were a partner for him to match. Heart rising up to meet his throat, he tugged at his earpiece.

"Come on, Schenn," he murmured. "You were always too good at this. You give me so little room to grow."

That had been the appeal of Qiao Sidhur's famous Asgørindad University: the relief of starting from the bottom of one of the Paths. He had spent most of his life achieving the sixth rank of Conquest, with some dabbling in the Arts that had lifted him to the third rank. While his status granted him the privilege of exploring all of the Paths at some point, it had been a long time since he started something new.

Philosophy had been an unexpected choice, one that his parents had met with substantial doubt. He had only just completed his Six-ing a few months ago—why would he stop now when his military career was just beginning? His argument had been shaky, but effective enough: there was always time to lead an army, always another war. And at nearly seventeen, he was the perfect age for university-level schooling. What was the harm? He could live with the common people, learn more about them. A prince for all Qiao Sidh. And Schenn—Schenn would like that, wouldn't he? It would be respectful, given the boy's low beginnings. It was a way for them to bond in their new situation, not everything had to be about mastering the arts of conquest. Most people never even made it to their Six-ing, most people—

A faint pull in his earpiece made him stumble. He cupped his hand over his ear with a gasp.

"Schenn?" he whispered, not daring to believe. "Schenn, is that—is that what you want? Tell me what you want."

Silence. Even a conjuring of the boy's voice failed him. He cursed, stabbing his blade into the earth. It snagged on a root, left him feeling like a child throwing a tantrum. In these moments, the distance between them was unbearable. How much longer would it take before they finally reconnected, his masters had promised—

The sound of wood snapping. Ahn turned around, a surge of what could have been either bloodlust or loneliness leaving him desperate for an opponent.

What he found instead was Hei.

They held the broken halves of a stick in each hand, watching him with the same critical eye as always. He wondered how long they had been there, deciding whether or not they would reveal themself to him. Such an enigma, with their dark looks and their animal language. Shame churned in his chest as they glanced at his sword, stuck out awkwardly from the ground.

"Good morning," he said, throat dry. Hei cocked an eyebrow at him, but made no move to respond. They were chewing on something.

Wind jostled the canopy above, shifting the light. Golden rays were breaking through the morning haze, the only sign to Ahn that any time had passed at all.

For a long moment, Hei said nothing. They tossed the broken stick aside, turning their gaze to the trees; even still, he could feel their focus locked on him. At last, they addressed him in a halting voice: "Not dead, yes?"

"I—sorry?"

"Seeing Ahn not dead." They gestured impatiently to the forest around them. "*Eiji.* Make Ahn dead easy."

"Oh—" Had Hei been concerned for his safety? The idea

left Ahn feeling out of his depth. He offered a bow of his head; back at Asgørindad, this show of deference had endeared him to the common people, shaped him as more of an equal. Hei appeared unmoved. "I am fine. Thank you. I was—practicing."

When they did not respond, he reached for his sword to illustrate his point. The moment it came loose from the earth, Hei leapt back, shoulders hunched defensively. Their lip was curled in a snarl, vivid eyes narrowed in suspicion.

Ahn exhaled slowly. He'd assumed that his posture was non-threatening enough, but apparently he was wrong. He smiled as he sheathed the blade. Entreatingly, he offered his open palms to them. "I will not hurt you. Or your sãoni."

Hei spat in the dirt, scowling. "No."

"No?"

"Sãoni. Not mine."

Ahn wasn't sure what to make of this. Hei's grasp on Dulpongpa only seemed to go as far as its similarities with Atengpa, and he was hardly fluent himself. Maybe there was a misunderstanding between them. Before he could ask for clarification, Hei started walking back toward the camp, leaving Ahn alone to wonder what had just happened.

He rubbed his thumb over the sword's pommel, watching them retreat through the forest. He tried to shake off the strange interaction, to return to practicing his forms—what would his sister say if he returned to the campaign looking sloppy? But each passing second seemed intent on working against him, until the sword felt impossibly heavy on his hip. Dread built and blossomed, muting the rainforest around him until he was blanketed in oppressive silence.

When he decided to follow Hei, the crunch of the ground beneath his feet was profoundly soothing.

They noticed him immediately, of course. Based on their expression, they hadn't expected the company. That was fair enough—without Sohmeng there as intermediary, their conversational opportunities were limited. Still, Ahn figured it was worth it to try. Hei was different from most people he had met, but Ahn had attended plenty of dinners and balls in the past. He could do small talk.

"So!" he said, "how long you have lived in Eiji?"

They glanced over their shoulder, squinting at him. Despite Ahn's struggles to keep up—the jungle floor seemed determined to break his ankles—they showed no sign of slowing down.

"Or lived with, with sãoni? You are very skilled—" His elbow made contact with a fat mushroom on one of the trees. It burst immediately, releasing loose fluffy spores that made him sneeze.

In a flash, Hei was at his side, dumping their water gourd over the floating fungus. The particles fell to the ground as Hei snarled something unintelligible. Ahn reddened; he didn't need a shared language to know that had been a close call. He stepped back, trying to get out of the way. "Thank y—"

Hei interrupted him with a loud shout, arm darting out to grab him by the ankle. Ahn hopped in place, bewildered, and looked down to see the tiny cluster of eggs he had nearly trampled. "... oh. Thank you, I—sorry. Sorry."

He wanted to explain that he wasn't usually this much of a walking disaster. Back in Qiao Sidh, he didn't have to worry about snakes in the river, or which pieces of firewood were full of stinging insects. It was the *rainforest*, not him! But he doubted Hei was interested in hearing it. They released their hold on him with a furious look, clicking and rubbing their forehead. Thoroughly chastised, Ahn didn't complain when they grabbed him by the shirt and half-dragged him the rest of the way back to camp.

Sohmeng was still asleep when they returned, as were most of the sãoni, who had not stirred much past the stage of drowsy rumbling. With a heavy sigh, Hei dropped down beside the stump where they had hidden their bags for the night and pulled out a few unfamiliar, brightly coloured fruits. They squeezed them, presumably testing for ripeness, and began the hard work of pretending that Ahn wasn't there.

Guilt twisted in his chest. He was so far out of his element, trapped with two people who had plenty of reasons to leave him to die. If he could make himself useful, his odds of survival would increase. And considering how far he had strayed from Qiao Sidh's camp, the three of them might be stuck together for some time. It would be better, he decided, to ease some of the tension early on. To establish some sort of relationship with these new travelling companions.

Of course it would be a little rocky. New friendships were rarely smooth at first, and this was more of an alliance, really. But all he could do was his best, and hope they would meet him halfway.

Ahn took a breath, steeled himself, and sat down beside Hei, choosing not to take their alarmed squawk personally. He gestured to the fruit. "What is this?"

Hei blinked at him warily.

"The, the fruit—" Ahn reached for one, trying to clarify, and was met with a full-body hiss. He winced, lowering his hand and trying again, slower this time. "What is this fruit you have?"

For a long, painful moment, they said nothing. Then, cautiously, they picked one up, dropping it into his lap. It was about the same size as a pear, but lighter to the touch. He bounced it in his hand with a smile. "Yes! This—what is it? What is . . . " He frowned. Repeating himself wasn't going to get them very far. There had to be a better strategy.

He cleared his throat, holding out the fruit and looking at it very seriously. "Hello, fruit," he said in his most regal voice. "My name is Ahn. And you?"

Hei stared at him, clicking very slowly.

He held the fruit to his ear, leaning in like he was listening for a response. When the fruit said nothing, he held it out to Hei in mock concern. "Name?"

For all that Hei was continuing to look at him like he was absolutely insane—which he might be, trying this out—they seemed to follow his question. "*Saka*," they eventually said, cutting into their own fruit with their sãoni claw.

"Saka," he repeated, feeling the shape of the word in his mouth.

"Sa*ka*," Hei said once more, correcting his emphasis and popping a piece of the saka fruit's flesh into their mouth. It looked delicious.

Pleased with his success, Ahn gave both Hei and the fruit a cordial nod. "Pleased to meet you, Saka," he said, and took a bite. For a second, Hei stopped eating, staring at him with wide eyes. He chewed on the tangy skin; a little tough, but tasty! After a beat, Hei simply sighed, shrugging to themself as they continued with their own breakfast.

It wasn't exactly a warm exchange, but it made Ahn brighten anyway. Maybe they were uncertain about him, but they had conceded to a meal together. It made him feel hopeful—many legendary alliances had begun at a banquet table. Around them, the sãoni woke one by one, stumbling through camp in such a way that even the most vicious of them seemed gentle. Sohmeng was just as slow to wake, pulling a large leaf over her eyes to block out the growing light. She had mentioned that she grew up inside a cave—it must have been an adjustment, coming into a world such as this. But she seemed happy enough.

Despite all of his fears, Ahn was surprised to discover a hint of his own happiness this morning. He wanted nothing more than to return to his sister's side, but that did not mean he had to spend every moment drenched in terror—what a lousy story that would make when he finally returned home. Generals weren't supposed to cower and philosophers weren't supposed to be closed-minded, and Ahn was meant to play both of those roles.

So while it was true that he did not belong here, Ahn allowed himself to relax as much as he could manage. He finished his saka fruit and leaned back against the tree, settling in to watch the sun shift the colour of the world around him.

The vomiting started about an hour later.

Four

WHEN THE MORNING BEGAN with the unmistakable sound of puking, the rest of the day didn't look too promising. Sohmeng was crouched at the scene of the crime, holding back Ahn's hair and doing her best not to lose her mind. When Hei had offered Sohmeng her own saka fruit, it hadn't taken much to figure out what had happened.

"You fed him the *skin*?!" Sohmeng hissed through gritted teeth. "Are you kidding me, Hei?"

"I didn't feed it to him," they said calmly. "He bit the fruit himself. It is not my fault he didn't realize it would make him sick."

"You could have told him! He's not even from here!" One of the hatchlings was scurrying over to investigate the new treat Ahn had splattered onto the ground. Sohmeng grimaced, waving a free hand at Hei. "Hei, would you please—"

"He didn't ask." Hei scooped up the hatchling, willing

to be helpful on at least one front. "Besides, I don't speak Dulpongpa."

"Godless—" Sohmeng rubbed Ahn's back with a little more force, willing herself not to scream. Even if Hei hadn't literally force fed him the saka, Sohmeng wasn't naïve enough to think that they were innocent. "Tell me he didn't eat more than one." She turned to the sputtering Ahn, quickly swapping languages. "How many did you eat?"

Ahn's bronze skin had gone remarkably green-toned. He gagged, managing to hold up one finger before returning to fertilizing the soil. Poor guy. At least he wasn't in danger of actually dying. Sohmeng patted him sympathetically, fixing Hei with her best impression of her brother's *Soh-how-could-you* face. It seemed to work, as they had the decency to look at least a little less smug.

Behind them, Mama let out a low bellow, shuffling forward curiously. She and the other sãoni tended to be more tolerant of Ahn when Sohmeng was near him, even more so when she touched his hair. They were naturally suspicious of the silver and black, which resembled the silvertongue plant that could kill them faster than Sohmeng could say *it doesn't smell like the plant though you idiots.*

Ahn groaned, leaning back against Sohmeng. His skin was clammy to the touch. "I'm—I'm sorry," he said. "This is very . . ." He gave up on the word, saying it in his mother tongue with a defeated wave of his hand.

"It's not your fault," Sohmeng insisted, pushing back his hair and reaching for the water gourd. Of course it was empty, as, apparently, was Hei's. She passed him the spare, wishing they had stopped to fill it all the way the day before. "Just drink this, okay? We'll get you more soon."

Leaves rained down on them as Mama sat against an enormous tree. Sohmeng wasn't sure she'd seen the sãoni get this close to Ahn before; maybe that adoption habit was kicking in again. Having the alpha on their side would certainly make life easier for as long as Ahn remained with them. Then all they'd need to do is get Green Bites off his power trip.

"... I think he'll be okay," Hei said, as though their opinion on the matter was the deciding factor.

"I think you should go get some water and have a long think about the concept of hospitality," Sohmeng retorted. "We'll talk later."

They let out an irritable snarl but skulked off, leaving Sohmeng alone with Ahn and Mama, who was now patting the dirt near them with an inquisitive chirp. Further back, Green Bites was hissing quietly for good measure, apparently on Team Hei.

Sohmeng looked at Ahn, sighing heavily. The gods hadn't blessed her with any sort of nurturing instinct—scathing humour was much more her bag. But seeing as Ahn was still working on mastering the basics of Atengpa, she doubted her jokes would land right now.

She stroked his hair, catching herself before she chirped out of habit. It was something she had gotten used to with Hei and she was still remembering how to act with someone who wasn't used to running with a six-legged crowd.

"I think . . . I think I'm done," Ahn said, nodding slightly to himself. "I'm sorry again—"

"I already told you to stuff it the first time," Sohmeng said, really nailing the whole nurturing thing. "It isn't your fault. Come here. Looking at it probably isn't going to make you feel any better you know."

She half-dragged Ahn over to a shady spot near Mama. Despite the fact that he was pure muscle and nearly a head taller than her, he felt light against her body, more fragile than she expected. He looked wary at the sight of the sãoni so close by; Sohmeng placed herself between them as a barrier.

What was she supposed to say to him now? This whole poisoning situation wasn't in any way her fault, but she couldn't help but feel responsible for Hei's behaviour. They were her partner, her mate, and as much as she was dreading the conversation, it looked like she needed to lay down some serious boundaries on Ahn's behalf.

Once he was looking a little less miserable, Ahn broke the silence. "Was it the . . . " He paused, struggling for the word. "On the saka fruit, the—?"

His poor excuse of a pantomime was a sight to behold. "The skin. Yeah."

"*Skin!*" Ahn said with a hum. Somehow, he made it seem like the new word was more important than the context in which he'd learned it. "The saka skin."

"I'm sorry," Sohmeng said, uncomfortable. "Hei should have told you. I don't know why they didn't."

Concern creased Ahn's brow. Sweat was still beaded

on his forehead. "No," he insisted. "No, no! Not Hei's fault, I did not know. I have done this, when I got lost. And in Qiao Sidh. I am bad alone in the wild, eating bad things."

Sohmeng could not figure out for the life of her why he was trying to be reassuring. His level of accomodation was actually bordering on offensive. "Okay, but Hei—"

"No, no, no!" He waved his hands at her, as if trying to brush the situation off. Mama watched them move, resting her throat on the ground. "I understand. A joke, right? Funny joke." He smiled weakly. "Hei did a joke."

Hei had never willingly done a joke in their life. At least, not outside of the few shy attempts they'd made to impress Sohmeng, and none of those had involved making her lose her lunch. She had to wonder what kind of jokes Ahn was used to if he thought this sort of thing was normal. Her disbelief must have come through in her expression, because he tried again, resting a hand on her arm. It was shaking.

"No need to upset, Sohmeng," he insisted. Godless night. She'd eat saka skin herself if he wasn't born under a super masculine lunar phase—how non-confrontational could a person get? It was a miracle he could even *lift* a sword.

"Kind of need to upset, Ahnschen," she said, looking out in the direction Hei had gone.

"My . . . " A bubble of a laugh escaped his lips. "You said it right."

"Of course I did. I'm the best." She stood up, brushing off her knees, and gave him one last lookover to be sure he wouldn't croak while she was gone. This conversation might take a while. "I'm going to get you more water, okay?"

Sensing her departure, Mama leaned in to Sohmeng with a friendly rumble. Sohmeng sighed, rubbing the sãoni's cheeks; they felt warm, their texture lumpier than usual. She'd have to ask Hei about it when she was done explaining that not killing people was a key part of *being decent*. The sãoni inched closer to Ahn, and Sohmeng took the opportunity to rub her face into his hair one last time, chirping out an affectionate sound. It wasn't quite a bite, but it had done her well so far.

To his credit, Ahn didn't pull back. In fact, he seemed to lean in, going along with the motion. He really knew how to roll with the punches, or maybe he was just feeling overwhelmed enough from the week he'd had that even her ungainly attempts at caregiving were working. Sohmeng looked back at Mama, leaning in and speaking in conspiratorial Atengpa: "Seriously, seriously, *please* do not eat this man while I am gone. I mean it. Not even a nibble."

Mama chirped, bumping against her belly. She'd have to assume that was a yes.

"Sohmeng?" Ahn craned his neck to look at her, exposing the ridge on his throat. He was made of sharp lines, perpetually softened by his good-natured demeanour. With the armour off and the sword away, it was easier with every passing day to see that he did not mean them any harm.

"I'll be back in a little bit," she said. "Mama will look

out for you—just stay close to her and there shouldn't be anything to worry about." The colony hadn't eaten him yet, after all—and his hair was an ongoing deterrent. "Drink that water. And try to get some rest."

Pushing through low-hanging vines, Sohmeng headed in the direction of the freshwater stream she and Hei had scouted out. She had memorized the route in landmarks: through the first wide clearing, past the toothed plants that were not to be touched under *any* circumstance, a left before the sour smelling anthills, and toward the gossiping gurgle of moving water. She took her time as she walked, fidgeting with the string of wovenstone beads she had taken from Sodão Dangde. The plan was to sew some of them onto Hei's vest, but for now they were nice to hold in her hand, a piece of an old home to ground her in the new.

It was hard to feel grounded right now—her head was spinning with hurt and frustration. The two of them had *just* discussed Ahn's treatment the previous night. How had it gone so wrong?

There would be no fixing anything if she stormed over yelling right now; she needed to cool down first. It stung to feel betrayed, but while Hei could be hot-headed, they weren't one to lie or suddenly go back on their word. There had to be something she was missing.

She counted through the cycles under her breath, swaying her arms in the long ferns. Eventually, a sour smell made her wrinkle her nose. But before she could go any further, there was Hei.

They were standing in front of a plant with massive curved leaves, folding them and decanting dew into a gourd. The two of them had drunk from those leaves before, slurping from the curve of them and marveling at the sweet, clear taste—better than stream water by far. It was a nice gesture, for them to be collecting it now for Ahn. She pulled her own gourd out to help them. It was always easier to talk about hard things when they were both using their hands.

Hei clicked quietly at her, and she returned the sound to the best of her ability. For a while, neither of them spoke. Sohmeng had gone in with her usual gusto the night before, and it hadn't worked; this time, she would wait to see what Hei had to say first.

Several empty leaves and heavy sighs later, they finally spoke.

"I don't know that word," they said.

"What?" Sohmeng was confused. "What word?"

"Hospitality," Hei said carefully. Their eyes met hers briefly, at once inquiring and shy. "What does it mean?"

"Oh." She paused her work, taken aback. She was used to explaining words to Ahn, not Hei. But she was glad they had apparently taken her words to heart. "It's like . . . being good to someone on a communal level. Treating them properly when they're a guest in your home. I guess it isn't used as much in Ateng because we're all in each other's business all the time, but it's a really important notion for traders. The word for it, *kejangar*, is used a lot in Dulpongpa."

"Why?"

"Why?" Sohmeng laughed, crouching for a lower leaf. The dewy water shimmered at her in the light. "It's about trust, isn't it? Letting strangers into your home, or entering a place where you don't know anyone? The hmun network might have its peace agreements, but people do bad things sometimes. Both parties need to know their kindness isn't going to get them killed."

"... I wasn't trying to kill him, Sohmeng," they said, clicking a little defensively.

"But you made him sick, Hei." She thought of Ahn's expression, his eagerness to excuse the whole thing as some prank. "That wasn't funny."

"I wasn't trying to be funny."

"Then what happened?" Sohmeng asked, trying not to sound exasperated. "I'm just confused, Hei. I'm trying to understand."

"He's so—" Hei cut themself off with a sãoni growl. She could see the way their fingers clenched around the water gourd, the way they tensed their jaw as they searched for the right words. "Like a loud little monkey, jumping around. Calling danger and causing problems."

"I don't think he's trying to, Hei."

"I agree." Sohmeng tried not to look too surprised. "You are, you are *right*, Sohmeng. He does not mean to be so much trouble, he does not try to hurt us on purpose, but he does it anyway. Careless." They rubbed their temples, smearing their makeup beneath their fingers. "Careless. And I tried to be nice, I tried to behave as you asked, but everywhere he walks is trouble, and it makes me *angry.* I feel angry to look at him here, when his hmun has broken so much. So when he picked up the saka and bit into it before I could stop him . . ."

"You let it happen," Sohmeng finished.

"I would not have let him have more than one," Hei continued miserably. "Maybe I should not have let him have any at all. But I was angry, and I wanted him to learn, and so I was careless too. And now we are all unhappy."

Burning godseye, did Sohmeng understand this. It was so easy to make impulsive decisions when she was angry. The Grand Ones had enough stories of her past transgressions to get the hmun through a whole Jeji phase of storytelling. For all that she could be frustrated by what Hei had done, she also could empathize.

What was it the Grand Ones had said to her at Chehangma's Gate? *Being upset does not require you to have a reaction?*

Now that was shortsighted advice if she'd ever heard it. Feelings demanded to be felt, and reacting to them was inevitable, a simple matter of cause and effect. It was wrong to tell people to just ignore the signs their body was giving them—but it was also *really* wrong to poison people out of spite. As much as Sohmeng hated to admit it, big emotions weren't an excuse for bad behaviour. But they had to be worked with somehow.

Why had no one thought to teach her this? Did they not know how? Were her feelings truly so frightening that everyone had expected her to just stifle them completely? Look how far that had gotten Viunwei.

She sighed, taking Hei's hands in hers. She had no idea what she was doing, but she didn't want to leave them alone with this. "Thank you for explaining. I understand better now."

"Are you still mad?" they asked, looking up at her.

"I mean, kind of, yeah?" She laughed a little, nuzzling her cheek into theirs. "That was really uncool, Hei. It was mean. But I also want you to know that you're allowed to be upset, too. You're even allowed to show it! That's important. But sometimes there are consequences—" She wrinkled her nose at the word. What had she become? "And if the way you show that you're upset really hurts people . . . that's not okay. So be mad, if you need to be mad—but find a way to do it that doesn't put anyone in danger. Okay?"

They clicked quietly in understanding, not quite meeting her eye. Sohmeng leaned in, pressing their foreheads together firmly. She wished she could end the conversation there, with some half-decent advice and everything cleared up. Things would be so much easier if this was just about Ahn. But it wasn't.

"Hei, I need to know—" She stopped, distracted by the tension in her chest. It wasn't often that she was scared to ask questions. "The sãoni. They're hunters, and they—well, they . . . " Hei chirped at her, concerned. "Have you seen them eat people?"

Hei pulled back a little, their expression unreadable. Sohmeng had needed to ask this ever since she saw them all but set Green Bites on Ahn, since she watched how their fear could turn so easily to bloodlust.

"Other bahãokar," Sohmeng continued. "Or traders, or travellers like Ahn." *Or my parents.* She struggled against the thought even as it pushed down upon her, heavy as the currents of the Ãotul. It wasn't something she knew how to manage; it made her want to kick and scream like a child. "We're not the only people who walk Eiji, and I know that the sãoni are predators, and that things happen sometimes but . . . but have you been there? Have you let it happen before?"

"I couldn't stop them if I wanted to, Sohmeng." Their voice was very grave.

"Please answer the question."

When Hei spoke, it was careful, as though the wrong thing could shatter the very air around them. ". . . once before, we encountered an exile from another hmun. It did not end well. I didn't enjoy it." There was no shame in their voice, no despair. But Sohmeng could see the way the memory haunted them, this ghost of the humanity they could not shake completely away. "It is why I forced the colony's hand and marked you as a mate. I did not want to watch that happen again."

A pained laugh escaped Sohmeng. The relief she felt was indescribable, matched only by the fear that came from the grim reality: they could not mark everyone who got in the sãoni's path. "I don't ever want to see that, Hei. I don't want to kill people."

They spoke with nearly parental patience. "Nature is—"

"I know," she said, cutting them off. "I know, Hei. But

that, that's my boundary. That's too much for me." She remembered the waiting, the great quiet that came from Eiji after her parents left her. The phases passing into cycles into years, all the neighbours who never came home. The collective nightmares about the creatures she now fell asleep on. "Eiji is my home, but so is Ateng. I have human family and I have sãoni family, and I don't want them to hurt each other. I won't be a part of it."

Hei nodded, pulling her close. For a while they just held her, undemanding. This was usually the point where she'd crack a joke, pull away—but it was a relief, to let an old wound be nursed. She closed her eyes, nuzzling into their neck. *Feelings demand to be felt*, she thought once more, secretly wishing the sentiment could apply to everyone but her.

"This is hard," she admitted.

Hei clicked in agreement.

"I'm glad you're here with me."

"Me too, Sohmeng Minhal."

She smiled against their shoulder, a nervous jolt going through her to hear the name from their mouth. She had been trying it on in her head ever since that night in the caves, trying to reshape the notion of who she was. Sharing it with Ahn had been a huge step; she hadn't been sure if she'd wanted to sing or puke. But when Hei said it to her—*Sohmeng Minhal, are you listening?*—it felt wonderful. It made her feel real.

"Thank you for being so protective of everyone," she said, giving them a kiss. "It's really obvious how much you care." Hei's eyes went wide at the kiss, and she could imagine the way they flushed underneath their charcoal makeup. That never got old. She grinned, ready to go in for another, but they beat her to it, nearly tripping over themself in the process.

Sohmeng squeaked in surprise, laughing between kisses as they tumbled to the ground. It had been a while since the two of them had really had any time to themselves. *No harm in enjoying it now,* she thought, tugging at their sãoni skin vest.

It was only later, when she was reaching for the water gourd, that Sohmeng remembered Ahn.

"Oh godless night—" She fixed her hair frantically as the two of them barreled back toward the camp. A nearby sãoni raised its head at her, squawking curiously. "He's dead, he's *so* dead, I'm such a moron, he's probably halfway to Green Bites' lower intestine by now—"

"M-maybe not?" Hei offered helpfully.

"Godless night, burning freaking godseye Sohmeng Minhal!" she cursed at herself. All that talk about not wanting to see anyone get killed, and Ahn was probably a stain on the forest floor. Or chased up a tree and left to starve. Could he even climb? She stumbled back into the clearing, out of breath. "Ahn! Ahn, I'm so so—"

She skidded to a halt.

Just as Sohmeng could not have handled the sight of Ahn's mangled body, she wasn't sure anything could have prepared her for the even stranger reality before her: Ahn, cuddled against Mama, surrounded by broken eggshells.

He was sitting perfectly still as two tiny, still-slimy hatchlings crawled all over him, squeaking up a storm.

"Oh," she said. Behind her, Hei let out a sound that wasn't Sãonipa, but certainly didn't qualify as a word.

"I tried to call you," Ahn said, frozen as a tiny set of claws scrabbled at his hair. Mama growled happily, nosing at him. "But I don't think you heard?"

FIVE

BALANCING ON A CREATURE with three times as many legs as Ahn was used to had not failed to lose its novelty. The sãoni propelled themselves through the jungle, only stopping when they encountered something their powerful claws could not manage to climb over or shred through. Which was to say, not much at all. Ahn was thankful to be riding with Sohmeng on Singing Violet; it was easier with his arms around someone who knew how to properly hold onto their head spines. Plus, the company was friendly.

Hei rode beside them on Green Bites, Singing Violet's mate. While this particular sãoni seemed to be a troublemaker in general, Ahn could not shake the feeling that it was sizing him up. There were so many levels on which that wasn't necessary, but Ahn couldn't speak Sãonipa, so he mostly just kept his eyes ahead.

The colony had returned to the migration route this morning, after a couple phases—he was still getting used to their lunar calendar—of rest and good hunting. They had covered miles of land in a matter of hours, led by Mama and the four healthy hatchlings that clung to her. Getting them to detach from him had been difficult; in the days since they'd been born, the first two to hatch had been especially clingy with Ahn. Apparently this wasn't unusual—a stunned Hei had explained that sãoni tend to latch on to the creatures they see in the moments after they leave the egg. Ahn just happened to be the lucky party.

"I would like to be a father one day," he'd said, wincing as Sohmeng had uncurled the hatchlings' claws from his shoulder, "but this was not what I imagined."

From then on they were up and down his legs, nestled in his chestplate, even chewing on his hair. After a few frightening moments of squawking, the rest of the colony seemed to realize that it wasn't actually poison.

Lucky for him, they also appeared to have lost most interest in eating him. This was in no small part due to Mama's warmth toward his new role as resident governess for young lizards. He doubted they would be very receptive to the etiquette lessons he'd received in the Winter Palace at Hvallánzhou.

"Wait wait wait," Sohmeng said, laughing as he tried to explain the concept to her. It wasn't translating very well. "You had to get *lessons* on how not to behave like a meathead? What kind of a kid were you Ahn?"

"No! I was fine, very well-behaved—"

"Oh sure, me too," Sohmeng said, interrupting him with a cackle.

Even Hei seemed to be smiling along. They had been more tolerant of his presence lately. The wariness hadn't fully gone away, especially when he was holding the hatchlings, but they acknowledged his presence with a nod or a hum, and didn't play any more tricks on him. He was grateful to have stumbled into a truce.

"Okay, but seriously," Sohmeng started again. "You were taught how to . . . eat and talk?" She was trying not to snicker at him too openly. He was reminded of Schenn, mocking his Imperial accent and unwavering politeness.

"And other social skills," he replied with a nod.

"Couldn't you just learn from watching people? Like . . . no screaming in public unless something bad is happening? Or like, oh hey look no one is burping in their neighbour's face, better not do that either? This seems like basic sense, Ahnschen."

He laughed, holding tighter onto her as the sãoni went over a bump. Sohmeng had a funny way of saying things. "This learning—lessons, the lessons were more . . . " He shook his head, trying to figure out how to interpret the concepts of class and nobility. "Bigger. Not everyone needs them. But I did."

"Because you're a meathead," Sohmeng said sagely. She turned to Hei, quickly translating the conversation.

"No," Ahn said. "Because I'm a prince."

Sohmeng's translation abruptly stopped. "Wait, what?"

Maybe he should have mentioned this sooner; as the weeks had passed, it had become more awkward to imagine slipping it into conversation. He cleared his throat, trying to act casual about the whole thing. "I'm the Eleventh Prince of Qiao Sidh."

"WHAT—"

Singing Violet nearly veered into Green Bites as Sohmeng gave an involuntary yank on her head spines. For a moment all reptilian chaos broke out. Hei, who was nearly standing on Green Bites at this point, shot Ahn an accusatory look, shouting at Sohmeng, "Pay attention!"

But Sohmeng was undeterred, only pausing to offer her sãoni a consoling pat and squawk before looking over her shoulder at Ahn. Her expression was akin to a hostage situation.

"Okay," she said, narrowing her dark eyes at him. "One more time for the lizards in the back. You're a *prince?*"

"Yes?" he replied with a timid smile. "Eleventh born."

Hei whistled. Apparently numbers translated similarly in Dulpongpa and Atengpa.

Sohmeng was spluttering, throwing her hands in the air. Ahn reached forward, trying to hold onto Singing Violet himself. "A prince. A godless *prince.* Why didn't you tell us?!"

"It's . . . in my name?" he offered unhelpfully. "Éongrir is the name of the Imperial family."

"I'm not from Qiao Sidh, Ahn."

" . . . Eløndham?" he tried. "It translates to Eleventh Beloved—"

"Oh, obviously! Because I speak Qiao Sidhur!" she exclaimed, jabbing him with her elbow. Where the rest of her body was beautifully soft, those particular bones were painfully pointy. And she used them liberally. "Give up on social school, Ahn. You're unteachable."

In a place with entirely different cultural rules, that was probably true. Funny, how all his years of etiquette school amounted to pretty much nothing down in the jungles of the Untilled. Even his martial skills were of limited use when there was no real war to fight. Oddly enough, his time in academia on the Philosophy path seemed to be the only thing getting him through his daily helpings of culture shock. Asgørindad University was where he'd learned how to engage with people outside of social scripts. It was where he'd learned to put his wonder to good use, and how to reach all of the people he might one day be ruling. Unlikely. But possible.

"This is so wild!" Sohmeng continued. "I didn't know royalty even *existed* anymore—I've only heard about princes and stuff in the old stories. We haven't done anything like that here in thousands of years."

Ahn wasn't sure what to say to that. Perhaps he should have known—there had been a translation for his title up in Kongkempei, which meant they had the concept. A few of the Grand Ones had laughed when his sister explained that Ahn, young though he was, should be treated with as much deference as they.

"Why are you here?" To Ahn's surprise, the question had come from Hei, and it wasn't entirely hostile in tone.

"I . . ." He hesitated. The core of Hei's question was not an unfamiliar one, rich with many contexts: his new roommates at Asgørindad, gawking at him as he stood alone in the doorway to their apartment after he'd left his bags in the middle of the street, expecting a valet; Master Hvu, complaining that his signet ring was interfering with his harp playing; Schenn, lying back to back with him in their small cot, neither of them able to sleep; the Third Prince to the Empire, his brother, staring at him with open contempt on his sixth birthday.

Why are you here?

"It was a gift," Ahn said. He shifted in his seat, carefully adjusting his hold on Sohmeng. "I spent most of my life training in one of the, the . . ." Very little of his Dulpongpa vocabulary had prepared him for translating the cultural touchstone that was the Qiao Sidhur Paths of Mastery. He winced, unsure if it was worth it to try. "I am sorry. The words are . . ."

"We have time!" Sohmeng said encouragingly with a pat on his arm. "Go slow. Let's figure it out."

It took the better part of the afternoon to work through the translation together. Trial and error, translations from Qiao Sidhur to Dulpongpa to Atengpa—even snippets of the sãoni language were used to express emphasis. Even though he knew the animals around him were simply responding to Hei's noises, it was indescribably strange to feel as though they were being included in the discussion.

Soon the land around them was changing: the trees grew taller and thicker, and where the understory had once been decorated by hanging vines, sturdy branches now reached out like arms, twisting and gnarling into one other like the web of some impossibly large spider. Sunlight shone through in bold pockets, lighting up copper-haired marsupials that whistled high above. The sãoni's eyes followed them hungrily, but none broke from the travelling pack for as long as Mama was intent on moving forward. As far as generals went, Ahn had seen few better.

By the time they were passing around bananas to share for an afternoon snack, the three of them had found half-way decent translations of the nine Paths of Mastery: Conquest, Discernment, Health, Aesthetic, Arts, Philosophy, Advancement, Fertility, and Spirit. Originally named by philosopher Tseir Jin Zhadh as the essentials of a culture, these paths had been reinterpreted as the nine key ways to advance the Empire. To dedicate oneself to a path was to be in service to the expansion of Qiao Sidh.

"Each path has ten ranks," Ahn explained. "The higher your number, the greater your achievement." Each rank was harder to achieve than the last, with the tenth only awarded posthumously. Most people were fortunate if they even made it to rank seven in one of their lifetime's paths; anything higher added a certain degree of celebrity. "We include our ranking in our names, so everyone will know . . ." He paused. The concept struck him differently in translation, left him feeling uncentered and exposed. "How far we have come. Or, how hard we have worked. How to show respect."

"And you choose these paths?" Sohmeng asked, tossing a banana peel to Green Bites. The sound of two sets of teeth snapping echoed through the woods, making Ahn's arm throb in memory.

"We do, yes," he said.

"Huh." Sohmeng wiggled closer to him, thoughtful, and Ahn glanced at Hei, uncertain of where to put his hands. He had always been a very affectionate person, happiest when in close company with others—though the less educated around him often couldn't reconcile that with his asexuality. Considering some of the trouble he'd had explaining it to his own peers, he wasn't sure where to begin with people from an entirely different culture. Would bringing it up be inappropriate? It wasn't really their business, but given his close proximity to Sohmeng and the nature of her and Hei's relationship and all of the tension—

Hei let out a sharp whistle, shaking him from the thought. They looked at him expectantly, glancing to Sohmeng, and for one terrifying moment Ahn wondered if he had been thinking aloud.

"Ahn?" Sohmeng said, nudging him. "Still awake?"

"Yes," he replied a little too quickly. "Sorry. Translating is very . . ." He waved his hand around, trying to show how scatterbrained he was. It wasn't completely a lie; working to integrate all of those new words so rapidly into conversation was a headache.

With no warning, Hei tossed a gourd of water to him. Were it not for his reflexes, he would have been clubbed in the head and knocked off the sãoni; he offered a weak smile anyway. It had probably been a friendly gesture.

"I was just wondering if anyone has ever mastered all

the Paths! Like just really went for it and beat the whole system?" For someone who had just learned about the Paths today, Sohmeng sounded eager to give it a try herself. Ahn couldn't help but smile, glad to hear the way that desire seemed to be universal. It made home feel less far away.

"Shengdhru Allateinn. A legend—a hero. No one else. But many people balance two or three paths in their lives." In fact, it was crucial for certain vocations. Health and Advancement were vital for surgeons, and Ahn had never met a courtesan who didn't at least rank in Discernment, Aesthetic, and Arts.

Having grown up in the royal family, Ahn himself had achieved a preliminary first rank in all of the Paths before he was eight years old. During that time, he had learned very quickly which Paths he was naturally suited to, and which he would be wise to leave alone. Such choice was a privilege that came with his status; it made him uncomfortable to think about for too long, though he couldn't articulate why.

"So . . ." Sohmeng said, looking back at him expectantly.

Ahn blinked, unsure what she was waiting for. He glanced over at Hei for a hint, but their eyes were on the low canopy of trees. A frown creased their brow, then disappeared before he could follow their gaze.

"What about you?" Sohmeng asked, audacious as ever. "What's your path?"

Wouldn't we all like to know, Ahn thought, feeling the weight of Schenn's knucklebone nudging against his jaw.

"Conquest," he said carefully, "is where I have spent most of my life. But I took a break after I achieved sixth ranking."

Neither Hei nor Sohmeng nor the sãoni were remotely scandalized. Why would they be? They had no reference point for what a big deal that was. He wasn't even fully sure that "conquest" was being translated properly—he had thought it wise to minimize the brutality that often went into the process. So of course Hei and Sohmeng had no idea what a Six-ing entailed, what achieving that rank had cost him.

"I took a break," he repeated, nearly dizzy with the dissonance of his words and their non-reactions, "and returned to my path in Arts. I also started Philosophy. Now I rank third in Arts and second in Philosophy. That's part of my name—Sølshendasá, Siengunghvøs." Listing these achievements should have made him proud; it always had when he heard his name announced at formal gatherings. But this time, it brought up something young in him, the terror of receiving praise and being given opportunity, the secret certainty that he was undeserving. He squeezed his legs on Singing Violet, steadying himself as she lumbered over a log. "I was working on those paths when my parents surprised me for my birthday. They gifted me a role in this campaign with my sister."

"And that's how you got here," Sohmeng said, nodding to herself.

Ahn wondered if she would say more about it, if she would ask questions that would lead to difficult answers.

He wasn't much of a liar, but he also had the sense to know that explaining what happened in Kongkempei might ruin his chances of getting back home in one piece. It brought up a vague feeling of guilt, but Sohmeng did not ask further, and Ahn did not volunteer.

Hei took a different approach, speaking a single word: "Conquest." One of the most sacred parts of Ahn's identity, made sinister by their tongue. They looked at him with those piercing green eyes, unflinching. Ahn couldn't hold their gaze; his stomach felt weighted to the ground.

He looked to the land for distraction, but found that the branches that webbed above him made the sky feel tighter. The trunks served as pillars, spread out in artful intervals. Not far to his right, trees clustered closer together, appearing as one tangled mass. Mama lifted her nose, letting out a low rumble.

"Did you want it?" Sohmeng asked. "The campaign."

Ahn shrugged. "It was a choice." A choice that had led him miles and miles from home, unsure of how he would ever make his way back to his family, back to the university where he had begun to feel like himself again. A choice that forced him into actions he didn't like to think about. "I cannot take it back now."

Singing Violet lurched then, coming suddenly to a halt. The rest of the colony stopped alongside her, staying just behind Mama. Noise replaced motion, and soon all Ahn could hear was clicking and growling. Hei made a few clicks of their own, guiding Green Bites closer to him and Sohmeng.

"What is it?" Sohmeng asked, stroking Singing Violet.

Hei shook their head, pulling up their hood. Ahn could feel Sohmeng exhale against him; her back was tense against his chest. He gave her a squeeze that he hoped was reassuring and, cautiously, moved one hand to rest on the hilt of his sword. The jungle was full of dangers, but even still, it troubled him to imagine what could disturb predators like the sãoni.

He looked closer at the tight cluster of trees ahead of them, thick and unbreakable as any stone wall. Ahn had never seen anything like it, but where he would have once simply been curious, he now felt unease. Something was strange; something was wrong. Hei slipped off Green Bites, eyes on the ground as they searched for tracks.

"Godless night."

Sohmeng was the only one who thought to look up. She whacked Ahn in the thigh, clicking to get Hei's attention as she pointed.

Two humans were crouched in the canopy of branches, camouflaged and silent. Ahn scanned the trees, looking for more. How long had they been tracked for?

"Enemies?" he murmured. He gripped his sword tighter, slowing his breathing the way his masters had taught him. Hei clicked, crouching low to the ground.

Sohmeng grabbed Ahn's wrist. "Not unless you act like a meathead." As her eyes followed the humans in the trees, Ahn could see her trying to form a plan. He was about to suggest a hasty retreat when something changed in her expression. "Trust me, okay?"

Before he could ask for clarification, she dismounted Singing Violet. She strode past Hei with her jaw set, waving her arms at the strangers above. Ahn took one look at Hei and knew they were as uncertain about this as he was; even still, he did his best to remain steady and trust this girl who had already saved him once from death.

"Hey! Hi, hello!" Sohmeng called in Dulpongpa. "You, up in the trees!"

A spear landed at her feet with a heavy thunk. Ahn reached once more for his sword at the same moment Hei rose with a snarl, but Sohmeng held up a firm hand to stop them both.

"Kind of rude!" she shouted. Ahn could see her hands shaking, even if her voice remained calm. "I'm just trying to talk to you."

This time, a voice called down in response. "Not a step closer, stranger. What is your business? Why have you brought this danger to our door?"

Sohmeng had the audacity to smile. "No danger, swear on my grandmother. Look, I know this looks weird, but I'm going to need you to bring me to your Grand Ones, or whoever's in charge here. It's about the hmun network—and about your neighbours in Ateng. Trust me, you're going to want to hear this."

Part Two: Nona Fahang

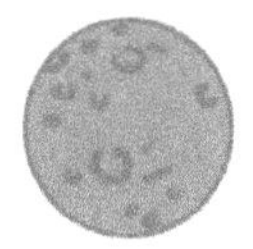

Six

EVEN AT SPEARPOINT, Sohmeng could not believe her good luck.

Stumbling into a hmun had been unexpected, but it raised opportunities galore. So much was broken in Eiji, and now she didn't have to face it alone. Despite the confidence she projected, Sohmeng had to admit that she'd felt in over her head since climbing Sodão Dangde. And as much as she wanted to believe she could personally fix the Sky Bridge and facilitate a conversation with Ahn's people, things suddenly seemed a lot more realistic with the support of another hmun.

After a good deal of back-and-forth, the scouts agreed to come down and talk properly once the sãoni were herded to a safe distance. Now she just had to work out the logistics with Ahn and Hei.

"It'll just be for tonight," Sohmeng insisted. "I'll go inside, fill the Grand Ones in about Ateng, and see what they can do to help. We'll be moving again by tomorrow."

Hei stood at Mama's side, clicking warily at the figures moving above. Around them, the sãoni were growling and shuffling. "Tomorrow," they repeated.

"I'll be back in the morning before the sãoni are even awake."

Ahn cleared his throat. Strangely enough, he looked more doubtful even than Hei. "It might be wise to continue on our way. How do you know that the Grand Ones will help you?"

"Why wouldn't they?" Sohmeng asked. "We're all part of the same network, even if we live far away from each other! We share ancestors and stuff."

"They threw a spear," Ahn said.

"Well, yeah, that wasn't cool," Sohmeng admitted. "But we look pretty scary with the sãoni, right? Once we show them we're not bringing in any danger, it'll be fine!" Ahn didn't look convinced. His eyes followed the strangers in the trees, his fingers flexing at his sides. Sohmeng attempted a reassuring smile. "Hey. We're still going to take you back to the Qiao Sidhur camp, if that's what you're worried about. This is just a detour, promise."

He still seemed pretty on edge, but Sohmeng could deal with that later. For now, she had to sort things out with Hei.

"It's close enough to nightfall that you shouldn't have too much trouble leading the sãoni away, yeah?" she asked. "But like, not too far away?"

Hei nodded, speaking carefully. "It is possible. How will you get back tomorrow?"

"I'll follow the tracks. I do pay attention to *some* of the stuff you say about hunting," Sohmeng teased. " . . . but if you could like, also leave a bunch of other obvious signs of where you are, that would be great. Just in case."

Hei sighed loudly. Sohmeng couldn't blame them. She was building this plan on the spot, trying to solve problems as fast as she thought of them.

Mama let out a low bellow, lifting her body from the ground; apparently she was done. The colony let out Sãonipa clicks of acknowledgment, readying themselves to move. Even Ahn's two attached hatchlings squeaked, urging him forward.

"I don't like this," murmured Hei, taking Sohmeng's forearms. "I don't like you being away from us."

"I'll come back to you," she said, nudging their nose with hers. After so much time spent with Hei, she also felt a little lost at the idea of being apart, even for an evening.

But this wasn't the jungle—this was a *hmun.* With people. And where Hei specialized in all things wilderness, Sohmeng had spent her whole life dealing with more human-shaped challenges. She could do this. She was Par—well, she had been Par before. Sort of. Her lunar identity felt lumpy and uncomfortable in its newness. She steadied herself, reframing the thought: *Fine, I'm Minhal. Let's cause some problems.*

A couple more scouts joined the party that was watching them from the treetops. One of them whistled for her attention. "Are they leaving or not?"

"Working on it," Sohmeng replied. She rubbed cheeks

with Hei for good measure; if this change of plan was making her nervous, she could only imagine how they felt.

"And him?" the scout asked.

Right. Ahn. He'd managed to keep his hands off the flaming sword, but he was emanating the same unflinching energy as the day they'd first met. It wasn't openly aggressive—he just looked too *ready* for Sohmeng's liking. She couldn't understand it; there wasn't any reason for this to be a fight.

Still, it seemed like a better idea to bring him inside than to leave him with Hei. Sohmeng had already learned her lesson on that front.

"He comes with me," Sohmeng called back, detaching the hatchlings from Ahn to put them back on Mama. Ahn rubbed the spot on his face where the little lizards had been affectionately gumming. He looked tense, pensive. For a second she thought he might refuse. ". . . that okay, Ahn?"

"I—yes," he said, tugging once on his piercing. "Of course. Sorry."

With that decided, Sohmeng gave Mama one last pat as Hei mounted her back. They reached down to pull her onto her toes for a kiss. "Don't have too much fun without me," Sohmeng said.

"Don't be silly," Hei replied, setting her feet gently back down on the jungle floor. "You know I'm no fun at all."

A whistle, a roar, the scrabbling of claws, and the colony disappeared into the jungle, slipping through the winding trees. Sohmeng took a deep breath, resisting some old, childlike urge to shout, to call them back to her. She had made her choice—now it was time to see what she could do with it.

The thicket of tall, slim trees began to shift, disturbing a flock of tiny jewel-bright birds hiding in the branches. Three scouts entered the clearing in cautious formation, holding spears not unlike the one that had landed at her feet. Sohmeng could understand their caution; even with the sãoni gone, these people had probably never seen any riders before.

Not that Sohmeng had much idea of what to expect from them, either. Though they were all descendents of the legendary civilization of Polhmun Ão, connected by ancient lineage, she had never seen a hmun outside Ateng. From a glance, this one's people looked to her like cousins: dark, straight hair, skin in shades of amber, sturdy legs and square palms. Their clothing, she noticed, had fewer layers than Ateng, but that made sense given the fact that they weren't stuck in the perpetual coolness of the caves.

With his slim frame, silvertongue hair, and solid two hands of height on everyone else, Ahn stood out. Even the bones of his face were different, his cheeks carved granite in comparison to the rounded pottery of Sohmeng's people. But it wasn't just appearances that highlighted the differences between them; it was the way the scouts gripped their weapons, eyeing him with distaste. Distrust.

One of them stepped over, an individual with a stern brow and grays in their short hair. "What is your business?" they asked. Sohmeng took them as the leader of the group. Their voice was naturally authoritative, and they had at least twenty years on the two scouts with them: a petite youth with two long braids, and another person with a scar on their cheek.

Sohmeng swallowed. Despite the extensive language practice she had gotten in with Ahn, all her Dulpongpa dried up in her throat, leaving her stumbling. "I—I am Sohmeng Par," she finally said. It was probably safest to claim Par right now; she couldn't risk them denying her entry if they thought she had been exiled. "Of the hmun Ateng. This is Ahnschen. He's . . . " She hesitated, watching the way Scar's hand flexed on their weapon.

"We know what he is," the leader said. "So I ask you again—what is your business here?"

Sohmeng stopped, glancing to Ahn. *What* he is? She had no idea what that was about, and the what in question remained still, revealing nothing.

"Do you need help?" Braids suddenly asked, looking at her worriedly. The leader shot them a look and they slunk back, apologetic.

Sohmeng pushed aside her confusion, grateful that someone had asked. "Yes!" she said to the woman in charge. The feminine 'I' the leader had used gave Sohmeng a pang of solidarity, left her wondering if she was Par, too—maybe that was a way she could appeal for help. "Yes, we need help. Like I said, I'm from Ateng—the hmun in the mountains, not too far south? We probably used to trade together, actually, but we haven't been able to because we've been trapped in Fochão Dangde, one of our mountains, for a few years because of an attack from the sãoni. Not, not the sãoni we just rode in on, but . . ."

This story was a little longer than she had initially considered. Despite her best efforts to summarize, the scouts didn't appear to be paying much attention, busy as they were sizing up Ahn. Sohmeng couldn't help but feel like her thunder was being stolen.

"Okay," she said slowly. "Um, look, I don't know if there's something I'm missing here, but I really need you to take us to your Grand Ones. This is sort of urgent."

Scar sneered, saying something to Leader in their hmunpa. It was too fast for Sohmeng to understand, but the tone didn't sound promising. Braids took Scar's arm, protesting, but they were quickly shaken off as their companion gestured furiously at her and Ahn.

This wasn't going how she'd planned.

"Ahn," she said quietly, doubt churning in her chest. "What's going on?"

Though the boy's face remained impassive, she caught the twitch of anxiety in his hand, an interrupted jerk of a motion. He wasn't going for his sword—he was trying to reach his ear.

Before he could answer, the scouts' attention was back on them. Leader stepped slightly closer to Sohmeng, her voice calm despite the rising tension. "Forgive my lack of hospitality, but I'm not sure if that can happen, Sohmeng Par."

"What—" Sohmeng couldn't tell if she was more confused or angry. Of all the complications she'd imagined, getting turned away had never even crossed her mind. "Why not?"

Leader ignored the question. "Are you a hostage?" she asked plainly.

"*What?*"

"A hostage," she repeated. "Are you with this man against your will?"

Braids was looking at Sohmeng with those big concerned eyes, glancing between her and Ahn like he was about to grow another sword out of his head. Meanwhile, he was just standing there and taking their animosity without so much as a word to defend himself. This was ridiculous.

"No," Sohmeng snapped. "Ahn's a—a friend. We found him in Eiji, he had gotten separated from his hmun—"

"His *hmun*," Scar spat, voice acidic. "Is that what he told you?"

Despite her better instincts, Sohmeng shot them a withering look of her own. "No, I used my mind-reading powers. Do you not have them here? They're a big thing in Ateng."

Sohmeng could practically hear Viunwei shrieking at her about pettiness, but she didn't care. Whoever this was, they had no right to talk to her like she was stupid. They didn't know anything about her. Maybe she didn't know everything about Ahn, but she and Hei had a pretty good sense of the bigger picture. Probably a better one than some closed-off hmun who started chucking spears on sight.

"Lita Soon . . ." Leader said placatingly, holding up a hand and switching back to their shared hmunpa. Despite her apparent authority in this group of scouts, the man didn't immediately back down.

Of course he's a Soon, Sohmeng thought, stifling a groan.

As the three scouts dissolved back into hushed arguing, Sohmeng felt a hand slip into her own. She looked to Ahn, whose eyes were on the tangle of branches above them. That's right—there were more scouts in the trees. It unsettled her to feel like she was being watched from all sides.

"Sohmeng," he said quietly. "Thank you for being kind to me. You and Hei."

Sohmeng blinked at him, taken aback. "What?" Where was this coming from? And since when had Hei ever been nice to him?

"I was very lost and you let me live." His hand was warm and dry in hers, but his voice wavered as he spoke. With a gentle squeeze, he looked at her, offering an apologetic smile. "I am grateful."

"That's . . . very sweet of you?" Sohmeng said. "But I'm not really loving this *last chance we have to speak* tone you've got going on."

The way he winced was too much. That was enough—Sohmeng was done with this cryptic nonsense. Whatever the issues were between Ahn and this hmun, she wasn't going to waste any more time standing around and being denied information.

She whistled sharply for attention. These people weren't Grand Ones; she didn't have to be deferential. She didn't even have to be *nice.* "If you aren't going to help us, are we good to go?"

Leader almost looked amused. "What happened to needing help?"

"Urgent help, actually," Sohmeng said, stepping right up to her and ignoring the way Lita Soon gripped his weapon. "So if you're going to waste our time, I have another hmun to go find." She wasn't sure when Ahn had moved so close to her, but she could feel that terrible calmness he carried. It did nothing to ease the strangers' tension, but it made her feel safe, to know someone else had her back when Hei wasn't there.

Braids looked to Leader, this time voicing their worries in Dulpongpa. "Polha Hiwei, he would want to know. We can't just—"

Hiwei, huh? Sohmeng could work with that; few signs hated a lost opportunity more than Hiwei children. She cocked an eyebrow at the group, feigning indifference. "Our sãoni are moving north anyway, we should find another by next Nor. Though I wonder if they would be curious about the fact that another member of the network shut their doors on a hmun in need."

The scout in charge, Polha Hiwei, looked once more between her and Ahn. "I believe your companion could tell you that the hmun up north have had troubles of their own."

Sohmeng went cold. "What do you mean—"

"But you're right," Polha continued over her, offering a conciliatory nod. "The hmun of Nona Fahang has had much reason as of late to open its gates to the troubled and the displaced. I will take you to our Grand Ones, and they can decide what is to be done about your situation." Her gaze landed pointedly on Ahn.

Sohmeng could not read the woman's intentions. For all she knew, this agreement was a punishment rather than a courtesy.

"Eakang," the woman said, nodding to the youth with the braids. "Go inform the Grand Ones of our guests' arrival."

"And—"

"Him too, yes. Now go."

Braids—rather, Eakang—turned on their heel and disappeared through the trees. With a whistle from Polha Hiwei, a slim wheel of rope was dropped from above. "Lita," she said, unwinding it. "Help me bind the man."

Sohmeng stepped in front of Ahn, protectiveness surging through her even as she struggled with what the woman had said. Logically she knew she couldn't protect him, but she couldn't just watch this happen either. He had travelled with their colony, the hatchlings cared about him, he had *just* thanked her for keeping him safe. "No," she snapped. "No, you can't—"

"Sohmeng." Ahn touched her shoulder. When she looked back at him, she could see genuine fear in his eyes. He squeezed them shut, cursed softly in Qiao Sidhur, and placed his sword upon the ground. Sohmeng could only stare. Why would he offer himself like this? "Please don't fight them—I don't want trouble for you."

"Ahn," Sohmeng asked, her own voice shaking, "what did you *do?*"

His face was drawn tight in what might have been shame; his answer came in Qiao Sidhur: "Qøngem."

Conquest.

It was a bad time to realize that she hadn't fully understood what that word meant.

"Your shell," said Lita coldly, his spear angled in Ahn's direction.

The man hesitated, then removed the few pieces of armour he kept on out of habit. The rest, including the helmet, had been left with the sãoni, too heavy to carry around all the time. Stripped down to his thin, loose shirt and dark pants, he held out his arms, inviting a search. Lita stayed firmly in place, but Polha patted him down. When she was satisfied, she passed the rope to Lita, who wasted no time forcing Ahn's hands behind his back.

Sohmeng wished Hei were here. She shouldn't have just let them leave like that; she thought she could handle it, she didn't realize they were walking straight into a hostile situation. What if she couldn't get back? What if—

Polha Hiwei took out a knife, stepping toward Ahn. Before Sohmeng could so much as shout, she sliced the blade through the low hem of his shirt, cutting off a thick ribbon of fabric. Ahn flinched at the sound, but the flash of skin beneath appeared unscathed.

"G-godless night," Sohmeng said as the woman tied it

tightly around Ahn's eyes. "Is this really necessary?"

"I'm afraid so." Polha held out a hand in invitation. "Come."

As they navigated through the wall of trees, Sohmeng became less and less convinced that Ahn needed to be blindfolded. It was a veritable maze of wood, so tall and dense that Sohmeng had no way of knowing which trees had grown which branches. Based on the scouts' careful steps, she figured there had to be some sort of route; one wrong step was probably enough to guide you into a corner too tight to wriggle out from.

Lita Soon was behind them with Ahn. Now and then Sohmeng heard the sound of his body making firm contact with the trunks. She clenched her fists, wishing desperately that she had more context, more information, *anything* to work with.

One step, then another.

The sound of her own breathing, a pained grunt from Ahn as his head was smacked into a branch. The cry of a bird, the creak of the trees.

One step. Another. And then—

The thicket opened, revealing the interior of Nona Fahang. From the inside, the forestry they had emerged from looked like a massive wall, surrounding a bustling village. Trees grew in clusters, woven into different structures: houses, archways, ladders. The overhead branches were shaped in such a way that the villagers were able to walk on them. She didn't know that people could live this way, all stacked on top of each other.

Despite all of her fear and uncertainty, Sohmeng granted herself a moment to appreciate the fact that she had made it. She was in another hmun. The first from Ateng since the Sky Bridge fell.

"Welcome to Nona Fahang," Polha Hiwei said, looking back at Sohmeng with unexpected warmth. She could see the pride on the woman's face.

People were beginning to gather, curious about the strangers that had been brought inside. They came from their homes in surprising amounts; just looking across the courtyard, Sohmeng already saw numbers far greater than that of Ateng.

"Straight to the Grand Ones?" Lita asked, nudging Ahn forward. His cheek was scraped where it had hit one of the trees, matching the scar on his captor's face. Sohmeng clenched her fists.

"I think that would be best," Polha agreed. "Before the whole hmun shows up."

Nona Fahang, Sohmeng thought, taking a moment to search through her parents' old stories. It was the fortress hmun, wasn't it? Built like a tree nut: miserable to get into, but wonderful once inside. A long-time trade partner with Ateng. Neighbourly.

Unless Ahn was the neighbour in question. The murmur of voices was building like the call of cicadas, whispers stacking on each other until they became a roar. Even as the villagers watched the scene, they kept their distance, save for the occasional wandering child who was yanked back by their parent. All around Sohmeng heard a word—*tsongkar, tsongkar.* She didn't know this word; she couldn't understand much of anything they were saying in Fahangpa. But it didn't sound like it meant anything good.

"*Tsongkar*?" she asked Polha.

"Not you," the woman said, a note of sympathy in her voice. "They're referring to your companion."

"But what does it mean?"

"Unwanted," Polha translated. "Uninvited. A guest who did not ask."

Conquest, Sohmeng thought numbly, and she suddenly understood why Ahn had seemed so ready to say his goodbyes. They wove through the crowd, approaching a gazebo at the center of town. From this distance, she could see the circle of chairs and the elderly bodies sat in them. The Grand Ones, out in public, attended to by the rest of the hmun. How strange, to see them so openly integrated in a community where the godseye shone on everyone.

She braced herself as she had done at Chehangma's Gate, those many phases ago. *Be better*, she thought. *Be something they won't hate. But be yourself, too.*

"Sohmeng?"

She stopped in her tracks at the sound of a voice in the crowd, calling her name.

"Sohmeng Par?"

Polha Hiwei was saying something to her, but she had already pulled away. The crowd parted for her as she looked around wildly, her own words catching in her throat. It seemed too dangerous to respond, like she might scare the possibility away by acknowledging its presence. She didn't dare to ask for this, she didn't dare to believe—

"Get out of the way," the voice insisted. "Move, please! That's my—Sohmeng, *Sohmeng!*"

The faces of the people blurred together into one unimportant mass. Everything disappeared but the sound of her name, which she followed until she came upon the voice that was calling it out like a new year's hymn. His hair had grown since she'd seen him last, and there was a new darkness around his eyes, like old bruises that had never quite recovered. But she would know him anywhere. How could she not know the man who had named her?

Even still, she asked: "Dad?"

"Sohmeng," he said once more, and she fell into his arms. Tonão Sol, her father, come alive once more in the jungles of Eiji.

Seven

DO YOU REMEMBER *what I told you about the Thousand Hour Siege?*

Ahn couldn't see how that was relevant. He couldn't see at all; the fabric that had been stretched over his eyes turned the world hazy and imperfect. Feeling the panic that threatened to overtake him, he leaned into his other senses.

This isn't a test, Ahn. It's a real question.

The language all around him was unfamiliar, buzzing cumbersome in his ears. If they were still speaking Dulpongpa, he wasn't sure he'd even be able to tell. And who knew if Sohmeng would help him anymore? His wrists tugged uselessly against the rope, earning him a sharp jab between the shoulder blades and an insult he could not understand.

You're not paying attention, are you?

Another shove from behind forced him to walking again, one step after another, uncertain of where he would land. He squared his shoulders, breathing slowly in through his nose and out through his mouth. He stumbled in the dirt, and told himself that he knew how to be fearless.

The heat in the back of his neck shifted, siphoning into his earlobe. It throbbed with old memory, and he bit back a groan.

That's more like it. While I have you, listen closely—no, stop that. Don't start wondering after me, you idiot. Listen to my words. Trust me.

Alright. So. The Thousand Hour Siege was the last strategic battle in the taking of Qiao Sidh. The Imperial army moved on Gurinn, the last remaining sovereign region on the continent. It had been a long and difficult harvest for Gurinn. People were hungry, and the feudal lords weren't feeling generous with their granaries; they were too busy keeping an eye on the oncoming army, saving up for themselves. And the army did come.

But the Empire did something unexpected: it approached the peasantry. This time, instead of terrorizing the lower classes, the invaders—sorry, the liberators—took care of them. They brought imported goods to soothe Gurinn's hungry. They built a magnificent road to open up trade with the rest of Qiao Sidh. They brought music, beautiful music. Soon, less and less of the lower class' taxes made it to the walled city of Jin Fóll, where the wealthy hoarded their bounty, and hid.

Of course, the peasant towns that remained loyal to Gurinn's feudal lords felt the pressure from the Imperial army. Embargos could pop up anywhere, and the punishment for stolen goats sure was steep that year. But that's Discernment for you, huh?

Ahn wondered where they had put his armour, if they had just left it out there in the trees. The thought was unexpectedly upsetting. He hadn't even wanted that armour, but his father had been so glad to gift it to him, he had looked so proud—

Pay attention, Ahn. I'm trying to keep you alive here.

By the time the Imperial force made it to Jin Fóll, the city had already begun to feel the farmers' ongoing lack of tribute. Even still, they refused to open their doors—and thus began the Thousand Hour Siege. It was brutal. At one point, the army allowed in a shipment of grain as a mercy, but it was rotten through. Then the water supply turned foul. Divine intervention. And while the wealthy lords suffered inside the city of Jin Fóll, the peasantry thrived in the countryside.

At least, until Imperial assistance stopped. The rations were halted. The road stopped being built. No more music, that's for sure. And it was all because Jin Fóll wouldn't open its gates to the invaders and give in to the force that had tilled the rest of the continent.

The Imperial army was organized and powerful. They could have taken Jin Fóll on their own and paid the blood price, but it was cheaper to motivate the farmers with hunger and propaganda. The rumours stoked by the Courtesan General—the wicked doings of the nobles, the feasts they made of their servants, their intention to punish the farmers who accepted Imperial aid—made the poor an army in their own right. Wasn't she a great-great-aunt of yours, or something?

Anyway, the city fell in one thousand hours. Ninety-eight years and one thousand hours, and Qiao Sidh had claimed

Gurinn, and the continent, for the Empire. Death at the prongs of a pitchfork rather than the edge of a blade.

"Why are you telling me this?" Ahn mumbled in Qiao Sidhur. He felt like a madman, drunk on information, on the pure sense of spirit coursing through him. He couldn't remember the last time the boy had come through so clearly. "You've been so quiet, Schenn. I thought that you—"

"Shut up tsongkar," snapped his captor, half-shoving him up a few bumpy stairs.

I'm telling you this because there's something you don't know, Éongrir Ahnschen—

The name jabbed at him, made him want to weep, made him hungry for his blade—

I grew up in Haojost, one of those peasant towns in the land my ancestors called Gurinn. No one alive remembers the world before Imperial rule, but we know the stories—the Empire's stories, and our own. We're not stupid, Ahn. We know how we were used, and to what end. We had little love for Jin Fóll, but the road Qiao Sidh built was only ever intended to lead to the heart of the Empire. A vein, not an artery.

Don't get me wrong, we get by. It's not so bad back home for the simple farm folk, smiling and waving when the royal parade comes through for the anniversary of our Imperial Adoption. New holidays, new language, aren't we oh-so-thankful. It's easy to smile at someone who only ever passes through town.

Sometimes I wonder how many years of loyalty you can buy with one thousand hours. I know, I know—the Empire is generous, and so the Empire is everlasting. Everyone loves the Empire, they say so in the books. And they built us a road.

But there are cracks in the road, Ahn. It wasn't put down even, not even at the start. Maybe you don't see them, but I thought you ought to know.

Better late than never, right?

The blindfold was yanked from his face.

Ahn blinked back the brightness. He had been brought onto a large, platformed gazebo and was surrounded on all sides by elders propped up in chairs. Their cheeks were tattooed, and their faces were not friendly. He could see townsfolk gathering, trying to peer in and get a look at him.

His hand flinched against the ropes again. He wanted to give Schenn another tap, to ask for advice that actually made sense. In response, he felt the bite of a spear against his back. Apparently Lita Soon had not yet left him.

The woman who had brought him in, Polha something, addressed the circle in her language. He didn't follow a word.

So it will be a trial then, Ahn thought, feeling far from himself. *A trial I can't participate in.*

Years of etiquette training just to die without getting a word in. Or else find a weapon and attempt to cut his way out. He wasn't sure which thought made him feel more sick. This was all wrong, he hadn't even wanted to come to Nona Fahang, he hadn't even wanted to come to this *continent.* He was supposed to go home, to finish his time at Asgørindad, to get married and have children and become a master one day. He was supposed to live enough of a life for him and Schenn both, not die alone in the Untilled.

"Ahn!" His head shot up at the sound of Sohmeng's voice. Maybe he wasn't completely alone. Not yet.

She ran over to him, trailed by a woman—well, maybe not, he hadn't heard their name yet—who seemed like they had been crying. Upon closer inspection, so did Sohmeng.

This was alarming, seeing as Sohmeng was decidedly not the crying type. He forced himself out of his self-pity, straightening up as best as he could with a spear ready to be embedded in his back. "Sohmeng," he said, looking her over for injury. "Are you alright? Did they hurt you?"

"No!" she insisted, laughing a little hysterically. "No, this is my—this is . . . " She trailed off, looking at the circle of elders, and quickly ducked her head in the closest approximation of respect that Ahn had ever seen on her. "Grand Ones, my greatest apologies for the intrusion on your Gate."

The person beside her shot out a translation, resting a familiar hand on her shoulder. As the elders spoke, they continued the task of translating, moving smoothly between languages.

"Our *gate*, as you call it, is open to all travellers of Gãepongwei," one of them said. Sohmeng frowned a little at the word, and Ahn wondered if she didn't recognize it either. "Though I must say, you are quite unlike any traveller I have met before. Wandering with a pack of sãoni! And with—"

"This tsongkar," another one of the elders said, looking at Ahn with distrust. He said nothing. It was probably wise not to speak unless spoken to.

"Honestly, we bumped into you completely by accident! Which I'm—I'm really grateful for." Sohmeng rested her hand overtop her translator's. "I really need your help. My hmun, *our* hmun, Ateng—it's in trouble. See, the Sky Bridge—"

"Your father has told us about Ateng's troubles," the elder interrupted. Ahn glanced at the translator, making the connection. He was glad he hadn't misgendered the man; that wouldn't have done much for an already ugly first impression. "And we would be glad to hear updates on your hmun's situation *after* you explain your connection to this young man."

Ahn could see the way Sohmeng's jaw was clenched, the way her fists balled in barely-contained frustration. It was a strange contrast to the quiet dread that had knocked the wind from him, leaving him numb.

"My partner and I found Ahn alone, separated from his people. We were hoping we could help each other out." She glanced at Ahn, a question on her face. He wanted so badly to explain to her that that much had not changed, but felt frozen in this public forum, his left ear still ringing. "See, his hmun—"

"I will stop you there, girl," an elder interrupted, leaning forward in their seat with a vicious glare that reminded Ahn of his first Discernment master. "He has no *hmun.* All in our network, in Gãepongwei, are hmun. He is an infection, a pest."

"Do you want to hear what I have to say or not?" Sohmeng

snapped. Her father was translating with an apologetic look, but Sohmeng made no move to soften her tone. "We found Ahn alone, and were planning on bringing him back to his campaign—the, the group of people he came here with. I thought that he could talk to whoever's in charge and explain that they interfered with the sãoni's migration route, and—"

"The sãoni are not our biggest problem right now," the elder retorted.

A deadly quiet seemed to overtake Sohmeng, and she took a moment before she spoke. " . . . you know, they kind of are, actually. Seeing as they destroyed my family's *life*."

Where many of the elders looked at the two of them with sympathy, the speaker was unmoved. "And now you cohabitate with them," they said. "And with him."

A nearby elder leaned forward, gesturing to Sohmeng. "Is that a ring of his you wear?"

"I got this from a bird!" Sohmeng shouted, pressing her palms to her eyes. The silver caught the light, sending a murmur through the gathered crowd. "I didn't even know Ahn back then!"

Ahn felt overcome by a nauseating sense of stage fright. Being raised in the royal family had gotten him used to being in the public eye, but he had never known how to manage the rare occasions when that eye turned critical. Now, he was literally in the center of a room that hated him.

There were too many voices for Sohmeng's father to keep up with. Soon, one rose above the rest, and the room quieted to hear it out. Apparently this congested form of communication was typical for this hmun.

The speaker shifted in their chair, as if trying to get a better look at them. "Thank you for your account, Sohmeng. As we have already said, we are glad to hear Ateng's troubles later. Your father has long been a member of our community, and we would not dismiss his daughter so quickly. But we must consider the more immediate trouble that stands before us."

Sohmeng seemed more than ready to continue arguing, but forced herself still. "Yes, Grandmother Pel."

Ahn kept his eyes to the ground, but he could feel the elder's attention fixed on him.

"What is your name, boy?" Grandmother Pel asked.

It had been a long time since anyone had referred to him as a boy. Since his Six-ing, Ahn had existed somewhere between man and walking myth, with expectations placed on him from both directions. He had taken great pains in university to let himself be seen as young again, and even then, Master Hvu was one of the only people who truly treated him as a novice. Hearing it now felt less like a shame tactic than it did a second chance. The young were always more easily forgiven.

"Éongrir Ahnschen-Eløndham, Qøngemzhir, Sølshendasá, Siengunghvøs—Eleventh Prince to the Qiao Sidhur Empire." He enunciated slowly and clearly. As he spoke, he got down on one knee before them. The act was disorienting; he had never kneeled to anyone but his royal parents. "You can call me Ahnschen, if it pleases you."

Simply *Ahn* would have been easier on their tongues, but he couldn't dismiss Schenn again, not after the first clear communication he had been given in months.

"...Ahn, get up," Sohmeng muttered, tugging at his shirtsleeve. "What are you doing?"

"It doesn't please us to call you much of anything, Ahnschen," Grandmother Pel said. "Might you know why?"

He hesitated. "The—the campaign, yes?"

"The invasion." *Invasion* wasn't a perfect translation for the word she was using. That word was more personal, intimate. A word meant for transgressions between neighbours rather than large-scale acts of domination. He had learned it back in the first hmun he had landed in. Invaded. "Over the past cycle, we have seen attacks on two hmun in the north—Hosaisi, and Kongkempei. Our trading partners, our cousins. Some have been forced to flee to Nona Fahang, to seek our protection from your—"

He didn't understand the last word she said. What he *did* understand was the sharp intake of breath from Sohmeng beside him, the pummeling disappointment.

But this was all wrong—this wasn't how it was supposed to have happened. He thought of long nights in the command tents with his sister, going over Qiao Sidhur historical strategies. They were supposed to first greet the people of the Untilled, to welcome them into the Empire. It was never supposed to have begun with violence. If their strategy was sound enough, any war they did wage would have been noble.

"That . . . that isn't right," he said weakly. The spear in his back pressed harder, forcing him forward to avoid being pierced. "We were supposed to talk first, to—"

He looked to Sohmeng out of habit, seeking her help in translating the concept of peaceful negotiation, friendly contact. But she kept her eyes on the ground. Something ached in Ahn's chest, but he lacked the language to explain it to her.

Her father spoke in her stead: "Negotiate?"

"Negotiate," Ahn repeated, feeling the hollowness of the syllables in his throat compared to the apparent truth of the matter. "We were supposed to negotiate. The Empire, Qiao Sidh, my—my home. We have a lot to offer, we . . ."

His explanation suddenly sounded ridiculous to his ears, a child's fantasy. Why would the people of the Untilled, of Eiji, care about the sacred expansion of some far-off empire? Why should his good intentions matter if they had only led to bloodshed? What did this rainforest owe to strangers who entered without asking?

I thought you ought to know. Better late than never, right?

"Ahnschen," Grandmother Pel said. "Seeing as you are their prince, I take it you have played a part in these invasions."

"Yes," he said softly.

"And now you enter our hmun," she continued. "Asking for . . . what, mercy?"

Ahn had not asked for anything. But he wanted it, and that seemed to count. "Yes," he said once more.

"Despite the harm you've caused."

"Yes."

"Despite those you've killed."

The spear at his back suddenly felt too sharp, too close. In his mind, it pushed itself straight through to his front, yanking down in an old imitation of the scar across his chest. He tasted the pink sands of the arena, the thick incense—

No, not that—

He saw Kongkempei, the hmun that had first welcomed them. He saw fires spreading through the clearing where they had shared so many meals. He heard his sister's voice and felt his own dread like an eel he'd swallowed alive, he saw the stranger turn on him, screaming in fear, saw his own sword raised again why must these things always end on the edge of his sword—

"Yes," he said, and he could hear the way his voice broke like a child's. The elders had asked for the name of a boy and been given the crimes of a man. It made him long for summer afternoons, for a roughened hand in his own. For more than a single fingerbone in consolation.

All was quiet in the circle of elders. Ahn heard nothing, felt nothing, but his own ragged breathing, bodily insistence that he was still, unbearably, alive. And so came the consequences.

"We sit under the final day of this cycle's Pel phase," spoke the grandmother who shared its name. "Do you know what that means?"

Ahn shook his head.

"It can be an uncomfortable time for our people," she explained. The people around her certainly looked uncomfortable, though they did not interrupt. "A time of sacrifice, and difficult decisions. Your arrival speaks to the gods' own sense of humour, or else their desire to challenge us." She paused, looking at him as though she might find the punchline to the joke. "It is also the phase I carry for our community, which gives me the final word on what we do with you. Had you arrived tomorrow, you would be in Grandmother Dongi's capable hands."

"I'd have fed you to the lizards," Dongi said flatly, rubbing her thumb over her walking stick.

"Grandmother Pel, please—" Sohmeng stepped forward, only to be silenced by a gesture from the Grandmother. Ahn could hear the blood pounding in his ears.

The old woman continued on as though there had been no interruption. "There are a few ways in which we could handle this situation: exile, execution, or reconciliation. Though exile might not be wise. We can't have you running back to your own and causing us even more trouble in the long run."

Ahn said nothing. Were their positions reversed, Qiao Sidh would not have even offered these people a trial.

"We are all eager to see justice carried out, boy. But you must understand, it is rare for Nona Fahang to manage the crimes of outsiders. This is not our way." Grandmother Pel paused, looking at him critically. "I do not think we yet know what justice looks like for someone like you. We do not know you. My decision is that we require more information to make a choice we will not regret. We will wait for a time that is more—"

"—auspicious," Sohmeng said breathlessly. And though Ahn did not believe in the gods of these people, this place, he realized that he had been saved. For now.

Grandmother Pel gave him a long look. "Judgment will be passed under the moons of Ginhãe. It is what the phase was made for. Until then, you stay in the walls of Nona Fahang, under close supervision. Explain yourself, if it's what you wish. Atone, if you know how. Or sit alone and rot. In roughly thirty days' time, once we have had a good look at what you are, we will decide what will become of you."

Thirty days. Thirty days to earn the right to his life. "Thank you, Grandmother Pel," he said, doing his best to appear humble.

"Hn. Thank the gods, not me." The woman turned her attention to Sohmeng. "As for you, Sohmeng Par—take the evening with your father. A reunion is long overdue. We will address your troubles tomorrow, but for now you are dismissed. Their watchful eyes upon you."

Sohmeng looked ready to protest, and turned to her father, gesturing to Ahn and speaking rapidly in Atengpa. She was visibly aggravated. Perhaps she had adjusted to living outside of a hmun, to carrying out her days without having to answer to anyone. It was not the sort of life he could imagine, but it suited her and Hei both.

Thirty days, he thought to himself. Would the sãoni have moved on by that time? If they did, would Sohmeng and Hei leave him in this place alone? How would he ever get home without them?

A firm hand on his arm, and he met the disapproving gaze of Sohmeng's father. "The scouts will find a place to hold you," he said warily. "A warrior will keep watch over you at all times. If you act out—"

"They'll kill you if you doing anything stupid, Ahn," Sohmeng said matter-of-factly. "So just . . . don't. Okay?" She started working at untying the ropes at his wrists despite the protests of the scout behind him. "No more bad choices."

"I understand," he said. She had not forgiven him, that much was clear. Frankly, there was no reason she *should*, given his connection to the campaign. But she had not dismissed him. His fingers tingled as the blood returned to his wrists, and he immediately reached for Schenn. "No more bad choices."

He tugged at the earpiece, searching for approval, for an explanation on how he might begin repairing the cracks in this long road. No sound came, none but the tap of flesh meeting bone.

Eight

THE LAST TIME SOHMENG had seen her father, he was preparing with his wife to descend Fochão Dangde with the rest of Ateng's best traders, trackers, and warriors. This was early after the fall of the Bridge, when the hmun hadn't yet learned to treat these expeditions as death sentences. Even still, the morning had been tense and tearful, one of the only times she could remember seeing Grandmother Mi look truly afraid.

Tonão Sol had donned his travelling garments, sleeves lined with dried silvertongue, and tied his hair back in a low bun. When it was time for him to go, Sohmeng could not think of a single thing to say, and simply squeezed him as tight as she could, as if that could keep him safe. The feeling of his arms around her nearly convinced her that things could be okay. Then, as she was hugging her mother, she heard the terrible sound of Viunwei sobbing. She watched his shaking shoulders, his fingers gripping tight to the man's shirt, and soon she was crying too.

Angry child that she was, she spent a few years convinced *that* was the reason her parents hadn't come back for her. She was young, and scared, and wandered her way into the belief that behaving like something was final would manifest that finality into reality. To be fearless, or else callous, was a Par-shaped personal prayer, a small act of storytelling to rebel against her own helplessness.

Had she ever really let that belief go? Maybe not.

Maybe that was why she could not bring herself to let loose the storm of screaming, raging love and hurt that had built up over the years. Perhaps that was what kept her calm as she followed her father, very much alive, into his new home. It was made of the same twisting trees that the rest of Nona Fahang used as architectural foundation. It was so different from their homes in Fochão and Sodão Dangde; no wovenstone, no too-low stone ceilings, no animal pelts to hold in the heat. Low evening light peered in through the wooden walls. There was a hammock, a chair, a small box for his things that also served as a table. Sweet-smelling herbs hung from the ceiling, plants that they never could have accessed back in Ateng. It was lovely, and well-cared for, and entirely unfamiliar.

"This is your house?" she asked. It was an obvious question, but when even the obvious was unbelievable, it seemed like a good place to start.

"My room," Tonão said, sitting down on the hammock with a little grunt. His left leg moved stiffly. "It's an extension of another family's house. They gave me this private space after they took me in. It belonged to a grandparent who had passed in the months before."

Normally curious, Sohmeng couldn't find it in her to question how a house like this was grown, or even to care about the people who lived just on the other side of the hanging, leafy curtain that separated the rooms.

"Dad . . ." she said, but her voice caught on the edge of all the questions she never expected to have the chance to ask. Tonão patted the spot beside him, and she sat, leaning against him and wondering how such a small room could hold so much empty space.

"I've imagined you here so many times," the man said. His voice wavered. "Playing with your dice in the corner, or arguing with your brother on the other side of the wall. Learning inappropriate songs from your mother—"

Sohmeng squeezed her eyes shut. "Mom?" she asked, the name a question and a plea.

She knew the answer in the way Tonão's shoulders fell, in the slow breath he took to steady himself. "She's gone, Sohmeng."

After so many years, Sohmeng thought she had learned the shape of her grief in full. She knew every inch of her anger, every ounce of her righteous fury, each and every pang of sorrow that had hit her at all hours of the day. But never had she imagined a world where Tonão Sol lived without Lahni Par at his side. It was a wrongness she hadn't prepared for, an unfairness she did not think the gods would stoop to.

"I hate that," she said, a bitter laugh rattling out of her chest. "I hate that so much, Dad."

Tonão just nodded. "Me too, little trouble. I hate it every day."

The nickname made her cover her mouth, made the hurt rise fuller and faster, demanding answers. "What happened?"

"Too many sãoni," he said. "Not enough of a plan. Your mother . . . was brave. Always brave. Braver than the rest of us, right up to the end." He stopped, taking a moment to compose himself. His eyes were circled, his smile a halting thing. "As far as I know, I was the only member of the party to make it to Nona Fahang. And even then, there was less of me than there was up in Ateng." He patted his shin, and it made a hollow sound.

Sohmeng's eyes widened as her father pulled up his pant leg to reveal a piece of wood where his lower leg used to be. It was smoothed down, carved into a vine-like pattern. Down the front were four lunar phases: Sol, Par, Soon, Par. She instinctively reached to touch it, then hesitated.

"Go ahead," Tonão said, and the way he laughed reminded her of what it was like when she was young, getting into everything without asking. "Handiwork of the best doctors and craftspeople in Nona Fahang. It's pretty, isn't it?"

"Does it hurt?" she asked.

"Not like it used to. And on days where the new limb digs in, I have people to help me with the padding." As he rolled the fabric back down, she caught sight of old scars on his arms, small points that had not been there before. She tried not to think about what he must have looked like, those many years ago. What her mother must have looked like, in the end. "This hmun saved my life, took care of me, body and mind. I've lived here since, trying to make my way. Trying to figure out how we could ever . . ."

He gestured to her, and she felt the four years between them, a gap greater than any mountain crossing. It felt tenuous and frightening to be trying so hard to bridge it now, like any wrong move could snap them apart once more. Her mind raced, searching for security, and found trouble in its stead.

"Nona Fahang knows about Sky Bridge," she said. "You told them."

"I did," Tonão said.

"And they know Ateng is stuck." The idea burned her up quicker than fire-sand. Another hmun had known about their predicament all this time. "Why haven't they come to help us?" she demanded.

Her father's expression softened. "They tried, Sohmeng. Three years ago, at my request. I went with them to try and map a long route to Sodão Dangde, but the sãoni at Fochão Dangde are territorial beyond what you'd see in the migrating colonies. We tried to navigate around them, but we were stalked at every turn, and I—I cannot ask Nona Fahang to send its people to die in droves as we have done in Ateng. It isn't fair."

"*Each to itself, but all in harmony*," Sohmeng quoted,

angry to have her distress met with reason. "There's no harmony if Ateng is trapped and starved, Dad. The batengmun are already dead, we don't want the rest of—"

She watched his face fall and immediately regretted her words. That wasn't how she'd wanted to tell him. The man in front of her seemed to have retained all of his gentleness, his kindness. But now he seemed fragile in a way she had never known. It was an unexpected pain, to meet her father this way, as a fellow adult.

"Dad, I . . . I didn't mean . . ." There was no backtracking. She tugged on her bangs, exhaling sharply. Burning godseye, this was so hard.

"They didn't make it, then," the man said.

"No," Sohmeng replied, trying not to think too hard about the figures huddled around the long-dead fire. "I'm sorry."

"Me too, Sohmeng." Tonão sounded exhausted. More than that, he sounded *guilty*, and Sohmeng had no idea what to say in response. "And—and everyone else? In Ateng, the family. Your brother, Grandmother Mi. Are they well? Are they alright?"

"Oh!" She took his hands, feeling selfish for not having told him immediately. "Yes! Dad, yes, they're fine. I mean, Viunwei is still Viunwei so take that as you will, but he's good. Tall and sullen. And Grandmother Mi is great, still causing trouble." Her smile wavered as she allowed herself to wonder how her own disappearance might have changed them. It was so much loss for one family to take. "At least that's how it was the last time I saw them."

"Which brings me to my next question." Sohmeng's father freed his hands from hers, reaching up instead to hold her cheeks like when she was little. His hands felt so much smaller now, made her realize just how much she had grown over the years. With a bewildered sigh, he shook his head. "How in two dark moons did you end up in Eiji?"

Sohmeng couldn't help the grin that spread across her face. She hadn't realized how eager she was to share her story, to spin what could have been a tragedy into the absolute marvel that it was. "When I figured out they wouldn't let me become a trader, I decided I had to take the long route."

She told him about the long route. The argument at Chehangma's Gate and Viunwei's remarkable inability to communicate with Jinho. The egg collecting and the fall, finding Hei and learning about the sãoni. It was strange to speak of the sãoni as found family, when she was looking at the literal harm they had done to her family of origin, but Tonão did not stop her. Rather, he looked at her with pride, with wonder. It was very similar, she imagined, to the way she used to stare at him when he told stories of trading down in Eiji.

She told him about the fight with Blacktooth, and the long ride up Sodão Dangde. She told him about the batengmun, and with every word felt the lonely weight of their deaths rest a little lighter on her heart. It was easier to bear with someone else listening, to have a witness to her own witnessing.

Hei's story she kept private and simple. She described them as an exile who had made their own way—anything beyond that was not hers to share.

"And this Hei," her father asked. He took her hand, examining the ring on her finger. "You two are . . . ?"

Sohmeng wrinkled her nose. One of the unexpectedly awkward parts of finding out her father was alive was explaining her relationship situation. She never understood why people had to make such a big deal about these things. "Yeah. I mean—yeah. We care about each other."

"And . . . ?" He raised an eyebrow so high she thought it would reach the ceiling.

"I don't know, Dad!" she said, throwing her hands in the air. "We're partners! Weird lizard partners! Happy?"

Tonão laughed loud enough to fill the room. "I am happy, little trouble. I'm so proud of you."

"For being someone's weird lizard partner?"

"For finding your *way*," he said. He pushed back a piece of hair that had fallen loose from her bun. The motion was so completely *parental* that it stopped her snark in its tracks, leaving her embarrassed and grateful all at once. "I don't care who you're courting, if you marry or not. I don't care if you're a trader or a builder or a cook. All I've ever wanted is for you to find your own way, Sohmeng. To become." He cracked a smile at his own pun, but it faded, muddying into a discomfort left nearly seventeen years unresolved. "Listen . . . I know that we, your mother and I—we didn't always give you the, the resources to—"

The privacy flap opened, startling away the rest of Tonão's thoughts. In the threshold stood the scout with the braided hair, holding an earthen teapot and two small wooden cups.

"Eakang," Tonão said with a wince of a smile. "What timing."

"Sorry to interrupt," they chirped in Dulpongpa, looking between Sohmeng and her father with an overly familiar smile. For some reason it made Sohmeng's skin crawl. "I brought you tea!"

Sohmeng followed her father's lead and took a cup. "Did you come here about Ahn? Is something wrong? Tell me he wasn't being a meathead."

They blinked at her. "No? I just thought you might be thirsty . . . ?"

"Ah." Tonão laughed a little. "I didn't explain—this house belongs to Eakang's family. They came to get me, when they heard someone from Ateng was at the door. When you gave them your name . . . "

"I had to meet you!" Eakang said, bright-eyed. "I've heard so much about you from your dad and I just couldn't believe you were really here, all the way from the mountains. Oh, sorry, I never properly introduced myself." They brought the teapot to her, filling her cup with another smile. "I'm Eakang Minhal."

Sohmeng dropped the cup, hissing as the hot tea hit her hand. She hardly felt it over the wave of shock, hardly heard the sound of Eakang rapidly apologizing and trying to clean up. *That can't be right*, she thought,

Minhal. They said their name was—

"Would you mind giving us a moment, Eakang?" her father said, taking Sohmeng's burned hand worriedly.

"Right," they said, quickly getting up. "No problem! Sorry, Damdão."

Damdão. *Damdão?*

Sohmeng stared at her father, all of the closure they had been reaching for suddenly tearing back open. Since when had her father been a surrogate to anyone? And since when had there been Minhals who weren't exiled?

She felt sick. She felt suddenly like she didn't exist, like she was falling upwards. She stood, shaking out her hand and trying to get her bearings.

"Oh, Sohmeng, this isn't how I wanted this to . . . " Tonão trailed off, looking at her with a pleading expression. She wondered if he could see it too, the nearly tangible space that had suddenly been cleaved between them. "Let me explain—"

"You replaced us?" she asked. It sounded petty even to her ears.

"Never," Tonão said vehemently, pulling himself to standing. "Eakang's family looked after me when I was still recovering, and I became close with their parents. Later, when Eakang's mother was having some fertility problems, I offered myself as their damwei. When I got pregnant, Eakang began calling me Damdão."

"But you never—" Sohmeng felt overwhelmed, trying to grapple with the history she was used to. "Mom carried me and Viunwei both. Why would you—"

To his credit, her father looked about as unprepared for this conversation as she felt. At least that was one thing they still had in common. "It was something my body could do, and I thought I would try. They had treated me as family, and I had come to see them that way too. After all they had done for me, the friendship they had extended when I was alone . . . it seemed like a kindness I could show."

"And Mom?" Sohmeng snapped, unable to stop herself.

"I will never love anyone in this world like I loved your mother," Tonão said, and the pain in his voice stung Sohmeng doubly for her own anger. "But I have found dear friends in this family, and it has been an honour to play a part in raising their children."

It was more than Sohmeng could handle. Despite her father's explanation, she felt betrayed. She turned away from the feeling, focusing instead on something she knew she had the right to be angry about.

"And Minhal, Dad?" she asked, hating the old fear that ran through her with speaking the phase name. "What about that?"

Her father bit his lip, guilt written all over his face. "Nona Fahang has a different belief system. Minhals aren't exiled here. They're . . . they're treated as harbingers of the unexpected, powerful forces of change. They even have a space for the Grand One." Sohmeng hadn't bothered to count the chairs in the Grand One's gate. Why would she? When she didn't see an empty place, she had simply assumed nothing was set for Minhals and turned her attention back to Ahn. "It's a different interpretation of the cycle,

Sohmeng. It . . . it varies, from hmun to hmun."

She covered her face. The room felt too small, suffocating. All the wonder of finding her father had distorted further with every complication, until she was being pressed on all sides by feelings she hadn't even been given time to put names to.

She realized her father was still talking. What was he saying? "—could tell them, if you wanted. They would be very—"

"I need some air," she said abruptly, turning to go.

"Sohmeng—"

She shook out her hands, trying to steady the unwieldy feeling of panic. It was so big, only familiar to her as an outsider, when she watched it overtake Hei. How did they do this so often? She wished they were here. Godless night, she wished she was back with them and the sãoni. Why had she sent them away? "I'm not—I'm not leaving you, Dad. I'll be back soon. I just . . . this is just—I need a minute."

She was out the door before she could hear whatever it was he had to say. On all sides she was surrounded by walls, lush and alive and keeping her trapped with a group of strangers. Even the sky above, gone dark save for the illumination of Ama and Chehang, felt like another form of confinement.

This afternoon, she had wandered into a lost piece of home completely by accident. And now here she was, desperate for space. Wishing herself an exile all over again, if only to find solace in a wrong she could understand.

NINE

AHN HAD SLEPT IN PLENTY of unusual places before, but none quite compared to the pygmy hog pen.

When the Grand Ones ordered Ahn to be kept under watch, they had failed to specify *where.* Sensing an opportunity, the scouts charged with his transport had dropped him in a cramped, stinky enclosure with dozens of small fuzzy animals, and minimal leg room. Ahn didn't dare protest. The throbbing scrape on his cheek was a reminder that it would be in his best interests to go along with their wishes.

Thus, the eleventh prince of Qiao Sidh spent the night trying his very best not to end up sat in a pile of poo. He squirmed, trying to find the most comfortable wooden pole to rest his spine against. And even when he managed to find a position that mostly kept the hogs from chewing at him—how did he manage to be considered *chewable* by so many species?—sleep did not come easily. Throughout the night he jumped awake at the sound of his overseers' voices, audible but unintelligible. Without the assistance of a translator, he was a prisoner of his own helpless tongue.

It would have been easier if Sohmeng was with him. His gratitude for her presence had quickly turned to anxiety over her absence. Who else in this place saw him as a person? Who else here cared if he lived or died? Sohmeng had sounded so certain when they were still outside the hmun's walls. She had promised to bring him home and, despite everything, he had dared to believe her.

Was it still possible? Would she even want to help him, after a night to think it over?

The Grand Ones' interrogation had rattled him. He always knew that the people of the Untilled might greet him with suspicion, but he was only just now beginning to understand why they might respond with *anger*. With hatred.

He watched the scurrying of nocturnal animals playing in the treetops; despite the bounty of food below, none of them dared venture too far down the high woven walls. Having grown up around plenty of wildlife on the western island of Hvallánzhou, Ahn knew that this was more a sign of healthy caution than respect, but the sight was still intriguing. In a world where human civilizations were so naturally integrated with the raw, untamed land, how did the animals have such a clear idea of what was and was not their space?

His eyes traced the treetops, seeking clear borders, but found none. Instead he caught sight of a seeking star, and his heart ached with old memories. Schenn knew all about seeking stars, celestial bodies by which shepherds and sailors and all manner of travellers found their way home. The boy had pointed them out, listing off their names with practiced ease, while Ahn had closed his eyes and imagined they were on a ship together, headed somewhere far away.

One of the pygmy hogs wiggled its chubby little body under the crook of his knee, seeking warmth. Ahn kept still, staring at the twinkling light above them. If he had ever known the name of this star or its constellation, it was long forgotten now.

"Look Schenn," he muttered in Qiao Sidhur. "It's like trying to share a bed with you. All he needs to do is take the blankets."

It shouldn't have surprised Ahn to find the silent treatment had returned. Even still, it stung. He curled against the side of the pen, using his hand as a pillow, hoping to keep the both of them as comfortable as he could.

He was awoken at sunrise by screeching from the trees, followed by a veritable explosion of feathers. Not exactly the royal, full body massage wake-up he longed for, but at least there wasn't any confusion about where he was. He pushed himself up with a groan, feeling the protest of his muscles. To the dismay of the blanket of pygmy hogs, he lifted himself to standing, grimacing at the smell clinging to his clothing. Somehow he doubted laundry service was included in the prisoner-of-war package, but it seemed worth it to ask. There was no point staying filthy if he didn't have to.

He ran his hands through his hair, trying to neaten it up before tying it into a ponytail. *A prisoner of war.* He supposed that was technically what he was now. Ólawen would never let him hear the end of it.

Out in the hmun, he could hear the sounds of people getting ready to begin the day. He rolled out his neck, eyeing the latch on the gate—

"Stay where you are, tsongkar trash."

—too suspiciously, apparently, according to Lita Soon. Ahn winced, bracing himself to face the man.

"Good morning," he said in Dulpongpa, attempting a cordial tone.

Lita glowered at him. Oddly enough, Ahn wasn't bothered by it. Weeks with Hei had prepared him for minor personal slights.

"I was wondering—"

"If you have to piss, do it with the other animals," the scout said, looking away from him.

Crass though it was, it answered one of Ahn's questions. Though it wasn't really the answer he was hoping for. "About that," he said. "The animals have . . . damaged my clothing. Might I wash it somewhere?"

Lita sneered, kicking at the pygmy hogs' trough.

"Is . . . is that really fair to the hogs?" Ahn asked.

The scout turned to face him, stepping right up to the fence. Fast though Lita was, Ahn didn't flinch back from the attempted intimidation. He held his own, choosing to meet the furious, exhausted gaze of the man in front of him. Because up close, it had to be said, Lita Soon really did look like he'd had a night as sleepless as Ahn's.

Was that what it was like, Ahn wondered, to be the kind of person who felt anger all the way through? He'd never managed it himself, always quick to forgive and pull back from conflict before it became too difficult to manage.

Perhaps that habit was what drove him, despite his better judgment, to apologize. "I think I may have wronged you in some way. I am sorry for that."

"You think?" Lita said, his voice deadly quiet. "You think you may have wronged me?"

"It seems so," Ahn responded, half a smile on his lips. It disappeared the second Lita's fist made hard contact with his jaw. He stumbled, but quickly righted himself before he could step on any of the tiny creatures at his feet.

"You really want to smirk at me right now, tsongkar? Little *prince*?"

Ahn touched his cheek gingerly, trying to control his expression. That nervous tic of a smile had gotten him in trouble before, but not like this. "I'm sorry," he said again, the words throbbing. "I was not trying to—"

"Soon!" another voice called. Lita abruptly stepped back from the fence, rage tugging at his scar. It still looked fresh. He looked like he wanted to say something more, but the voice called to him again in his hmunpa, and he quickly walked away, replaced by another scout.

Ahn thought about greeting them, about trying to start off on the right foot with *someone*, but they didn't so much as acknowledge him. He assumed they would have to say something eventually, but as the morning crept by, doubt crept in. Uncertain of what else there was to be done, Ahn settled back against the fence and watched the world go on without him.

He had never been good at stillness. The slower his body went, the faster his mind picked up speed in compensation. The best solution was to keep himself moving, or to spend time with other people. He wasn't necessarily chatty, but he thrived in social environments. It was part of what made his time at Asgørindad so satisfying: engaging as his studies were, he was also able to lose himself in the vibrant student life.

Once his suitemates got past the shock of sharing space with a member of the Imperial family, they had accepted him warmly into their friend group. He went with them to pub nights and shows, even joined a couple of student organizations. He wasn't naïve enough to imagine people really thought of him as ordinary, but their acceptance was enough. Once he'd heard one joke about his face being on the money, he'd heard them all—and it didn't hurt that he could occasionally use his status to pull favours. It was easy enough to be the other when it didn't come with ostracization.

It was different here in Nona Fahang, where his otherness earned him active malice. They hated him for participating in this campaign that had, apparently, gone much further than he realized. He had always known that war was central to Conquest; he had trained for the grim and glorious reality of it. But Conquest began first with discussion, negotiation—the agreement was meant to be beneficial to everybody, right? That was why he had prepared so studiously for the campaign, practicing what little Dulpongpa and local customs they had recorded from first contact over five years ago. The point was communication, not tyranny. They were spreading cultural values that other people would *want* to receive. It was an honourable thing, wasn't it?

The idea nagged at Ahn, made him inexplicably frustrated. He had so many questions for Ólawen, questions he feared he'd never have a chance to get answered. He wanted desperately to fix things, to shape the world back into something he understood. As he watched Nona Fahang carry out its daily life, he was overcome with the urge to explain that whatever had happened, it wasn't his *fault.* He hadn't planned for violence or wanted it or even participated half as much as they seemed to believe—

The thought unraveled like a silk thread. Each justification sounded more hollow than the last. Whether or not anyone *should* have been hurt didn't matter; it had happened, and there were consequences.

He took out his ponytail, replaced it with a braid. Unbraided. Did it again.

The hours passed, Ahn's stomach rumbled, and nothing made sense. He was getting ready to start stacking pygmy hogs when Sohmeng finally showed up.

"Burning godseye," she said, struggling with the latch of the pen. "They just left you here alone?"

"Not alone." Ahn stood up, trying to figure out how to

exit without setting the animals loose on Nona Fahang. "I had the hogs."

"Yeah, I can smell that." At the sight of the attempted jail break, a guard ran over to try and put a stop to things, but Sohmeng shut it down. "*Kept under close watch*, the Grand Ones said. Well *I'm* watching him now. If you've got an issue, take it up with them or shove it."

Based on how quickly they ran off, Ahn could only assume the guard went with option one. "Thank you," he said, hopping out of the pen and shutting the door to the sound of irritable squeaking.

"No, I'm sorry," Sohmeng said, sounding aggravated. "I should have . . . or—ugh, I don't know. Come on, let's clean you up and get you something to eat."

From what Ahn caught of the conversation, it took some persuasion for Sohmeng's father to allow the Qiao Sidhur prisoner into the family's shower stall. Once the man relented and left them alone, Sohmeng turned away from Ahn with a heavy sigh, holding out a hand. "Clothes," she said. "I'll try to wash them while you wash the rest of you. Just pull on the rope for water, soap's in the bowl."

The shower was a clever contraption: a hanging pump in the wooden stall released collected rainwater from a bucket overhead. It was much chillier than the heated baths he was used to back home, but he wasn't about to complain. Not when he smelled better than he had in weeks.

He scrubbed his body, sighing in relief at the fresh citrus smell. Through the small gaps in the wood, he could see Sohmeng sitting on a log and working at his clothes in a bucket. The fabric looked flimsy compared to the sãoni skin she wore.

As he started on his hair, Sohmeng blurted, "Look, can we talk about this whole invasion thing?"

Ahn froze. "If you would like."

"I mean, I wouldn't," she said, scrubbing harder at the fabric. "But I kind of need us to. Because even though we haven't known each other very long, I think you're a good person. And I've vouched for you a lot. So I'm feeling pretty messed up about the idea that you might have literally been murdering what amounts to my very distant cousins. Or anyone." Her voice lowered, and she muttered seemingly to herself: "I can't believe I've had to have this conversation *twice*."

Ahn tugged the rope for water, trying to let the chill steady his heart. "I understand. I'm sorry if you feel lied to."

"That's the issue, Ahn—I don't know what I feel. I'd just like to know what happened so I can decide."

It was a reasonable enough request. He owed her his life, after all; his honesty was the least he could give in return. "I told you my family gave me a role on this campaign, as a gift." It sounded grotesque now, when he thought about what it looked like from the other side. An uneven road that no one asked for. "I didn't want it, but I thought it wouldn't be long. I could spend time with my sister, actually use my sixth ranking, and still come home in time for my next session at school. When we first landed in Kongkempei, I spent a lot of time learning about culture, improving my language . . . We were supposed to negotiate about how the land would be managed."

"Managed," Sohmeng repeated.

Ahn winced, releasing more water to rinse with. The rivulets caught on the scar across his chest. "My home, my hmun, it is an . . . empire. A hmun that grows, and—and takes. We take." Her silence felt worse than any judgment she could have passed aloud. He wrung out his hair. "Do you have something to dry . . . ?"

"Yeah." She tossed a towel over the stall. Ahn patted himself down, unsure of how this story could possibly go on without making things worse. "You can just come out in the towel when you're done. Hei's pretty much desensitized me to nudity by now, and I kind of want to freak out my dad."

After a harrowing moment trying to figure out who he wanted to upset the least, Ahn obliged, stepping out of the stall with the towel around his waist. He sat beside Sohmeng, trying to pretend he didn't see her eyeing his scar.

"So?" she asked, scrubbing his pants with a stone. "Your empire didn't negotiate, then?"

"It seems not." He reached up, tugging at his earpiece with a twist in his belly. "One night something—happened. It was after dinner, I was feeding Lilin." Lilin. How he missed her. "There was, there was fire. Yelling. Swords. I did not know what made the fighting start, so I tried to find my sister. She was in charge, she always has answers.

But I found her fighting with one of the hmun's leaders and then—"

The world around him felt different then. He swallowed, trying to push back the sensation that he was underwater.

"Someone was behind me. They were yelling, and had a weapon, so—"

The foliage around them was blending together, creeping closer until he could nearly feel it prickling on the back of his neck. He twisted the fingerbone in his ear.

"—so I used my own and—"

Metal was supposed to be a heavy thing, but Ahn had always wielded it lightly. A second limb, an old friend, part of an elaborate dance that always ended in victory. He was good at winning, but winning didn't feel good. It felt like the sound of pulling the blade *out* after, like the iron in the air and the bile on his tongue. The pink sand gone red and thick, his masters watching him from the arena—

No wait, not the arena, the village, not the—

"Ahn? Hey, Ahnschen?" Sohmeng's voice cut through the memory.

Pressure released suddenly from Ahn's chest; he had been holding his breath. At some point he had let go of the earpiece and reached instead for the scar that crossed his heart. He was clutching it so hard his nails had dug in.

He smiled a little. An old habit. "Sorry," he said.

"For what?" She was looking at him in a way he couldn't understand, her face holding all of the discomfort he couldn't wear for himself. Slowly she took his hand, pulling it away from his chest. He let her, suddenly overcome with the fear of what would happen when she let go.

"I'm not very good at this," he murmured, a tight laugh escaping him.

"At what?"

"Talking," he said, focusing on the way she held his hand down by his leg. It almost seemed protective. "Explaining myself. Understanding others. Expanding the Empire."

Sohmeng snorted at that, giving him another one of those pointy elbow jabs. "Look, I get that this might be complicated for you. But I'm glad you suck at conquest, Ahn."

The elbow jab turned into half a hug, her arm sympathetic on his back. He leaned into her, feeling the air return to his lungs even as a frightening realization spread through him: he was glad, too. Everything he had worked for, everything he had lost—all to be struck with the knowledge of just how little he wanted it. He had no idea where that left him, what it meant for his future—for *Schenn's* future.

"Still with me, Ahnschen?"

He apologized once more, biting back a wince when he realized it had come out in Qiao Sidhur.

"It's okay," Sohmeng said. "Like, it makes sense to be scared."

"Scared?"

"Uh, yeah?" She laughed a little. "The Grand Ones are pretty intimidating, if you didn't notice? I'd be losing my mind if I was in your position right now."

Ahn had been afraid in his life. Of course he had. He had just never been given permission to express it openly. No fear, no doubt. Just acceptance, or else private adaptation. To admit to this shortcoming was a highly dangerous act, especially in the hands of someone positioned as an enemy—but he found it felt more like confessing something to a friend. This time, his longing for intimacy outweighed his survival instinct.

"I am scared," he said. And somehow, in the act of speaking his fear aloud, he found it weighed less heavy on his heart.

"Me too, Ahn." Sohmeng returned to scrubbing his clothing, her brow furrowed in thought. "Look, I don't like what I've learned about how Qiao Sidh has behaved in Eiji. I'm disappointed, and I'm confused, and it doesn't make *sense* given the kind of person you are. And looking at your face right now, I don't think you get it either. I think you made a mistake, and I think you *know* you made a mistake, and I think both you and Eiji deserve to see the mistake fixed." She pulled his shirt from the tub, looking it over for lingering stains. "It doesn't help anyone if they just—just exile you for it. It doesn't change anything."

"And if they decide to kill me?" Ahn asked softly. It was a reality worth considering.

"I won't let that happen," Sohmeng said, and the look on her face dared anyone to get in her way. "I refuse. Can you trust that, Ahn?"

"I—" The answer was no. Of course it was no. It should

have been no. There was no reason for him to believe Sohmeng would keep him safe, but his want overrode his doubt, and the answer he gave was: "Yes. I will trust you."

The flicker of surprise on Sohmeng's face immediately alerted him to the language discrepancy. His cheeks flushed, but all she did was nudge him with her elbow again as she replied, "Then I'll have to trust you, too."

Ten

OUT IN EIJI WITH the family of sãoni, Sohmeng had often found herself longing for the days of human language. When Mama got stubborn about her sense of direction, or when Green Bites kept play-stalking her through the woods, or when the hatchlings got into *everything*, she would moan to Hei about how much easier it would be if they could just *talk* to each other. Not in bites or growls, but in actual words. *Words made sense!* she had said. They simplified things, made communication run smoothly.

Three hours into meeting with the Grand Ones, she was beginning to reconsider.

Knowing that Nona Fahang had already tried and failed to help Ateng once before definitely made Sohmeng's request more complicated, but she refused to be disheartened. All she had to do was offer the Grand Ones a fresh perspective, help them understand the urgency of the situation. With that knowledge, how couldn't they help her?

In many ways, Nona Fahang's governmental system was similar to that of Ateng: the Grand Ones made the decisions, while the leaders of the community carried them out. Unlike Ateng, their decisions weren't made in private beneath the holy light of Chehangma's Gate. No, the people of Nona Fahang had their life-changing consultations right out in the square, where anyone could join in as an audience member. Where Ateng favoured ritual and sacred spaces, Nona Fahang's relationship to the Grand Ones was nearly casual.

A Sohmeng of the past would have loved the idea of such transparency—especially because it would have knocked her brother down a couple self-important pegs. But now, surrounded by twenty-five elderly strangers with trust issues, the last thing she wanted was even *more* judgmental eyes on her. Her very reasonable appeals suddenly sounded silly, her confidence slowly draining with each whisper she couldn't understand.

It didn't help that Grandmother Dongi was one tough nut to crack.

"And once more, your request for aid is unfeasible," the old woman said, drumming her fingers on her walking stick. Her exasperation was coming through loud and clear in Tonão's translation. "We simply cannot spare anyone for such a lengthy and complicated expedition."

"I don't think it would take that many people," Sohmeng insisted. "It's not quantity, just—capability! A few people who know Eiji."

"Our scouts, traders, warriors—they are already at their

limit keeping watch for the invaders, gathering resources in case of an attack. I cannot risk Nona Fahang's security for a venture that is likely to fail."

Sohmeng grit her teeth, choosing to ignore that last statement. "I know the timing is risky. It might take a few phases, but *when* we pull it off, you'll also have an ally in Ateng! We could support each other."

Sohmeng had learned a new word this morning: *Gãepongwei*, the name that was now being used to identify the connection between the many hmun of Eiji. When the Qiao Sidhur had asked the first hmun for the name of their 'nation', the concept had made little sense. The varying hmun had always lived individually, spread across Eiji, but they saw each other as distant relatives. Now, Nona Fahang and the other hmun in the network had apparently taken to using Gãepongwei, finding new closeness in the arrival of a common threat. "If things are really so dangerous right now, won't we be stronger together?"

From the other side of the circle, Nona Fahang's Grandmother Mi raised a hand. Sohmeng's heart tugged as she looked at the woman's tattooed cheeks. What she would do to see that mischievous smile right now, to know that someone had her back.

"Speak, Grandmother Mi," granted Grandmother Dongi. This was another difference between Ateng and Nona Fahang: instead of passing decisions through council-wide votes, the final word in this hmun belonged to whoever was the representative for the current ruling phase. Other Grand Ones could offer opinions and ideas, but their power was limited by the shape of the moons.

"Should we find a way to Ateng without trouble, there is still one matter you haven't covered," she said, tilting her head curiously. "How do you plan on fixing the Sky Bridge? Does Ateng have the capacity to help us help them? What part could they play in this aid?"

Sohmeng felt herself go red as the attending villagers ogled her, turning this ordeal into a miserable spectacle. "That . . . I, I mean . . . " She trailed off, uncertain of what to say. She had sort of been hoping that the leaders of Nona Fahang would be offering up ideas of their own by now. "Look, there's a lot of questions we all want answered—"

There it was: the old, familiar collective sigh of a group of people who didn't think she had any idea what she was doing. Muttering about all the ways this wasn't a good use of their time. It had been bad in Ateng, when she had been consistently denied opportunities based on her tengmun kar status, but this time it felt doubly unfair. She had been living as an adult for months now, doing her best to be a better community member. It stung to be dismissed all over again.

Maybe this time they were right, and she was in over her head. But wasn't that a good reason to collaborate instead of rub it in her face?

Grandmother Dongi knocked her walking stick against the platform, hushing the council and those listening in. "Sohmeng Par, it is clear that you are a very bright and strong-willed girl, and we have sympathy for your cause. Trust me when I say this isn't malicious, but we simply cannot extend ourselves to Ateng right now. Our walls keep back sãoni and hãokar and all sorts of predators—but they will do nothing against the kind of fire your companion wields. *That* is our first priority right now."

Sohmeng's shoulders dropped as she heard the finality in the woman's voice. She couldn't argue with that, but she also couldn't help but feel like they were holding Ahn's existence against her. "I thought all the hmun were supposed to work together."

"And we do," said Grandmother Dongi firmly. "Look around and meet refugees from Hosaisi, from Kongkempei. They will tell you of our shared desire for collaboration. Now, is there anything else you have to s—"

Something stirred the Grand Ones' audience. A young teenager ran up to the platform, out of breath, looking ready to apologize or else hit the ground.

"Excuse me," they said, stumbling to a stop beside Sohmeng. Tonão went to them as quickly as his leg allowed, ready to assist in translation. "I, there's—"

"Breathe, young Hiun," said Grandmother Dongi. "What do you need us for?"

"Not—not you, actually," they mumbled, looking at Sohmeng. "We need her, Tonão's girl, at the north wall."

"And why is that?" asked Dongi.

The messenger had gone pale, as though they didn't fully believe what they were saying. "There's a visitor asking, well sort of shouting, for her by name. And they—burning godseye, I thought Auntie Polha was just teasing, but they're riding a são—"

Before the word was out of their mouth, Sohmeng had broken into a run toward the wall. She could hear her father shouting behind her, but she wasn't about to waste any time explaining. The meeting had gone far longer than she expected—she'd been so focused on the Grand Ones that she'd completely lost track of time. The sãoni would have woken hours ago.

After some arguing with the guards, she managed to convince someone to guide her through the trees. She could hear Hei's voice, loud and insistent and stubborn as anything.

"I don't want to speak to you," they were yelling at the people above in Atengpa. This was only made more intimidating by the sãoni growling right alongside them. "I'm looking for Sohmeng. Bring me Sohmeng now, and also please stop talking."

When she saw the exit, Sohmeng squeezed past her guide, calling out Hei's name in Sãonipa, three clicks and a chirp over and over until she emerged from the trees. At the sight of her, Hei launched themself from their sãoni and into her arms. Clicking wildly, they rubbed their cheeks against hers, looking her over to make sure she was in one piece.

"You're late," Hei said. "Why are you late? Why did this happen?"

Sohmeng hugged them tightly, allowing their makeup to get smeared on her cheeks. "I'm okay, I promise—things just went a little long."

"I was worried," Hei replied gravely, bumping their

forehead into hers. "You said you'd be back before the sãoni woke up."

"I'm sorry," Sohmeng said. Still, she couldn't help but smile a little. She felt bad that they'd been so concerned, but it was also nice to see just how much they cared. "And I can take care of myself, you know."

"I would prefer to share the labour." Hei took her hands in theirs, glancing up at the scouts in the trees.

She was enjoying the feeling of their thumbs kneading her palms when she got a closer look at the sãoni Hei had rode in on. It wasn't Green Bites, but one of the younger, more timid ones who usually kept to the outskirts of the pack. "Wait, where is—"

"Mating season," Hei said flatly.

"Oh." Sohmeng laughed a little. "Well that's... auspicious!"

"No it isn't. Now we're going to be stuck here until it ends and they calm down. The colony spread a little—space means less snapping at each other." They paused, flexing their fingers in their sãoni claws. "... you should tell this hmun's travellers to be careful for the next few phases."

Sohmeng clicked in gratitude, bumping cheeks with Hei one more time. "I will. Thank you." The sãoni beside them let out a little rumble, pressing his striped throat to the ground and examining Sohmeng. She approached him slowly and offered a hand, which he nudged. This one was sweet; she ought to pay him more attention. Give him a silly name or something.

"So?" Hei asked. "Did your plan work? Can you come back to the colony yet?"

The question pulled Sohmeng in so many directions. The magnetism of her wants used to be so clear, like the compass Ahn carried with him. But now she felt almost disoriented by all her conflicting desires; she wanted to catch up on lost time with her father, and persuade Nona Fahang to help fix the Sky Bridge, and figure out how to negotiate with the Qiao Sidhur, *and* hide with Hei and the family in Eiji and avoid all of these problems altogether.

"I—" she hesitated, unsure of where to start. "Well, things have turned out to be more complicated than I thought."

To Hei's credit, their clicking only sounded a little bit like a *told-you-so.*

"I asked the Grand Ones if they would help with Ateng, but they refused—at least, they've refused for now." She said the words quickly, unwilling to take them as final. She wasn't ready to accept the idea that the hmun would just abandon each other in a moment of crisis. "It's the Qiao Sidhur campaign. They've been attacking other hmun, and things have gotten really ugly, and apparently Nona Fahang can't spare the resources to fix the Bridge."

Hei didn't have much love for human society, but they still glowered at the revelation. "Ahnschen?"

"No, not Ahn—well, sort of."

It didn't feel good to explain the details of the interrogation that had played out. It felt even worse to explain that awaiting the final sentencing would mean a minimum of thirty days apart. Sohmeng could see the crease in Hei's brow, the way they chewed their lip. She was asking for a lot.

"Thirty days," Hei repeated, running a hand through their messy crop of hair.

"I can't leave Ahn here alone, Hei. He's . . ." Sohmeng didn't really know how to describe what was going on with Ahnschen. The powerful warrior they had first encountered in the jungle seemed different, like every passing day she was allowed to pull off another plate of armour and see the uncertain man underneath. Sure, he was deadly with a sword, but the more time she spent with him, the more she began to think of that skill as a reflex, an old habit. "I don't know, Hei. I promised I wouldn't abandon him. I think he knows he messed up, and he wants to make it right. And if we're going to talk to Qiao Sidh about backing out of Eiji, we need him as an ally."

Hei clicked quietly. Sohmeng could see how fast their mind was moving, could see the brilliance and doubt reflected in their green eyes. There were so many ways this plan might not work. She braced herself, waiting to see which one it was they would bring up.

But all they eventually said was, "Mating season should buy us some time. I guess it is auspicious."

"Hei! Burning godseye, thank you—" Sohmeng threw her arms around them, flooded with relief. They caught her with a little squawk of confusion.

"Why are you thanking me? I was always going to

help you, Sohmeng. It just needs to work with the sãoni. I would never leave you alone."

She squeezed them tighter, grateful beyond words. Mid-hug, she nearly popped them as another memory struck her, another very important reason she couldn't leave Nona Fahang just yet. "Also my, my *dad*. I need to tell you about my dad! He's—Hei you're not going to believe this, but he's alive."

"Your father?" Hei leaned in close, as if they had somehow misheard her.

"Yeah," Sohmeng said, laughing a little. Despite the whirlwind of complicated feelings she'd been dealing with, it still felt sort of magical to say the words aloud. "He's here, in Nona Fahang."

She expected an onslaught of questions, but Hei seemed more focused on how she was feeling than what more she had to say. They took her hands, ran their thumbs over her wrists to feel for tension; it made her feel listened to, even if she hadn't said much at all.

Sohmeng sighed, watching the patterns their clawed fingers traced on her forearms. ". . . it isn't fair that I have to choose like this. I want to be with you and the colony, but also be in Nona Fahang."

"The sãoni cannot get through the wall," Hei said with a frown. "And also that would be a horrible idea."

"No I *know* that, dummy." Sohmeng bonked her head against theirs. "And you know I'd never ask you to be with all of those people. That wouldn't be fair."

Hei clicked quietly, relief softening their features.

"I just wish you were a little closer. I want to be able to go in and out as I please, but I'm already not on the best terms with the Grand Ones. They'd probably dismiss me forever if I asked to keep a literal pack of sãoni camped outside their door." Sohmeng snorted, glancing up at the scouts. They were eyeing the sãoni Hei had brought with something between caution and wonder. The lizard seemed to feel much the same, pawing at the ground. "I can hear it now: *Does Ateng raise their children to be chronically inconsiderate? We've already warned you about the invaders like, a billion times! We have to keep them out, protect our walls, not surround them with—*"

Sohmeng stopped talking so quickly that she nearly choked on her words, pulling back from Hei to get a better look at the walls. They had served Nona Fahang faithfully for this long, hadn't they? And mating season had spread the colony thinner than usual, and the scouts hardly ever touched the ground anyway. A bit of silvertongue would be an additional safety precaution, but it wasn't entirely unfeasible. It would solve any immediate danger posed by the Qiao Sidhur, wouldn't it?

"Sohmeng . . . ?" Hei let out a wary Sãonipa growl. Given Sohmeng's current thought process and slightly maniacal grin, it was more than warranted.

"Hei," she said, nearly daunted by her own genius, "I have a really bad idea."

Eleven

AHN NEVER THOUGHT he would be grateful for a private moment with the sãoni. His first meeting with the creatures had been a fight for his life, a battle against an opponent he had never been trained against. After that, he was kept in a constant state of vigilance, expecting the colony to turn on him at any moment. But now, outside of the walls of Nona Fahang, the sounds of the alpha's rumbling mostly meant he was at a safe distance from any other humans who wished him ill.

"Stay in our line of sight, tsongkar!" shouted one of the scouts from the canopy. Their neighbour shot out a comment in Fahangpa that made everyone laugh. The joke was lost on Ahn.

After Sohmeng managed to get her plan approved by the Grand Ones, Ahn's new assignment had been explained at spearpoint in halting Dulpongpa: while Sohmeng was working with Nona Fahang's leadership on the logistics of camping sãoni outside the walls, and Hei was retrieving any of the creatures that weren't participating in mating season, Ahn would be on silvertongue duty, applying the plant to all of the weak points in Nona Fahang's walls. If the animals happened to turn him into lunch, it was no real loss.

The few sãoni that had followed Mama were watching him closely with those big eerie eyes. Some of them were making threatening noises, but Ahn told himself it was just because of the sack of silvertongue he was carrying. Over the past few weeks, he had developed a certain fondness for the plant; without it, he probably wouldn't be alive. That and his hair, mild embarrassment to the Imperial family though it was.

A loud whoop came from above as a heavy fruit smashed on the ground beside him, earning the attention of the sãoni and more laughs all around. Ahn grit his teeth. Not that he wanted to hurt the sãoni, but if the scouts were going to provoke the creatures, they could have at least given him a sword.

He was moving to tie the velvety leaves to more trees when another fruit dropped down, this time slamming into his arm and spraying juice everywhere. So much for the change of clothes he'd been given. He rolled out his shoulder with a wince.

"What, you don't like your lunch?" taunted one of the scouts. "Open your mouth next time, it might taste better."

Given the size of the melon they dropped next, Ahn imagined that he mostly would be tasting the remnants of his own teeth. Which was probably what they were getting at. Outside of his siblings' sniping, which felt more political than personal, Ahn's status had protected him from bullying for most of his life. So far, he wasn't enjoying it.

He thought about trying to engage again, to do what he could to get on their good side. But the throbbing bruise Lita Soon had left on his cheek said the effort came with its own risks. Perhaps if he just did a good job here they would give him a break, and he could try to show them he wasn't the person they thought he was.

Two more fruits dropped around him, agitating the sãoni and forcing Ahn to jump out of the way before he got knocked on the head. He looked up, trying to figure out where they were being thrown from, when a horrible noise came from behind him.

Three of the adolescent sãoni jumped at the branches. They couldn't reach the humans above, but still they snapped and snarled, frightening the scouts into losing the rest of their fruit. Satisfied, the creatures ate through the smashed pulp on the ground.

Heart pounding, Ahn leaned back against the trees and smiled weakly at the sãoni. Then he saw Hei, slinking up behind them and looking disapprovingly at the scouts above. Had they set the sãoni on them?

"Hei—" Their name was out of his mouth before he could remember how much they also didn't like him. He gripped the bag of silvertongue tighter, losing whatever he was going to say when their green eyes locked on him. " . . . hello."

They nodded what amounted to a greeting and turned their attention to Mama and her hatchlings. The little lizards were wiggling up a storm squeaking at Ahn. He felt bad; they clearly wanted his attention, but the smell of the silvertongue was repellant. Once he was done and had his hands washed, maybe he would be allowed to go hold them. Apparently his people-pleasing now extended across species.

After a moment of trying to calm the hatchlings, Hei sighed heavily and trudged over to Ahn.

One of the scouts took a break from arguing about the ruined food long enough to notice. "Hey!" they yelled. "You! He has to stay here!"

Hei ignored them entirely, stuffing their hand into his bag and pulling out the silvertongue with a look of distaste. They seemed to have spent enough time with the sãoni that they were put off by the plant by association.

"I'm talking to you," the scout continued, thumping their spear once against the branches.

Ahn looked up at them, clearing his throat and doing his best to sound amicable. "They don't speak Dulpongpa very well."

"Then tell them what I said!"

"I don't—I don't speak Atengpa, either." He paused. "Or Sãonipa."

"São—" The scout stopped themself, rubbing their temples. It looked like a few of the others had gone back to the village for more fruit. "If you bolt, we have our orders. Remember that, tsongkar."

Ahn nodded, continued tying the leaves. The young sãoni had finished the fallen fruit and were now exploring the clearing, snuffling for any bits they might have missed. Mama growled something at them, but they refused to settle down.

"*Tsongkar.*" To Ahn's surprise, the word came from Hei. They muttered to themself irritably, tying off the leaves they had taken. "Tsongkar, hãokar. All same. Kar, kar, kar." They spat into the earth.

Ahn had absolutely no idea what they meant, but for once it didn't seem like they were mad at him. He worked on his own silvertongue, listening to the calls of the sãoni and not daring to say a word that might interrupt the tentative peace between them.

Despite his claims, Ahn had to wonder how much Dulpongpa Hei actually followed. He had a feeling that they listened to a lot more than they let on, used their quiet as a way to follow the rest of the world more closely. Even with Sohmeng, they weren't a creature of many words.

"Kar, kar, kar," Hei mumbled again, making a sãoni noise of frustration. Mama squawked in concern, but they countered it with a sound that Ahn assumed was supposed to be reassuring. It was remarkable to watch.

"You are very clever—" he began, then stopped when their eyes narrowed at the word. Perhaps they didn't understand. "Skilled—" Not quite. " . . . familiar, with the sãoni."

Hei kept their eyes away from him, hands busy with the silvertongue. "Familiar? Yes. They are family."

Ahn smiled at the way they spoke, like this was the most obvious thing in the world and he was foolish to question it, nevermind pay them a compliment. Sohmeng was brazen with him in a way that reminded him nearly of Schenn, but Hei was different. They made it clear that they didn't need him, or need to like him. And, absurdly, that made him determined to *be* liked by them.

Beyond his impact on the ecosystem, Hei didn't care who he was or where he was from, which meant the only thing they could judge him on was his character. Their frankness made him want to be his best self, and to see if he was worth being liked, or disliked, for exactly who he was.

Hei let out a small, threatening growl; Ahn reddened, realizing he had been staring. He started to sputter an apology, but Hei had already stepped close to him. They lifted one of their clawed fingers and, more gently than he could have imagined, tapped the bruise on his cheek. Despite himself, he flinched.

They jerked their chin in the direction of the scouts. "They do this?"

"Yes," Ahn said, inexplicable hesitation in his voice. "They did."

"You did wrong?" Hei's eyes scanned the rest of him, seeking any other injuries.

"I think so," Ahn said softly. For a moment, their gaze caught; the hungry snag of a thorn on an old winter cloak. It tore at him a little when they broke away to return to their task, saying nothing else.

Silence stretched between them, louder than the chatter that came from above, louder even than the sãoni in the clearing. Ahn turned his focus to looping silvertongue into knots around the banyan branches. It felt more like decoration than defense.

"Ahnschen," Hei said, tying a leaf to a high branch. It was the first time they had ever used his name.

"Yes?"

"Sohmeng likes you. I do not like you." Hei spoke the words firmly, yanking on their leaf with a little more force than necessary. They reached into his bag, pulling out more of the silvertongue, offering him one more cursory glance. "But I will not hit you."

"Only poison me?" he asked, unable to hold back a grin.

Hei's eyes went the size of pastry trays. Ahn wasn't sure which of them squawked louder.

"Wait, no—" He put his hands in the air, trying to shake away his ridiculous comment. "It was, I mean—it's a joke! I was making a joke, it's okay!"

" . . . oh." Hei clicked cautiously, rubbing at their nose. If Ahn didn't know better, he'd think they were embarrassed. "Bad at jokes."

"Me too, it seems," he replied with a small smile.

Hei sighed loudly. "Bad at *many* things, Ahnschen." He couldn't argue that, even if it was strange to hear someone say it so directly. They rested a hand on the tree in front of them, thumbing the thin, papery bark with a pensive expression on their charcoal-smeared face. "But good, too."

"Pardon?" Ahn asked.

"Good too, Ahnschen," Hei repeated, looking at him with resignation that was nearly companionable. He had no idea what to make of such a look. "Sohmeng likes you. Be good. Okay?"

The limits of their shared language made it impossible for him to ask for further clarification. And even if they could understand each other more clearly, he had a feeling that Hei wasn't interested in offering anything more than what they believed was necessary.

They clicked at him with a tilt of their chin, waiting.

"Okay," he said, nodding a little. Somehow, it was enough for Hei. They chirped, satisfied, and left to wash their hands and return to the sãoni. Their arm brushed his as they walked past; a small concession to his presence, or else a peace offering.

Be good.

Ahn had been trying to do this for his whole life. Back home, it meant something entirely different—being good at something was simply a stepping stone to becoming the best at it. Whatever path he walked, there was no doing it halfway if he wanted to bring pride to his family. That was the cultural expectation of Qiao Sidh: step into the legends that will follow you through death and life again.

How naïve he'd been. A prince of the Empire, oblivious to the knowledge that greatness came with consequences far beyond himself. Now, as he began to face them, a new question arose: what did it mean to be good, or at least to simply be *better*, in a place so different from home? Beyond that, what did it mean to be good without being good *at* something?

It made a novice of him. But one thing was clear: for the sake of a kind word from Hei, Sohmeng's hand on his back, the forgiveness of strangers, Schenn's voice in his ear . . . he could try to figure it out. He could learn again. That much, at least, remained the same.

TWELVE

DESPITE THE COUNTLESS WAYS in which Sohmeng's plan could have gone immediately and dramatically wrong, the sãoni were settling well outside Nona Fahang. The silvertongue prevented them from getting too close to the walls, Mama found a cozy tree to scratch her back on, and Ahn had even come up with a brilliant feeding plan. Once a day, the scouts dropped food scraps, keeping the colony content as they became more accustomed to human presence.

Hei had been wary of the idea, at first. They didn't like humans getting too close to the sãoni, and made sure Sohmeng passed the scouts a list of things the creatures could not stomach. Luckily, the list was very short, and the relationship seemed on course to being mutualistic.

All was well outside of the hmun. Inside was a different story.

Problem-solving challenged Sohmeng, but it also made her feel in her element. But now, sitting at a dinner table with her father's new family, all she felt was out of place. Bubbly Jaea Won and statuesque Pimchuang Ker sat on opposite ends of the table, passing food back and forth as Eakang Minhal tickled baby Kuei Fua, who was squirming in Tonão's lap. Everyone had their own stools, including Tonão. Sohmeng had needed to borrow one from the neighbours; it felt stiff beneath her as she watched him coo over Kuei. Being the youngest child in her family, she had never before seen this baby-bouncing incarnation of her father. She wasn't sure how she felt about it.

The table had been filled with a whole variety of sliced fruit and steamed buns, along with a dark, spicy spread that she didn't have a name for. It had surprised her to learn that communal meals only happened during holidays here, that families took their suppers together privately. Instead of having the space to mingle and work out what she was feeling, Sohmeng was locked in proximity to these new people.

"Do you want—" Pimchuang gestured to Tonão, who took over translating her words into Dulpongpa, "—tea, or would you prefer juice?"

"Tea's fine," Sohmeng said, ignoring a phantom sting in her hand as she watched Pimchuang pour. The woman was taller than Tonão by a couple finger lengths, long-legged and flat-chested, with a curve to her brow that gave her the appearance of constant consideration. Or maybe she was just sizing up Sohmeng.

Meanwhile, Jaea Won smiled excitedly at her, chattering at Tonão in Fahangpa. She was round as Sohmeng, with the same bright eyes as Eakang and a clear, ringing voice that Tonão rapidly translated. He'd barely gotten a bite of food in.

"Please, eat something!" Jaea exclaimed, gesturing to the table. "You've never had cooking like Pim's, I'm sure. It's even good enough for our picky little Kuei Fua—oh, darling *please* let go of your Damdão's hair—" The translation cut out for a moment as Tonão laughed, passing off the baby to Jaea. "And I heard you've already met Eakang Minhal?"

"Not—not formally, exactly," Sohmeng said haltingly. She could feel their eyes on her like a blackfly buzzing around her ear. "Just outside of the walls." And when they barged into her conversation with her father.

"Then let's introduce you both properly," Tonão said. He sat between her and Eakang. "Sohmeng, this is Eakang Minhal. Being Kuei's sibling, they've become very much a stepchild to me. Eakang . . . " He looked at them with the kind of smile that said this was an important moment for both of them, something they must have talked about before. Some special old story, come suddenly to life after nearly four years of hearing it told. Sohmeng clenched her fists. "This is my daughter, Sohmeng P—"

"Minhal."

The word was out before Sohmeng fully registered having made the choice to say it.

The energy in the room seemed to contract. Pimchuang's gaze turned to Tonão, sympathetic but unsurprised. It was like Sohmeng thought, then: these people already knew about her. At the very least, Jaea and Pim did. Eakang looked ready to launch through the roof.

"Sohmeng Minhal," Tonão said, voice wavering. She wondered when the last time was that he had said her gods-given name aloud, admitted to the truth of who and what she was—

No. This was getting to be too much. She wasn't going to get into this here, in front of these strangers. If Minhals were allowed to exist in Nona Fahang, then that's what she'd do. Exist. No need to harp on the past. "It's nice to meet you all," she said in Dulpongpa. "Thank you for taking care of my father."

The meal was delicious, the people were fine. She learned about their lives and listened to their stories, picking at the food with a tight stomach. Pimchuang aided in organizing communal festivals; Jaea was involved with banyan maintenance. One time, Jaea looked away from Kuei for just one second, and he had climbed a tree. And Eakang? They were Minhal. Just like her.

"Have you seen your father's weaving yet, Sohmeng?" Jaea asked, squeezing the man's shoulder. "He's made some beautiful things, especially this past year!"

Since when did her father weave? He'd never shown any interest back in Ateng. "Not yet, no."

"Jaea, please." Tonão looked almost bashful, but Sohmeng could spot the pride in his expression. The joy. Given everything he had gone through, it surprised Sohmeng to see how easily he smiled here. There was a rhythm to this home, a natural way of life that left

Sohmeng feeling smaller and smaller as the night progressed.

It had been a while since she was surrounded by so many humans; maybe she had forgotten how to engage with them. Granted, she had spent most of her time in Ateng being chastised, but it was a role she had learned to fill. Here, she didn't even speak the hmunpa. She felt more sãoni than human.

The next day, Tonão accompanied her to the Grand Ones, where she self-consciously announced her new phase name. They took the change easily, gracefully; the worst of it was the pitying looks some of them gave her. And just like that, she was back in the community as Sohmeng Minhal, no questions asked.

She was supposed to be relieved—when the alternative was exile, she was supposed to be *overjoyed*. She grit her teeth against the anticlimax of it all, forced her head high when she felt like curling up with it between her knees. This was meant to be a lucky thing. A fresh start, where her father was alive and her very existence wasn't cause for shame.

It makes sense that I feel weird, she thought to herself. *But I don't need to act weird. This is uncomfortable, but I can handle it. I can handle all of this.*

And that might have even been true, if it hadn't been for Eakang.

Eakang Minhal was completely insufferable. They were always gawking at her, or else finding a way into her business. At first it had just been during meals, when they accosted her with questions: *what's it like in Ateng? Is your brother still there? How big do the sãoni get? Do you want new clothes, Sohmeng? Aren't those sãoni skin clothes itchy, Sohmeng? You can borrow mine if you want, Sohmeng!*

Given that Eakang was about half her size, Sohmeng had no idea what they were playing at with that ridiculous suggestion. Still, she let it go—they were a couple years younger than her, immature. They didn't know better.

"Minhal children do a little bit of everything in Nona Fahang!" Eakang explained at one point. They had taken it upon themself to play the role of Junior Grand One. "We drift through different roles until we find one we like, but we're never really expected to stay anywhere too long. We're like butterflies, or chameleons!"

It got worse when they started introducing her to the other Minhals, showing off how special and unique they all were because of the free reign they were given in Nona Fahang. Luckily most of the others weren't too bad, but Sohmeng couldn't stand the way they all buzzed around Eakang like they were a big pink dung flower.

"Sohmeng's *so* cool," Eakang said one afternoon to their phase-mates. This was the same day they'd forgone their signature braids in favour of a bun, beaming at Sohmeng all the while. "They ride sãoni, I even saw them doing it!"

"Wow," said another Minhal breathlessly. "I can't even imagine. Those things are so scary."

"Yeah but Sohmeng is *super* brave. Like their dad, but even more!"

Sohmeng bristled; how many times had she used the

feminine *I* in front of them? Just because she was going by Minhal didn't mean she was changing her entire identity. But no matter how many times she made the correction, they never seemed to take the hint.

"I'd love to try it one day," Eakang said, looking embarrassingly hopeful. "Maybe you could teach me?"

Not on your life, Sohmeng thought.

"Mrr," Sohmeng said, and mumbled some excuse about having somewhere to be.

But everywhere Sohmeng went, Eakang seemed to follow—asking questions, making useless commentary, or just sticking that big goofy smile in her face like it was the best day of their life. Which she supposed it was, given how much everyone seemed to adore them. It was truly shocking that no one else had noticed how annoying they were, every hour of the day.

"Ahn, I'm serious," she groaned to her captive audience. "They're the worst. Verifiably the worst person in Eiji, possibly on the planet. Does anyone suck this much in Qiao Sidh?"

"Hard to say," Ahn replied, grunting as he dug out a latrine. "I haven't met everyone."

"Don't take their side," Sohmeng hissed, peering from behind the house Ahn was digging for. After his work with the silvertongue had been successful, she'd persuaded the Grand Ones to let him do some manual labour for the community. He looked calmer when he had something to do, and it seemed like a good way to build goodwill. "It's so obnoxious! They follow me everywhere, talk to me about absolutely nothing, try to pull me into their stupid little club. I'm going to strangle them with their own braids, I swear on both the gods."

"It sounds like they really admire you," Ahn commented, yanking at an enormous rock that was caught in the soil. "Like a younger sibling would. I used to trail my siblings all over the palace."

"Please don't make me send you back to the hogs."

As the phases passed from Dongi into Se into Won, Sohmeng did what she could to keep busy and turn the tides in her favour. To her dismay, the Grand Ones didn't budge on their position regarding Ateng. Their reasoning was relentless, and impossible for Sohmeng to effectively argue against. What if the sãoni at the base of Fochão Dangde decided to stalk them during the journey? What if the Qiao Sidhur attacked and scouts returned to find their home destroyed? How much could go wrong in the time it would take to repair the Sky Bridge?

It was exhausting. It made sense. It made Sohmeng want to scream. She had always believed that all the hmun of Gãepongwei would show up for each other—it sucked to have that belief challenged. She wanted to keep fighting, to find the magic words that would make the Grand Ones behave in a way that made sense to her. But as the days passed and the rejections piled up, she was forced to admit those words didn't exist. For as long as the Qiao Sidhur invasion remained a threat, help for Ateng would not come from Nona Fahang.

So Sohmeng changed tactics, and focused her attention

on Ahn. If she could find a way to turn the trial in his favour, then they could get back on the road to Qiao Sidh and return to their original plan. Bargaining felt more complicated now that she understood the violence that had occured in the northern hmun, but it wasn't impossible. If Ahn could understand he'd made a mistake, why couldn't his sister? All Sohmeng needed to do was get everyone to the camp in one piece—and that meant using this thirty-day window wisely. Her pleas to the Grand Ones for Ateng became reports on Ahn's good behaviour, and she did what she could to find work he would excel at. She was confident that Ahn regretted what had happened—he just needed a way to make it right. *To atone*, like Grandmother Pel had said.

It worked out sometimes. Often, he was regarded with disdain. It would have been easier to judge people's distrust if she hadn't met the refugees from Hosaisi and Kongkempei. Some had integrated with the community, but many kept to themselves, their grief still fresh on their faces. Looking at them sometimes made Sohmeng feel like she was advocating for a cause even more impossible than securing aid for Ateng. But for the sake of Eiji, she kept going, only able to hope that she wasn't making things worse.

Sohmeng felt her legs ache with every leap forward, every step back. The days felt at once too long and too short, and the stress began to grate.

The final straw came one evening when she was alone with Eakang, helping to prepare dinner.

Eakang had been battering her with questions about Ateng, asking about everything from the language to the holidays to their Tengmunji practices. Thinking of the bodies she had found, Sohmeng's answers got more clipped with each passing minute. It made sense for Eakang to be curious about other hmun, but she wished they could give her a day off, or at least be less in her face about the whole thing.

"So they just all vote instead of going with the person with the dominant phase?" they asked.

"Yup."

"That's so weird!"

"Mhm."

"How do they know they're making the right choice?" Eakang pressed.

"They're the Grand Ones," Sohmeng said, passing them a thick ginger root as encouragement to get back to work. "What they say goes."

"That must be so frustrating." Eakang sighed, peeling and grating the root into a bowl. "Especially with how harsh they are, right?"

Sohmeng stiffened.

"Like the exiling and all that? That's so messed up. Like not even because you're a criminal, just because you're . . . " They trailed off, glancing at Sohmeng with a look they must have thought was sympathetic.

All at once, Sohmeng's distaste hardened into something unnamable. She hated the way they were looking at her, waiting for some personal response, some Minhal camaraderie despite their vastly different experiences. It made her *burn.* No one in her hmun had ever had the right to this information, and yet this absolute stranger somehow felt entitled to her privacy, to her life. Was it not enough that they'd already gotten her father?

"Sohmeng?" Eakang turned to face her, the smile on their face an indicator of just how oblivious they were. "I just wanted to say that I think it's great that you're also Minhal. It's so unfair that Ateng would have exiled you, but I'm really glad you can be yourself here."

Be herself? They didn't even know her! She stared at them, stunned into silence.

"Like I can't even imagine what you've been through." They bit their lip, having the nerve to genuinely look upset. Like it was their problem. "I was wondering though, um, your friend? They also speak Atengpa, right? But they don't seem like they're from your hmun, so I was just wondering if they were also—"

Sohmeng slammed her knife into the waste bucket, the sound of it nearly knocking Eakang flat on their butt. That was far enough. "That's not your business."

"Oh!" Eakang stared at her, stumbling over their words. They looked embarrassed, aware that they had overstepped, but Sohmeng wasn't in the mood for an apology. "I shouldn't have—"

"No," she said coldly. "You shouldn't have."

She stood up, brushing off her pants and abandoning her work. Eakang was trying to backtrack, but Sohmeng cut them off with a sharp Sãonipa snarl. "Tell my father

I'm not staying for dinner."

"I didn't mean to—"

"I don't care," Sohmeng snapped, and she found that she meant it. She didn't care what Eakang Minhal had intended—she cared that they had crossed a line. It was one thing to bother her day in and day out with questions; it was another to drag Hei into a conversation they weren't even present for.

She stormed out the door before things could go into territory she'd have to apologize for, keeping her head down until she made her way outside Nona Fahang's walls and into the colony's territory. The moment Hei saw her, they jumped up, clicking in alarm.

Ignoring the calls of the scouts above, she went straight into their arms, hugging them tightly and simmering with anger. Hei guided her to Mama, who nosed her worriedly as the hatchlings scrabbled at her feet, squeaking up a storm. Unable to find words to describe her frustration, and sick to death of jumping between two inadequate languages, Sohmeng made every furious Sãonipa snarl she knew. The creatures around her clicked in what might have been confusion, but she chose to take it as solidarity. Hei held her closer, not pushing for an explanation.

It only made Sohmeng burn deeper, thinking of how casually Eakang had asked about Hei. As if the idea of them getting exiled was some far-off myth rather than an actual tragedy that had happened to an actual person. Actual people. She buried her face in Hei's shoulder, breathing slowly and counting off the phases in her head.

Par Go Hiwei Fua Tang Sol—

It wasn't fair.

Jão Pel Dongi Se Won Nor—

It wasn't fair that Eakang had gotten to steal her father for four years.

Chisong Heng Li Ginhãe Mi—

It wasn't fair that she was angry at her father for finding joy outside of her own family.

Ker Hiun Ãofe Soon Nai Tos Jeji—

It wasn't fair, but it was so hard to stop.

How could she tolerate being around Eakang when they had lived such vastly different lives? How was she supposed to handle the fact that they were celebrated while she had to spend her childhood hiding who she was? Why were they treated so differently when they were both—

Minhal.

Sohmeng exhaled, rolling her forehead against Hei's collarbone. If only Ateng's Grand Ones could see her now, containing her anger just the way they'd always wanted. Exiting the stressful situation before she could blow up at innocent bystanders. Would they finally see her as an adult?

Hei chirped softly, nuzzling Sohmeng's cheek until she felt the unmistakable sensation of charcoal clinging to her skin.

"I don't know how to behave with other people," she mumbled into Hei's shoulder. The teeth sewn to their clothing bit lightly against her skin. "It would be easier if they knew how to behave with *me*. If they'd meet me halfway."

"Humans are difficult."

It was true. Sohmeng's opinion of other people had improved after so many months away from them. She had forgotten how complicated it was to communicate, how she always felt at least a little bit like an outsider. A new phase name wouldn't fix that.

Up above, the gods shone with Won's influence. It hit Sohmeng then—it had been a full lunar cycle since she'd entered Eiji. Just over one hundred days, a quarter of a calendar year.

Merging her two lives felt like pulling down the sky to touch the earth, like trying to wear the skin of both past and future iterations of herself. There was no story to guide her, no map to consult. She felt for the first time like maybe she didn't know how to be an adult after all. She didn't know how to access whatever secrets adults had that enabled them to do so little, to let the world stay so wrong—and she didn't want to. Growing up was supposed to make her feel *less* helpless, wasn't it?

Hei was right—humans were *difficult*. She sat beside her partner, trying to reimagine herself into a person who knew how to manage this situation. Who could be determined, and patient, and fair. Who could fix problems she hadn't even caused herself.

Thirteen

AHN WAS NOT USED TO feeling dangerous. Back in Qiao Sidh, his sword was a symbol of devotion, his rank a sign of the depths of his caring. Even the bone in his ear was something tender, a physical manifestation of love and loyalty.

In Nona Fahang, things were different. As he awaited his trial, time passed in a series of tasks, none of them pleasant: digging latrines, doing Nona Fahang's literal heavy lifting, providing ongoing waste disposal. Much of the work put him into close contact with the very community that despised him. More than once, he wondered if being put in a prison would have made them trust him more or less.

Outside of Sohmeng and Hei, Tonão Sol had been the closest thing to hospitable that Ahn had found, allowing him use of the family's shower stall. One of the women of the house also offered him food on occasion, but they never spoke much beyond that. It was probably difficult to relax around someone who was constantly flanked by at least one guard. So Ahn did his best to ease the burden of his own presence; he worked hard and quietly, smiled at the children who dared run up to get a look at him. When someone engaged with him, he was polite, and never overstayed the interaction. Slowly, many of the fearful looks he received mellowed into mere unease, and he counted that as success.

But his good behaviour made no difference when it came to Lita Soon.

Ahn was making the rounds collecting entrails for the sãoni, hefting the pole up onto his shoulders and trying to balance the foul-smelling buckets on either side. In a moment of community organizing genius, Sohmeng had suggested using peoples' cooking scraps as motivation for the sãoni to stay near the walls. It was an easy waste disposal system, and it kept Nona Fahang from having to use up too many of their resources on the creatures' appetites. It was also disgusting, making Ahn the obvious candidate for the job.

He was just finishing up when Lita Soon approached him. "You missed something," the man said, tapping his spear against the ground.

Ahn looked behind him, worried he had dropped one of the bird carcasses. Just like that, the scout's spear took a shot at the bucket to his right, tipping out half of the filthy contents within. They landed with a horrible splat at Ahn's feet, viscera staining the ground outside the small home.

"Right there," Lita said, his voice falsely sweet. "Do you see?"

It was a childish trick. One that made Ahn look careless. The woman he had collected these from had actually greeted him this morning, and now— "I see. Thank you."

Ahn took a slow breath, lowering the pole back to the ground before the left bucket lost balance and made even more of a mess. He stood over the guts spread on the ground, fingers flexing in hesitation. Beside him, the butt of the spear tapped once more, a casual threat.

Schenn used to joke that Ahn's fuse was long enough to catch fish with. And it was true—he hated getting angry, found the feeling frightening and unmanageable. But something twitched at the end of the line.

"There a problem, little prince?" Lita taunted. "I figured you were used to getting your hands dirty."

Tension struck like lightning through Ahn's body. His shoulders pulled back, his chest locked tightly around his heart. "I would like to know what I have done to you," he said, his voice as even as he could manage. "And if you would allow it, I would like to find a way to make things right."

Lita Soon scoffed. "Just clean up your mess, tsongkar."

Ahn saw the spear rise, ready to take a swat at him. Before he could stop himself, his arm shot out and caught it. The Soon man's eyes went wide.

"I am *trying.*" Ahn stepped over the blood at his feet. How was he supposed to be non-threatening when he was constantly being forced to defend himself? "It is clear that I have caused you pain, or else you just get some sort of thrill from exercising control over others. But based on the way you look at me, I can only assume it's personal." Lita tried to wrest the spear out of his hands, but Ahn held tight. He had trained his whole life not to be knocked down. "So I ask you, kindly, to tell me how I might settle this grudge."

Watch yourself, Ahn. No, watch him—you're scaring him. Let go of the spear.

The warning from his earpiece made Ahn gasp audibly. He released his hold so quickly that it felt like a spasm in his fingers, and Lita stumbled. When the man righted himself, he was looking at Ahn with pure disdain.

Ahn took a shaky breath, stepping back with his hand cupped over his ear. His heel squished in something warm and wet.

"You want to know what you did to me?" Lita Soon asked, his voice shaking. The lack of control made him look so young. Only a few years older than Ahn, a few years younger than Ólawen. Full of such rage. "*Kongkempei.*"

Ahn faced the accusation with as much poise as he could manage, but the truth shone through on his face.

"That's what I thought," Lita said. "Of course you don't remember me. But I remember you—how could I forget the face of the prince? The spoiled little boy whose people burned down my home. I saw you run away that night—your sister butchered my neighbours, and you fled on your beast."

"I—" Ahn's voice caught. When he spoke, the words sounded weak even to his ears. "I'm sorry. I didn't—"

"How *dare* you." The man laughed, furious. "You were

there. You were there, and you did nothing to stop it, and now you try to pretend you feel remorse? You try to placate me?" Ahn's eyes went to the scar on Lita's face, a mark of the pain that marred each of their interactions. "You want to make it right, Éongrir? Here—"

The man switched abruptly into words Ahn didn't know. He winced, saying nothing.

"Well?" Lita pushed. "How about it?"

"I don't—I don't understand."

"And why's that?"

"I don't speak Fahangpa."

Lita barked out another harsh laugh. "That was Kongkempeipa, tsongkar. Going on about how you want to *fix things* when you can't even tell the difference."

Ahn closed his eyes for a moment, his chest tight with embarrassment—no, with shame. Even now, he was struggling against the instinct to defend himself, to insist that these acts of violence had not been his doing. He did not start the feuding that had apparently been working its way through the rainforest. And his relation to Ólawen did not mean he had any say over her orders—though he was desperate to try and understand them, to know why she would move so brutally on these people who were just trying to live their lives.

But he had been there, and he had done nothing. That much was true. He felt nauseous, unable to face the pain he had caused.

He crouched down, picking up the viscera on the ground and throwing it into the buckets. When it was all tidied and his hands were slick and foul, he hoisted the pole back onto his shoulders. "I'm going to bring this to the sãoni," he said quietly.

"Run and I'll kill you," Lita said. "I have my orders."

Ahn gripped the pole tightly; his voice was harsh to his ears. "Where I am from, we do not announce our orders. We simply act on them. So kill me already or save your breath." Before the man could respond, Ahn turned on his heel and walked. Some frantic thing in him braced for the sensation of the spear through his back, skewering him like fresh fruit. But it never came.

Éongrir Ahnschen walked out of Nona Fahang in a fog, vaguely hearing the whispering around him, feeling the creeping press of strangers' eyes. As he passed into the sãoni's territory, he was struck with a peculiar disappointment to find himself whole. It would have been easier, he thought, to face the spear. Easier than another stretch of days with the loathing, the dread.

This wasn't how he was supposed to feel, was it?

He dropped the buckets of carnage at the sãoni's many feet, reminding himself to step back when they lunged in to feed. A few of them growled at him suspiciously, but a low rumble from the alpha settled it down quickly enough. A soft pressure scrabbled up his legs, his torso—the hatchlings had come to see him again. They gummed at his fingers, cleaning up the worst of the filth that had layered on his skin. Their nubby teeth poked at him, but it didn't matter so long as the blood was gone. He couldn't stand the stickiness on his knuckles, the way it creased and cracked, the way the priestess's sponges had chafed at his skin and the healer's sinew had pulled so tightly at his chest—

"Ahn?"

The sound of his name was like a punch, forcing him back into the moment. The hatchlings were squeaking at him for more food. How had he not heard them?

Sohmeng and Hei were sitting together by Mama, a dirt map scratched out in front of them. He must have missed them when he walked out here. Sohmeng was frowning. "You okay?"

Ahn's mouth twitched into a smile. "I'm fine."

Sohmeng didn't bother to hide her skepticism, but she didn't push. "You want some water for your hands?" She passed him a gourd before he could reply and he accepted out of reflex. His body did not feel like his own. "How did they even get so dirty?"

"I was careless." He did his best to wash off all that the hatchlings had not licked away. "Please don't let me interrupt you. I just needed a moment."

"Um, sure." She was quiet a beat longer, obviously leaving space for him to talk in case he changed his mind. Even Hei was quiet, their gaze flickering over him.

When Ahn turned his attention back to the hatchlings, scratching their chins and adjusting their claws on his bare arms, Sohmeng and Hei went back to their conversation. From what he could see, they were talking over the map, likely discussing the migration route again. He wondered where they would go next, once they were rid of him. Wondered what would be left of their route, if his sister was apparently on a warpath.

When he thought about it, Ahn couldn't deny that things had been tense when they first landed in Kongkempei. That wasn't entirely a surprise; Conquest was often met with struggle early on. The hmun was wary of Qiao Sidhur presence, having heard about the previous invasions four years back, the multiple attempts to set up colonies in the lower continent. Those attempts had been unsuccessful; between the sãoni, the insects, the illness, and the terrain, most of the soldiers who survived the first journeys called the land uninhabitable. But after encountering the native peoples, the conquering general determined that it must be possible to claim the Untilled as Qiao Sidh had claimed the upper continent. They would improve it, even.

After that general died of dysentery, Ólawen took up the work with her father the Emperor's blessing. This time, they would not move carelessly. This time, they would study all they had learned of the land, form alliances with the people who dwelled there. They would expand gradually, aiming for peaceful annexation whenever possible to counter the unforgiving ecosystem. Perhaps they would build a road.

Ahn sat hard on the ground, choking on a bitter laugh.

Schenn had come through earlier, Ahn swore it had happened. That was three times now, three times since landing in the Untilled. Three more times than Ahn had ever heard him back in Qiao Sidh.

Run.

There are cracks in the road.

You're scaring him.

He rolled the rounded end of the bone between his fingers; it was smooth against the stretched hole in his ear, but it did not soothe him. In Kørno Wan, his masters had promised the students that their partners would be able to speak to them after death. They would pass messages from the bilateral realm, and the grief of their Six-ings would transform into a new kind of connection.

Ahn didn't feel connected. Ahn felt afraid.

Had he truly accessed Schenn's voice, or was it simply Ahn's best impression of the boy, mimicked under stress? Had something gone wrong during their Six-ing, was that why things were so quiet? Or was Schenn just angry with him? If his Conquest masters were wrong about expanding the Empire, if invasion was never a kindness, what were his Spirit masters wrong about? How deep were the failings of his culture?

Darkness rose in Ahn's chest, suffocating him from the inside. *Help me, Schenn,* he silently pled. *I don't know what to do. I don't know what I've done.*

He pressed his forehead into his knees. Both he and Schenn had consented to their Six-ing; a major condition of the ritual was that either party could call it off at any time. Their partnership was matched, it was equal—except no, it wasn't. It wasn't, because if Schenn backed out, he would have spent the rest of his life as the coward who denied Éongrir Ahnschen a Six-ing. If Ahn had backed out, it would be seen as nothing more than the whims of a flighty royal. At worst, it would have cost him a throne he never expected anyway.

The fight to the death had always been fair. They were equally trained and evenly matched. The fight had been fair, but the choice to enter the arena hadn't. Ahn thought of the long nights before their Six-ing, the way he and Schenn had held each other in the dark. Each and every talk that had died midway when Ahn dared wonder aloud at what would happen if they didn't follow through. Schenn's staunch belief that it had to be done. The polishing of the blades, the blood soaking the sand, his sister's insistence that everyone felt a little complicated about it but that didn't mean it was bad, he was fine, he would be fine—

I'm sorry, he prayed frantically, twisting his earpiece. He did not know what to do with all this power he had not asked for, the power he wielded even now, clumsy as a child. *Schenn, I'm sorry. That day on the beach, I didn't mean to rub it in. I didn't mean for any of this—*

He yelped at the feeling of a hand on his wrist. Hei was crouched beside him, their claws pressed to the flesh of his arm.

"Sorry," he gasped. "Sorry, I'm sorry."

Hei gave him a long look, a single click.

"What Hei said," Sohmeng agreed. She sat down on the other side of him. "You look awful. Do you want to let go of your ear?"

It was throbbing where Ahn had been pulling at it; he hadn't realized until Sohmeng pointed it out. He released the bone, shaken by the image of the lobe tearing, cutting off any chance at connection that he hadn't already ruined.

Hei's knuckles brushed his forehead, his cheek, checking for fever. Their eyes moved from his face to his earpiece, and he resisted the urge to shrink back from them. Everyone back in Qiao Sidh knew what he had done the moment they saw the bone, which protected him from questions. The thought of explaining it aloud made him want to cry.

"No sick," Hei said. They tapped his chest, meeting his eye with a look that might have been sympathetic. "Breathing, Ahnschen."

He breathed. The oxygen made him dizzy. Sohmeng patted his shoulder encouragingly, dropping an escaped hatchling back in his lap. The way it wiggled reminded him of the day one of the hunting dogs at Hvallánzhou had given birth. He'd been a child himself, giggling as a puppy squirmed in his arms.

"So . . . looks like you're freaking out a little," Sohmeng said carefully. Ahn stroked the little sãoni's back, trying to calm down. "Makes sense."

Ahn felt his body lock up, his breathing cut off. "What do you mean?"

Sohmeng tugged at her bangs, looking a little uncomfortable. Beside her, Hei simply watched them, saying nothing. "Well, the trial's coming up, yeah?"

The trial. The *trial*, of course how had Ahn forgotten the trial?

"Oh," he said. "That—yes, that. No, I'm fine. I'm fine."

Hei clicked again. It was more of a snort, actually.

"I'm fine," Ahn echoed. His fingers had found their way back to his earpiece.

"... sure," Sohmeng said. "But just for the sake of argument, what if you weren't fine? I know thirty days is better than none, but it isn't actually that long, and we don't know what the Grand Ones are going to say, and—"

"I think they'll kill me." The words came out easy. From far away, Ahn could hear the relief in his voice. "It would be the right thing to do."

Silence grew between them, filling rapidly with the life of the rainforest. Sãoni chirps and insect chitters and the distant voices of the scouts. The space expanded, and Ahn felt smaller. Felt like himself in the smallness.

Sohmeng broke first. "Ahn—"

"It's true, Sohmeng." Twice now he had cut her off. On top of everything else, he was losing his good manners. "If my people had never showed up, Eiji would be safe. Ateng would be safe. The sãoni would be migrating the way they should. This never would have happened if I had been the one who—"

The fight had been so close. The tear of the blade through Ahn's chest had shocked him and Schenn both. Despite the burning pain, the dizziness of bloodloss, that shock had given Ahn's body the power to retaliate. To finish it.

"That's Qiao Sidh, Ahn," Sohmeng snapped. "That's not you. You weren't even there when they first landed! What were you doing when you were like, what, fourteen?"

Nearly fifteen. He was still at Kørno Wan with Schenn. "Nothing—nothing good, Sohmeng."

"I don't believe that. No one can do *nothing* good."

Sohmeng looked over to Hei, seemingly trying to get them to take her side. They scratched at the dirt with their sãoni claw. "Look, it's true that if Qiao Sidh had never invaded, everything would be better. And you've messed up, you really have, but you're not responsible for your entire empire!"

"I'm the prince."

"*Eleventh born*," Sohmeng spat. "How many times have you said that to me? Besides, you're not just some prince, you're our *friend*." Ahn could see the complexity of the anger that twisted in her; they both knew it wasn't her job to defend him. But she wouldn't back down. "You know what? Enough. This is—this is ridiculous. I'm going to talk to the Grand Ones. You've been doing everything you can, they need to see that!"

Before anyone could argue, Sohmeng was storming back into Nona Fahang. He watched her walk away with her fists clenched and her chin held high.

After a moment, Hei rose as well. Ahn's hand dropped from his ear as he braced himself for another afternoon alone with his swarming thoughts—but then Hei sat back down. Their back brushed his, light as breath. The hint of contact made him want to weep, and despite his best judgment, he pressed back.

Hei allowed it, saying nothing. They sat with him for a long time, holding space for all the ways in which they did not yet know how to touch.

FOURTEEN

ONE AFTERNOON, when Sohmeng was pacing the perimeter of Nona Fahang, things went from bad to worse. The hmun was preparing for a festival honouring the Chisong phase, and Eakang wanted to tell her *all* about it. She was avoiding them—and trying to plan her way out of attending the upcoming party—when she heard the sound.

It was one she would have recognized anywhere, a sound from her worst dreams: human screaming, sãoni snarling. An attack.

Eakang quickly became the least of her worries. Sohmeng bolted for the exit, her mind rushing through worst-case scenarios. She and Hei had been so careful, the sãoni had been adjusting so well. She had promised the Grand Ones that the colony would be a helpful force and not a dangerous one—

A group of scouts were gathered outside Nona Fahang's primary exit, spears in hand, keeping back any curious villagers. They were shouting back and forth with their comrades above, the banyan platform shifting with the rush of footsteps. Arguing with them would take too much time—she had to get through. Sohmeng steeled herself, ready to start shoving, when a firm hand took hold of her arm.

"Good," said Polha Hiwei. "You're here."

"What happened?" Sohmeng demanded. "Is anyone hurt? Where's Hei? You need to get a healer, you need to—"

"I need you to slow down, Minhal," Polha interrupted. Being addressed by her phase name startled Sohmeng into silence, and the leader of the scouts took the opportunity to continue. "No one is hurt, but a sãoni took a snap at one of my scouts."

Sohmeng paled. "I'm—I'm sorry. I'm so sorry. That wasn't supposed to happen."

"That's right it wasn't," Polha agreed, shooting a glare upwards. Even in the ruckus, Sohmeng noticed that the scouts were keeping a wide berth from their leader. "A few of my own decided now would be the time to show off and tease the creatures, like they're shoulder monkeys and not *apex predators.* Didn't think I had to explain that one to grown adults, but here we are."

Sohmeng did not envy the scouts who had pushed their luck. She wanted to be angry, but frankly, she was just grateful it hadn't been worse. "So it's okay, then?"

"Not quite. The issue isn't with the sãoni. It's Hei."

This, Sohmeng was not expecting. "Hei? What are you talking about?"

"When the sãoni lunged, one of the scouts threw down

a spear in defense. She missed, but that didn't stop Hei from picking it up and throwing it right back up at her. Nearly skewered the poor woman, and not so much as an apology."

Sohmeng froze. What was she supposed to say? She could feel the other scouts listening in, waiting for an excuse. "I . . ."

Polha sighed, pulling Sohmeng aside. To her surprise, the woman looked sympathetic. "This was the fault of my scouts, and I apologize. But people are going to talk about Hei's behaviour today, and I can't stop that."

"They're not a bad person," Sohmeng insisted.

"I believe you. At the very least, I trust that Hei is less dangerous than the tsongkar." Polha glanced over her shoulder. "But if they lash out and hurt one of my scouts, there's going to be a problem. Up until now, the sãoni have been a helpful presence, but I need to know that if they get aggressive, Hei will think first of Nona Fahang."

That was absolutely not something Sohmeng could promise. "I'll talk to them."

"It would be more effective if Hei spoke for themself, you know." Polha took Sohmeng's shoulder, looking at her firmly. "Whatever it is you see in them, all the rest of Nona Fahang knows is that they're a wild human who commands sãoni, and just so happened to ride in with a Qiao Sidhur prince."

"I was also there," Sohmeng said tersely. "And I haven't done anything wrong."

"This is true. But it doesn't change the fact that there

is much to fear about Hei. Should the tsongkar's trial go your way, I imagine you'll need Hei and the sãoni to get him back to his people—it would benefit all of you to make introductions. Build some trust with the Grand Ones so they don't send the colony away at the next sign of trouble."

Sohmeng nodded numbly. The logic stood; it just felt impossible.

"Consider it. And send Hei my apologies." With a final pat on Sohmeng's arm, Polha whistled for the scouts to move aside.

A few phases of daily back-and-forth had helped Sohmeng memorize the route. The steps usually felt like a meditative lead-up to seeing her partner, but this time, she felt little but dread as she stepped into the clearing.

Hei was there, and they were furious. They were fussing over one of the adolescent sãoni, holding a spear. It looked freshly made, like one of the pikes they had used to take down Blacktooth. A short distance away, Mama was growling at the treetops. The rest of the colony seemed equally restless.

Sohmeng took a deep breath. "Hei—"

"They were supposed to leave the sãoni be, Sohmeng." Their voice was harsh, impatient. "That was the agreement."

"Polha Hiwei, the leader of the scouts, she wanted me to send her apologies—"

"What do I do with an apology? I do not care about words, I care about actions." Hei pointed a clawed finger at the canopy, their other hand rested protectively on the adolescent sãoni's back. The little creature snuffled at Sohmeng, and she felt a pang of anxiety. This could have been so much worse. "This is their fault. Their mistake."

"I agree. Polha agrees. It was a mistake but—but you threw a *spear* at them, Hei! They're scared of you." She did not like the way that seemed to satisfy them. This wasn't the animal world; being frightening often invited more trouble than it prevented. "We need to focus on calming everyone down. Do you think you could . . . " It was a long shot, but it was all she had. "Would you introduce yourself to the Grand Ones?"

Hei let out a sãoni noise of disbelief, loud enough to make Mama growl. Sohmeng tried to ignore the way the scouts rustled the leaves above them.

"I know," she said, tugging at her bangs in frustration. "I *know*, but if you could just try, if you could tell them that you're on Nona Fahang's side—"

"I am not on Nona Fahang's side."

"Ateng's side, then!"

"*Your* side!" Hei snapped back. "I am on your side, and the side of the sãoni. That is all."

"Then as someone who's on my side, would you please compromise with me on this one thing? For Ahn's sake, for the sake of our plan—"

"*This one thing?*" Hei barked out a laugh, throwing their hands in the air. The sounds they made felt equivalent to curses, which set the rest of the colony to rumbling unhappily. "I am compromising every day, Sohmeng! For your sake, I compromise. I deal with these *people* stomping above me, I encourage the sãoni to be stagnant and lazy and eat from the hand of Nona Fahang."

"Thirty days," Sohmeng said weakly. "I asked for thirty days. It's been seventeen, we're more than halfway through. You said mating season would slow them down."

"Yes—and when it's *over*, half the colony will have new bad habits. What if Mama decides it's easier to stay off the route, less dangerous for her family? They get *treats* on top of their hunting here, don't they? We'd be one more colony gone wrong, eating through the local ecosystem until it eventually ends up even worse than Fochão Dangde."

"Mama's smarter than that," Sohmeng argued. She didn't know if that was true, but she wanted to believe it.

"Then another antsy sãoni claims the alpha title, and there's a rift in the colony."

Sohmeng remembered what it had looked like the night Mama's colony had gone head-to-head with Blacktooth's. She and Hei still wore the skins as proof. The idea of that happening within the group of sãoni she had come to know and care for was devastating.

She had been relying on Hei to be a stabilizing force during the past several phases, trusting them to handle the sãoni so she could focus on the humans. She was asking too much of them, but she didn't know how to manage if they gave her anything less. It was a horrible, helpless feeling. Sitting with it was too heavy to bear, and she grasped at the first idea that came to mind.

"What if—what if I talk to the Grand Ones for you?" she asked. "I could tell them some of your story, that way you don't have to! Just enough so they know you're not a spy for Qiao Sidh. Not, not everything, obviously . . . "

It was the wrong thing to say. It was clumsy and inconsiderate. Hei didn't even respond; they simply stared at her with hurt in their eyes, waiting for her words to run out.

"What would you have me do instead?" Sohmeng asked softly.

"Leave with me," Hei said. They sounded so certain that it was almost tempting. "Now. Tonight. Let Nona Fahang solve its own problems. We can find another way to help Ateng—this hmun wasn't even part of your original plan."

"What about Ahn? He's the reason we're waiting, Hei."

Hei hesitated for only a moment, their brow creased as they came to a decision. "We take him. We steal him away and we all leave together. I can—I can go into Nona Fahang if it's just to get Ahnschen. I won't need to talk to anyone."

Their answer surprised Sohmeng. Hei and Ahn seemed to be tolerating each other more, but she hadn't expected this level of solidarity. At least one thing was going right. Still, for so many reasons, this fantasy was impossible. "I'm sorry, Hei. I don't . . . I don't think that's a good idea. How will they ever trust Ahn in the future if he runs away now?"

Hei frowned, searching for an argument.

"Besides," Sohmeng said, tucking a stray hair behind her ear, "I couldn't leave my dad behind that way."

Hei looked away at the mention of Tonão, and Sohmeng bit down on her disappointment. They had not yet addressed this issue head-on. Considering what her father had gone through with the sãoni, and what Hei had gone through with humans, there wasn't any clear path to their finding a way to meet. While it felt small compared to all the existential challenges they were both facing, it was another glaring reminder of the irreconcilability of Sohmeng's two worlds.

Hei reached out and touched her cheek. Their hand lingered there, present and tender and tired.

"Will you please wait for me? Thirteen more days, that's all." All she could do was hope that Ahn would still be alive by then, that whatever plan they were going with wouldn't be soured by grief.

"I can wait. But if the sãoni are endangered, or interfered with, then . . ." Hei trailed off, biting their lip. Sohmeng understood. It was the right thing to do, even though the idea made her heart hurt.

"I don't want to give up our life together, Hei."

Hei clicked in agreement, pressing their forehead to hers.

Both of their boundaries were necessary, and impossible. They had laid out their individual needs, only to find that neither of them could be fully met. It didn't feel much like compromise when no one was getting what they wanted, but given their current situation, she wasn't sure what alternatives they had.

When Sohmeng returned to Nona Fahang, the Grand Ones saw her immediately. Polha Hiwei translated her apologies and explanations into Fahangpa: what happened with Hei and the sãoni was a mistake. They were terribly sorry, both of them. Yes, everyone had the hmun's best interests at heart. The spear? A misunderstanding, of course. A moment of fear and frustration, but unacceptable. Hei was sorry, really.

It was nothing but empty platitudes and outright lies. Sohmeng left the gazebo exhausted.

She kept her head down as she walked through the hmun, trying her best not to make eye contact with anyone. She could feel the way people were watching her with some awful combination of pity and distrust. Before Eakang could leap out of a shrub to express their condolences, she found her way to Ahn. He was carrying a barrel on his shoulder, flanked by two guards; apparently he had been recruited into setting up tents and seating areas for the Chisong festival.

"Are you alright?" he asked. "I heard there was trouble with the sãoni."

"Yeah, you and the rest of the hmun." Sohmeng grimaced. That wasn't fair. "... sorry. That's not what I meant."

"It's alright." Ahn adjusted the barrel, glancing back at the guards. "I have a few more runs before lunch. Walk with me?"

Sohmeng took him up on the offer, glad for the company of someone who didn't seem interested in judging her. She even helped carry a few things. Lugging around the tents and poles gave her body something to do as she explained what had happened with Hei and the scouts.

As they sat at the table they'd assembled together and shared a pot of soup, she finished her story: "I thought

Hei had a handle on things. I know the sãoni aren't easy to control, but I just needed *one thing* to work out. It's felt like such a mess since we got here, and now the Grand Ones are worried that the sãoni are too dangerous to keep around. And between dealing with my dad's family and—" She caught herself. It probably was kind of tactless to talk to Ahn about the stress of the trial.

He caught her meaning anyway. He poked at his bowl, not quite meeting her eye. "I'm sorry. I know how much trouble I've caused."

"We've been over this, Ahnschen, and I don't want to do it again." She stole a chunk of meat from his bowl, vowing to take another every time he got that self-pitying look on his face. "I'm not interested in the guilt, I just want us to make this right."

"I—I understand." The weight of the whole *they should kill me* conversation still hung unresolved between them. It had scared her to hear Ahn talk that way—she had never encountered such despair in another person. With the added complication of how Ahn's empire had harmed her home, she had no idea how to talk to him about those feelings. It was easier to focus on making a plan. "May I ask you a question?"

"You just did, but go nuts."

"Why wait for me? For the trial?" he asked. "When you found Nona Fahang, it was supposed to be an opportunity to help your home. Now all it is doing is wasting your time. Why not leave and look for help elsewhere? I—I would not be angry, if you left. I would understand."

Sohmeng sucked her teeth. Between her earlier conversation with Hei and now this, her resolve was seriously getting tested. "Aside from the fact that I need you to tell your sister to step off my rainforest?"

Ahn's mouth quirked up in a smile. "Aside from that."

"I know what it feels like to be an exile." It never stopped feeling vulnerable to share this part of her life. Ahn had been filled in on the basic details when she changed her name, but up until now, she had not felt ready to say much more. "I know what it's like to live in fear of being judged poorly. Disowned. Left by myself. And I wouldn't wish that on a friend. I already promised that I would get you out of here—do I look like the kind of person who breaks my promises?"

"No," Ahn said. There was something in his voice she couldn't fully understand. "You do not."

Sohmeng cleared her throat, taking another slurp of soup. "Plus, if your sister found out that I had just left you to die here—not that you're going to die, don't make that face—my bid for negotiation would get shut down pretty fast. I wouldn't work with anyone who hurt my brother, and he's the worst." She thought of Eakang, and quickly reevaluated. "...well. Almost the worst."

Ahn tapped his spoon against his bowl, smiling. "Discernment," he said.

"Hm?"

"You'd do well on the Discernment path, I think."

Sohmeng blinked, taken aback by the change of topic. The Paths of Mastery had intrigued her since she'd first learned of them; she had never imagined that someone's social roles could be so gamified. It sure sounded like a lot more fun than being assigned to them at birth. "What would my name be?"

"You don't really do surnames here, but it seems like your phases hold the same weight as our family lineages, so . . . Minhal Sohmeng Idhrenhvøs." He nodded, satisfied. "I gave you second-ranking to start."

"Benefits of being friends with the prince, huh?" Sohmeng teased, and her shoulders relaxed at the sound of Ahn's laughter. After the ongoing stress they had both been managing, this felt easy. "Why Discernment, though?"

"You're clever," Ahn said. "Incredibly clever. You have a mind for planning, and you always have an eye on the bigger picture." He hesitated. The look on his face could have belonged to Hei; tender and gentle and wild. "You remind me of someone I used to know."

Sohmeng didn't know what to do with that look. She tried to play it off as a joke. "Someone you liked, I hope."

"I loved him with all my heart."

Oh. Well.

Sohmeng opened her mouth. Closed it again. Watched Ahn turn red as a parrot's belly.

" . . . that's not, not what I meant to—" He stumbled over his words, clearly mortified. "Not that I, I mean, you—that's not why I hang out with you."

"Yeah," Sohmeng snorted. "You hang out with me because you're trapped with me."

The joke didn't seem to do much to get Ahn out of

whatever existential vortex he had worked himself into. He rubbed his face, speaking through his fingers. "No, but even if I wasn't trapped, I would still like you. Not because you remind me of him, but because you remind me of—you. You're you, and I like you for who you are. I like being your friend."

Sohmeng would have liked to have said something nice in turn, but Ahn's reaction of combined embarrassment and sincerity seemed to have unlocked something terrible in her. Instead of *that's sweet!* or *I like being your friend too!* or *Ahn are you making this weird?* her mouth decided to blurt out: "Ahn, you're gorgeous and I'd love to, but how would I ever know if you were only offering because of the looming threat of death?"

Ahn laughed, surfacing from his hands. "That's not what I mean! And that wouldn't be—like me."

"What, not allowed to mess around with anyone until you graduate from meathead school?"

"No, no!" Ahn replied. "I'm just not very interested in people that way."

Sohmeng squinted. Sure, she was pretty new to the world of sexual intimacy, but had found it incredibly rewarding so far. She glanced over her shoulder, making sure the guards weren't eavesdropping. "But have you like . . . tried?"

Ahn took another sip of his soup. "A few times, with a few partners. The act itself is almost always nice—like how a massage is nice? I just don't really think about other people that way. Unless they're interested, and there's nothing better to do . . . " He shrugged, smiling a little. "There's a word for it in Qiao Sidhur: *zhørmozhør.*"

Sohmeng did her best to repeat the word back, trying to wrap her brain around the concept. Ahn seemed happy, comfortable with himself. " . . . I hope it hasn't bothered you when I, y'know." She pantomimed squeezing his bicep. "It's just supposed to be for fun, but I wouldn't want to make you feel weird."

"It doesn't bother me," he said, and snagged a bite of meat back from her bowl.

She swatted him, smiling as she returned to her own meal. The conversation reminded her of her early days with Hei; even then, despite the challenges of their circumstances, there had always been time to indulge in playful company.

When was the last time she had felt truly playful? Nona Fahang had left so little room for the easy joy that had defined her days walking Eiji. She was unbelievably grateful to have her father back, but rewriting her history and reimagining her future took a massive amount of energy. She wanted to skip ahead to the part where Eiji was safe, where she could simply bask in the enjoyment of her new life.

Taking an hour to sit with Ahn and laugh about all the ways they were different did not bring her any closer to fixing the world, but it reminded her of what she was fighting for. It made the future feel just a little more possible.

Fifteen

"UP!"

The hatchlings popped up onto their hind legs, little fore-claws raised to the sky. One of them wobbled, squeaking.

"Up!" Ahn repeated firmly. He held his palm above them, slivers of meat tucked between his fingers. The creatures balanced, holding their pose, and he lowered his hand once more. "At rest."

They dropped down, chirping at him hopefully until he passed over the treats. After many attempts and no small amount of unhappy gumming, the hatchlings were finally beginning to catch on to his training methods.

"Well done," he murmured, stroking their heads one by one. "Very clever."

The idea had come to him after his conversation with Sohmeng. She was stressed, trying to satisfy so many people at once, and none of them seemed to appreciate the work she was putting in.

Considering how much of this balancing act was on Ahn's behalf, he owed it to her to ease the burden. There wasn't much he could do about the Grand Ones' refusal to help Ateng, and his word that Sohmeng wasn't a Qiao Sidhur spy would probably be the opposite of helpful, but keeping the sãoni in line—oddly enough, that was something he *could* help with.

Being raised in the royal family, part of his early education in the Fertility path had included raising animals. Despite the fact that the sãoni were gigantic reptilian predators, they seemed receptive to the same training as hunting dogs or raptor mounts. It helped that the hatchlings were still small, and quite attached to him. His relationship with Lilin had been built much the same way. If he could get the sãoni to respond to some basic commands, Sohmeng could prove to the Grand Ones that she and Hei had them under control.

"Up!" he called again, firmly enough that some of the other sãoni paid attention. Luckily, none of them seemed troubled by his actions, simply curious.

The hatchlings moved more smoothly with each run of the obedience exercise. Even though it made him feel a little silly, he tried to imitate one of their happy sounds to show his pride in them. It mostly seemed to confuse them—maybe Hei or Sohmeng would show him how to do it later.

He smiled to himself, feeling hope rise within him for the first time in a while. Despite the unease that had lingered in his gut since talking to Lita Soon, the other guards seemed to be getting less prickly around him. After all of his tasks were completed, he was allowed out with the sãoni; the scouts in the trees were omnipresent, but they weren't dropping melons on him anymore, and that was a marked improvement on his experience.

"Up!" he called again to the hatchlings. They were quicker this time, sharper-eyed. He would have to give them a break soon, so they would be at their best when he showed this new trick to Sohmeng. He wanted to prove to her that he was worth the time she was putting in for him, that he was capable of more than just destroying things. He wanted this like he wanted Hei to judge him positively, like he wanted to make things right with Nona Fahang. With all of Gãepongwei. Everything felt so out of his control, but he could try to be a decent person. A regular person, rather than some foreign prince of an invasive empire. People could see him as something better than he was, and maybe Sohmeng—

"At rest." The hatchlings dropped down, eyes locked on him for their reward. Ahn swallowed, reining in his thoughts before they drifted into dangerous territory.

Behind him, Mama chirped loudly. He tossed her the rest of the food without a word. Training the alpha seemed risky, far beyond his capabilities; he wasn't sure how much work he could even do on a creature of Mama's age and status.

He turned back to the hatchlings, raising a hand without any treats in it. Moment of truth. "Up!" he called to them, and they rose.

"At rest," he said, and they sat. Though they chirped quietly, they accepted his stroking as reward enough, and he felt himself glow with pride at his work.

" . . . what you are doing, Ahnschen?"

Ahn was abruptly jolted from his pride, nearly poking one of the hatchlings in the eye. With a little tut of apology, he looked up to see Hei watching him with their arms crossed.

"Sorry," he said, smiling sheepishly. "You startled me."

They didn't return the warmth. On the contrary, they were looking at him with more hostility than he had seen in weeks. He resisted the urge to take it personally; of course they would be tense after the sãoni's altercation with the scouts.

With a single click, they nodded their chin in the direction of the little sãoni. "What is this?"

"Oh!" He stood up. Maybe showing them the new trick would help lift their mood. "I'm glad you're here. I've—I've actually been working at it all afternoon. Look, let me show you. Up!"

With well-practiced movements, he bade the hatchlings rise and rest, not even needing meat as a motivator this time. They moved with his hand, their bodies synchronized in a perfect demonstration of his training abilities. To his delight, he noticed that some of the other sãoni were paying attention. Perhaps the older ones wouldn't be so difficult to work with after all.

He looked back at Hei, smiling brightly. "You see? They're so clever, they picked it up so—"

Hei was not smiling back. Ahn's enthusiasm faltered, his hands dropping to his sides.

"Is something wrong . . . ?" he asked. One of the hatchlings jumped up at his hand, nosing between his fingers for where the meat used to be.

Hei stepped forward, making a sharp sãoni noise that sent the hatchlings scurrying away. They growled something Ahn couldn't understand, then followed it up in Dulpongpa. "No more. No more . . . this!"

"What?" Ahn's shoulders fell. He couldn't understand what they were so angry about. "What did I do?"

Hei gestured aggressively at the sãoni. "*Animals.* Not, not *games.* Not for—" The imitated his motions, only seeming to get more frustrated by their inability to share the language. "Not *yours.*"

"Animals play plenty of games," Ahn said tersely. He could feel the tension that had eased from him this afternoon returning, putting him on the defensive. Vaguely, he wondered why that was the first thing he had thought to say.

"Not your games," Hei retorted.

Ahn wasn't sure what they meant by that, but he didn't appreciate their tone. Why—after all of these weeks of struggling to understand each other, after the hard-earned nights where they had finally been able to sit side-by-side without Sohmeng as a barrier—why were they treating him with so much distrust? He had been so sure that somewhere along the way they had come to an understanding.

"It's not just for fun, Hei," Ahn said. "I'm—I want to see if we can train them. I want to help."

"Help?" Hei spat, turning their back to him. "No help. Just trouble, more big trouble."

"How is training them trouble?"

"Human games! Sãoni not—not *for* humans."

The creatures around him were paying even more attention now, alarmed by Hei's raised voice. Ahn doubted his own frustration was doing much to help, and he tried once more to keep it in check. He tugged at his earpiece. "Well speaking as a human, I think we would all feel a bit more reassured to know that they could be tamed."

Hei squinted, missing the word. "Tamed? What is tamed?"

It should have been obvious that he would have to explain this. "Not wild. Not dangerous. Still animals, but they listen to humans. Tame."

Hei let out what must have been the Sãonipa equivalent of a curse, a hiss loud and vicious enough that Mama rose with a warning growl. They advanced on him, the fury in their eyes burning hot enough to intimidate despite the several inches he had on them. Briefly, he wondered if they were going to go back on their word and hit him.

"Not being *good*," they said, voice shaking. "Just like all others—other humans. Worse. Sãoni tsongkar."

The word hit him with surprising force, falling like a stone in his stomach. He had gotten used to hearing it flung around by the residents of Nona Fahang, but this was different. It hurt in a way he could not explain, to be met with such disgust by someone he was coming to think of as a friend.

Ahn had made plenty of mistakes, but he did not think this was one of them. So instead of shrinking back, he held his ground. "The sãoni don't seem to mind."

"What?" Hei snapped.

"You don't like it," Ahn said slowly, "but they have not complained. UP."

With a sharp lift of his hand, the hatchlings were up on their hind legs again, squeaking at him nervously. Despite the fact that this colony had been prepared to eat him not a Qiao Sidhur month before, the rest of the sãoni made no move against him. Even the alpha simply watched, growling in a way that Ahn did not fully believe was directed at him alone.

He narrowed his eyes at Hei, emboldened by the proof around him. "At rest," he said, the words a warning to them both.

Hei wasn't interested in heeding it. With another Sãonipa snarl, they lunged—

—only to be stopped by a swat from Mama. They struggled against her powerful legs, her pressing nose. Ahn would have stumbled out of the scuffle, but the giant lizard had pinned him with one of her back legs, and the hatchlings were using the opportunity to jump all over him in search of more food.

"You—!" Hei shouted, but their voice was drowned out by the squawks of the alpha.

The commotion only got louder when Sohmeng came

running through the entrance to Nona Fahang. She was out of breath, frazzled; a piece of bark was caught in her bun.

"Whoa!" she shouted, looking at the scene before her. "Whoa, whoa, what in two dark moons—"

Hei let out an unintelligible sãoni noise, still fighting against the powerful hold of the alpha, whose concerned nosing had all but knocked them on their back. With a careful roll, Ahn pulled himself out from under the cage of claws, panting with effort.

"Sohmeng," he said, quickly trying to compose himself. Given the interspecies brawl that he was currently involved in, it probably wasn't very convincing. "I didn't, I didn't see you there—"

Sohmeng rushed over to Hei, trying to calm them down alongside Mama. "Yeah, funny that. Anyone want to explain why one of our watchmen just came rushing over, insisting I *come out here quick, before they kill each other*? Hei, please stop—"

Ahn's heart dropped. This wasn't how today was supposed to go.

Hei barked something in Atengpa as Sohmeng coaxed Mama away from them.

"Get him out? Hei, what are you talking about? What *happened*?" She looked at Ahn, bewilderment in her eyes. Even with the trouble between him and Hei early on, it had never looked anything like this. "What did you do?"

Before Ahn could defend himself, Hei was speaking rapidly in Atengpa, pointing their clawed knuckle at Ahn in accusation. It was unbelievably frustrating to be left out of the conversation.

Sohmeng, at least, was reasonable. She put her hands on Hei's shoulders and pressed cheeks with them, trying to calm them down. It worked, and soon the only sounds around them were her voice murmuring Atengpa and the curious chirps of the sãoni who had gathered to watch the scene, like it was some schoolyard grudge match.

Mama nudged him with her tail, and much to Ahn's surprise, it made him feel a little less alone.

"Okay," Sohmeng said in Dulpongpa, stroking Hei's hair. "So I caught about half of that. *What* were you doing with the hatchlings?"

"It—it was supposed to be a surprise," Ahn said.

"Well I certainly am surprised," she said flatly. "Now, details please?"

Ahn's voice crumpled in his throat. It was like being young again, caught by his Discernment master without any answers. He swallowed, trying to calm himself, to speak in that self-assured way that had gotten him through his brief foray into adult court life. "You said the Grand Ones might feel safer if they knew we had a strong handle on the sãoni. So I was—I was trying to teach them some tricks, some training . . ." He pushed his hair from his eyes, feeling foolish. "Could I show you? It's easier if you see."

After a tense exchange with Hei, Sohmeng agreed.

Ahn whistled the hatchlings over, waving his palm at them. Peeping excitably, they climbed over Mama and settled at his feet. Ahn squared his shoulders, raised his hand.

"Up," he said, and the little creatures rose up without hesitation. Despite the hours he had put into this, it looked so much less impressive now. Hardly worth the trouble it had caused, trouble he could still barely comprehend. "At rest." Down the trio dropped, chirping at each other happily.

Don't you see? Ahn wanted to ask Hei. *It's harmless.*

Instead, he turned his attention to Sohmeng, who did in fact look surprised for a moment before she covered her face and groaned.

"Ahn," she said, voice strained. "You should have told me. Or asked, or something."

Ahn's shoulders dropped. "I didn't think it would be a problem."

"No," Sohmeng muttered, rubbing her temples. "No, of course not. You wouldn't understand—"

Whatever else she was going to say was drowned out by Hei, who had returned to their stream of hostile Atengpa. Ahn wished they would switch over to Dulpongpa; maybe it wasn't their first language, or even their preferred one, but it was the one they shared. Ahn had been forcing it into his head with such intensity that he'd gone to bed with a headache nearly every night since he'd shown up. But they insisted on locking him out of the conversation.

He was getting ready to walk himself straight back to the pygmy hogs when Sohmeng suddenly made a sãoni noise loud enough to make him jump. Hei tried to counter it with a hiss of their own, but Sohmeng stood her ground.

"I want him *out*," Hei said, this time in pointed Dulpongpa. "Not with sãoni. No Ahn with sãoni, no more *humans* with sãoni. I say before Sohmeng, I say again now—no more humans!"

"Hei, this is not helping!" Sohmeng responded. "He didn't mean—"

"OUT."

"FINE." Sohmeng pointed at Ahn with a frustrated shout. "You—come with me. We're going inside." She said something else to Hei in Atengpa that earned her a glare, but ended their yelling. She grabbed his hand in hers and tugged him through the banyan maze, where a scout was waiting to accompany them.

The bustle of Nona Fahang should have drowned out the fight, especially seeing as everyone was preparing for the Chisong moon festival, but Ahn couldn't shake the feeling that people were staring at him. He felt hyperconscious of his disheveled appearance, the dirt smeared on his clothes and the hair come loose from his braid. A scout had come for Sohmeng—what had they told the others? Did everyone think this was his fault now, too?

Ahn had just wanted to help. To show that he wasn't dangerous—no, that he was an ally! The thought that his ridiculous plan might have just ruined both of their chances of ever getting home made him feel sick.

"Come here," snapped Sohmeng.

Ahn blinked, and realized she had brought him to her

father's home, where Ahn usually came to use the shower. Ahn swallowed the knot in his throat, trying to ask if this was a good idea, but Sohmeng dragged him inside.

"Dad!" she said in Dulpongpa, nearly sending Tonão Sol to the floor in surprise.

"Sohmeng?" The man looked between the two of them with confusion. "Is everything—"

"Ahnschen is staying with us."

Ahn blanched. That didn't sound like a request. "Sohmeng," he said in an undertone, "that isn't necessary—"

"Shut up, Ahn," Sohmeng replied.

Ahn shut up.

"Sohmeng," Tonão said cautiously, looking at Ahn. "I'm not sure what's happened, but perhaps we should talk about this."

"You want to talk?" Sohmeng asked. "Fine. This is Ahnschen whatever-the-phase, eleventh prince of Qiao Sidh. Please, call him Ahn. Now, you might know him as the incredibly toned prisoner who sometimes uses your shower after he's gotten covered in crap, or guts, or whatever other horrible thing he stumbles into. He's good at a million things, but right now everyone's real caught up on how well he swings a sword. Ahn and I have both had a difficult day, and having him stay with my impossibly stubborn partner is not an option right now. So I am asking you, as your daughter, to please let him stay here before I scream so loudly that I *bring down the moons.*"

Tonão and Ahn shared a brief look, the kind of

camaraderie that can only exist between two people who are deeply afraid of a third.

"Of course, Sohmeng," the man said after a moment. "I'll—I'll go talk to Jaea and Pim."

"Thank you."

Things got a little bit surreal after that. After some more arguing from across the privacy flap, Tonão returned with a hammock for Ahn to hang outside. He took it gratefully, but kept his talking to a minimum, not wanting to disturb Sohmeng, who had not finished seething in her own hammock. Later, Tonão briefly introduced him to the women of the house. One of them, Jaea Won, came in with a baby on one hip and a new set of clothes for him under her arm. Without a shared language, all she could offer him was a pat on the arm, but he appreciated it.

The other woman, Pimchuang Ker, was not so welcoming. When she dropped off two bowls of leafy salad, she avoided Ahn's gaze. Apparently her ease with him was reserved for outside of the home. He struggled not to taste her bitterness in the meal.

Aside from offering Ahn some after-dinner lemongrass to chew, Tonão stayed out of their way. Eventually, Sohmeng broke the silence.

"Come with me to the Chisong festival tomorrow."

Ahn looked up from the empty bowl he had been scratching at with his fork. "Sorry?"

"The Chisong festival," Sohmeng repeated, swinging in her hammock. Ahn hadn't yet moved outside to his own, not wanting to be by himself. "It's one of the lunar phases, double full moon. We're not supposed to rank the phases in terms of importance, but we totally do, and Chisong is a big deal. Kids born under it are basically guaranteed rank, just like ones born under Minhal are booted for being its opposite." Tension sang in the quiet that followed. "Well. In Ateng they are, anyway."

Ahn had heard a little about Sohmeng's experience with the phases, and knew she had recently changed her own to Minhal. But he hadn't been given much insight into how she felt about it. In general, she didn't seem overly inclined to share feelings.

"You've been setting it up for the past few days. You might as well come in and enjoy the food. Dance a little. I don't know." She rubbed her face. "The whole thing seems a little show-offy to me, but whatever."

"I see," Ahn said carefully. He straightened up, trying to get a better look at her in the hammock. "I appreciate the, the explanation, but . . ."

"But what?"

"Is it really a good idea for me to go?" Kind though the invitation was, the image of him celebrating with the village currently deliberating on his death sentence felt a little gauche.

"What?" Sohmeng sat up. "It's a great idea! You're never supposed to be left alone, and getting stuck with me definitely keeps that from happening. Plus it lets your regular guards relax during the festival, which might make them look on you more favourably. I'm sure Lita Soon will be crushed, but he can find someone else to antagonize for a night."

Ahn laughed a little at that, but his doubts remained. "What about everyone else?" he asked. "I've done what I can to give back to the community, but they all mostly think I'm just . . ."

"A dirty, no good tsongkar?" Sohmeng rolled her eyes. "They can get over it."

It would have been easy to take Sohmeng's apparent forgiveness and hold it above everyone else's wariness. But much as he liked her, she didn't have the final word on how others were supposed to feel. "I don't know, Sohmeng. It seems a little . . . insensitive?"

"What, so you just hide away forever? They already know you're here, Ahn! They won't like you either way so you might as well—" She sighed loudly, struggling for a moment to find her words. "Look, do you want this war campaign to continue?"

"No." The word came out so abruptly, with such vehemence, that he surprised himself. Even still, he stood by it. "I don't. If—when, *when* I get back to my sister, I'll do everything I can to make her stop." That wasn't good enough. He swallowed, tried again. "I will make her stop. And when I return to Qiao Sidh, I will talk to my parents and be sure this never happens again."

"Good," Sohmeng said firmly. "You want peace, so show Nona Fahang peace. No one said you couldn't go, so you might as well take the opportunity, Ahnschen. You've already cleaned up their garbage and not murdered them all in their sleep, so smiling at a party should be no problem."

"You're—you're right," he conceded. It was a bizarre approach, but a diplomatic one. And Sohmeng did have a better head for this kind of thing than he did. "This could be a turning point."

Sohmeng flopped back down into the hammock with a sigh. "And then I don't have to be there alone, which is also a big freaking plus."

It seemed strange to Ahn that Sohmeng would feel like she was going alone when her father and his family would also be there. Then again, things were hardly ever that simple. Despite how much he had always enjoyed social events, Ahn knew the feeling of being lonely in a crowd, of laughing with friends while trying to ignore the impossible chasm between everyone's life experiences.

He could not understand what it was like to be Sohmeng Minhal. But if she considered his company at the Chisong festival worthwhile, he wanted to prove her right. Instead of coming up with ways to impress her, it would be wiser—and more respectful—to simply do as he was asked.

"...thank you," Ahn said quietly. "For giving me another chance."

"Yeah, Ahn. No problem."

"Really," he insisted. "Your company has been—I mean it's really—"

"Don't you get mushy on me now, Ahnschen," she interrupted, pushing off the wall with her foot to make the hammock sway. "The moonless void of my heart cannot handle any more feelings tonight."

Ahn doubted that, but he didn't push it any further.

He took a bite of the lemongrass Tonão had left for him, savouring the pop of flavour on his tongue. It cleared the bad taste today had left in his mouth, refreshing and resetting. He imagined the festival. For one night, he could be a stranger at a party rather than a prisoner from a far-off land.

Ahn fell asleep to dreams of dancing. In the dream, he was floating across a dance hall in the winter palace, spinning from partner to partner. First, he was a child, dancing with imaginary siblings who laughed with him and pinched his cheeks. Then, he was back at Asgørindad, pressed close to friends who had forgotten his title, who wanted nothing more than to tell him jokes and fall asleep on his shoulder during lectures.

There was someone else he danced with in that dream—a partner with a sheathed sword at his hip. A boy whose face remained hidden. Ahn craned his neck as he twirled the boy, trying to get a closer look. Just when Ahn thought he had it, the boy turned to sand in his hands. It glittered in his palms, ran through his fingers. Left Ahn wondering when the music had stopped.

Sixteen

SOHMENG MINHAL TOOK A DEEP BREATH, steadying herself to face her opponent. She had withstood many an injustice in her sixteen and a half years, but this was really, *really* pushing it. Even still, it had to be done. She would not back down from a challenge, no matter how distasteful.

"Hey Eakang!" she said, smiling as brightly as her teeth could bear.

The young Minhal jumped. "S-Sohmeng! I didn't see you there." They tucked their hands behind their back, glancing at Ahn, who was standing quietly by Sohmeng's side. "Um, what's up?"

Sohmeng forced her smile a little wider, trying to counter their nervous energy. Of course they were nervous—she had ripped them a new lunar phase the last time they were alone together. Deserved as it had been, she couldn't let old problems get in the way of her new mission.

"Oh, I just wanted to say hi before the Chisong festival

tonight! I'm sure you'll be *so* busy, so I figured I'd wish you a watchful eye now." Ahn cleared his throat, nudging her. Yeah, she was laying it on a little thick.

Eakang smiled a little. "That's really nice of you. If, if you wanted to hang out during it we could totally—"

"Have you met Ahn?" Sohmeng asked, pushing the man forward. "I don't know if you've had the chance to be introduced!"

"I mean, I was one of the scouts who brought you both in—"

"Of course, of course," Sohmeng said, waving her hand at them. "But I don't think you've really had a chance to *talk*, to get to know each other!"

Some part of Sohmeng knew, deep down, that this was not her most shining moment. And under Chisong, at that. She justified it with some vague thought about Minhal and opposites and *intentions aren't everything just let me live okay* and decided to work on being a more honest person later.

"Let me do the honours," she said. "Ahn, this is Eakang Minhal. My father's—stepchild. Eakang, this is Ahnschen, eleventh prince of Qiao Sidh and a very good friend of mine!"

Ahn inclined his head at Eakang with a warm smile, but didn't tap his unpierced left earlobe; Sohmeng had told him to leave out the Qiao Sidhur greetings for now. "It is my pleasure to meet you, Eakang Minhal."

"Um, you too, Ahnschen!" To Sohmeng's surprise, Eakang offered a tentative smile of their own, and a hand for him to grasp. Good. The less anxious they were, the easier this would be.

"Ahn's coming with me to the Chisong festival this evening!" Sohmeng announced, linking arms with the man.

Eakang's brows raised. "Is he?"

"He really is." Sohmeng gripped Ahn's arm a little tighter, daring him to run away at the last minute. She'd been talking him out of his stage fright on-off throughout the day. With her best pass at a winsome sigh, Sohmeng amped up her own performance. "I just . . . I really hope that he's able to have a nice time. That we all are! This festival is *so* important, and such a *great* way to share in culture and community. It would be so devastating if people let their own grudges get in the way of everyone having a nice time, don't you think?"

"It is supposed to be a special time for everyone," they agreed carefully.

"And Ahnschen has wanted so badly to learn more about Nona Fahang. Sure, the circumstances that brought him here were kinda complicated, but he . . . well, he—" Sohmeng jabbed him in the side. "Tell Eakang what you said."

"What I said?"

"Just this morning. About Nona Fahang." Sohmeng blinked at him slowly. Was this man seriously in the running to become an emperor? "How you feel about Nona Fahang."

"Ah!" Took him long enough. "I am sorry, my Dulpongpa is not very . . ." Ahn shrugged apologetically. "It is one thing I want to learn more of. I would like to see true peace between our, our cultures—and that comes from learning each other. But I know I have hurt people, and they don't have much reason to trust me. So it is hard to make things right, even though I want to be—to be good."

"Be better," Sohmeng agreed, nodding emphatically. The genuine guilt in Ahn's voice was a nice touch—and a reassurance that she was doing the right thing. "He just hasn't had much opportunity, you know? So I *sure do hope* people give him a chance tonight."

"It—it's important to try to make things right after causing harm," Eakang agreed, looking at Ahn with newfound sympathy.

"And *I* know that Ahn's a decent guy," Sohmeng said, squeezing his bicep for good measure. Like an unripe melon. "But I don't think anyone will listen to me. I'm an outsider, after all."

Much to Sohmeng's delight, understanding dawned on Eakang's big dumb face.

"You know what?" they said, pushing one of their braids over their shoulder with a look of determination. "I can help."

"*Really*?" Sohmeng asked. This was too easy. "But *how*?"

"I can talk to people," Eakang insisted. "I can tell them that Ahn's a really good guy, and that he's trying his best to get to know everybody. I don't want to brag, but I've used my Minhal standing to try out a lot of things in the hmun, and I know a lot of people. Maybe they'll listen to me!"

Sohmeng pressed her hands to her cheeks, dragging

Ahn's arm along for the ride. "Wow! That's such a great idea, Eakang! I *never* would have thought of it!"

Eakang beamed, bouncing on their toes. "I should go get ready! And then I'll get right to it. You can—you can count on me, Sohmeng! And you too, Ahnschen. I won't let you down!"

As they ran off to spread the good word of Éongrir Ahnschen, Sohmeng marvelled at her own brilliance. In one fell swoop, she'd found a way to build goodwill for Ahn *and* keep Eakang out of her hair during the Chisong festival. Maybe tonight wouldn't be so bad after all.

"Told you it would work," she said smugly.

"You were right, but . . ."

"But what?" Sohmeng laughed. "I didn't also manage to snag a Grand One's seat?"

"Eakang might not be your favourite person, but they're a good kid," Ahn said gently. "I bet they would have agreed to help if you'd just asked."

The words churned uncomfortably in Sohmeng's gut. That was probably true. But with everything else going on, the additional task of being *nice* was one thing too many to juggle.

"We should get ready too," Sohmeng said. "All this work won't go anywhere if we show up to the party looking like something the sãoni dragged in."

As the two of them took their turns in the shower stall and changed into fresh clothes, they could hear the sounds of people and music filling the hmun's main square. Sohmeng tied her hair up into two buns, one for each of the moons; it was different from what she was used to, but it was nice to feel a little festive. As she rubbed crushed plumeria petals onto her neck, she tried to push back her nerves.

In contrast, Ahn appeared to be leaning into the social mood in the air. Despite the fact that he was far from home in a stranger's set of clothes, surrounded by people who did not care for him, he readied himself for the event with quiet poise. Sohmeng supposed he had gone to plenty of parties before, being a prince and all.

"Do you want help with your hair?" she asked, watching him braid the long strands of black and silver. It seemed like a nice thing to offer. A reminder that they were in this together.

He looked up at her, surprised. "If—if you'd like?"

Sohmeng decided she would. She sat behind him, finishing the braid and twisting it into a little bun. It was nice, pulled back from his face. Her gaze wandered briefly to the exposed piercing in his ear. She poked it, curious. "What is this?"

Ahn jumped slightly at the touch, bringing his fingers up to the jewelry. The motion seemed almost protective, as though she had poked a healing wound. "It—it's a piece of home."

Nosy though she was, Sohmeng could hear the hesitancy in his voice, and decided not to press. "It's nice," was all she said. She secured her sãoni skin wrist cuffs, now decorated with some of the wovenstone beads she had taken from Sodão Dangde. She understood the comfort of the familiar.

Ateng had several holidays, so Sohmeng was no stranger to the concept of parties. But Nona Fahang put one on like she had never seen. It looked like the entire hmun had flooded the square, a swirling mass of red and white in celebration of the moons. Everyone's cheeks were painted according to their birth phases in imitation of the Grand Ones' tattoos. As far as she could tell, they had also coordinated their outfits according to gender, with the men in white dresses, the women in red, and the bigender in mixes of both. It was unusual to see people wearing these visual identifiers; usually gender was expressed through language, not appearance. Still, she was suddenly thankful for the attention with which Jaea Won had dropped off their own clothing, colouring Ahn in the masculine and Sohmeng in the feminine. She would have to thank her later.

Two enormous bonfires had been put up in the square, and people danced around them in circles, hand-in-hand. The Grand Ones clapped along with the musicians, the more mobile ones getting up to join the dancing while the seated were attended to by party-goers. Long tables were laid with food, almost all of it symbolically circular: stacked cross-sections of fruit glazed in honey, thick steamed buns sprinkled with seeds, bowls of mint water, and pungent, spiced berry wine. People helped themselves to generous portions, and for each item that was taken, two more seemed to appear in its place. Pimchuang Ker was refilling a bowl of candied flower buds, laughing with her neighbours.

Sohmeng squeezed Ahn's hand in her own, feeling very far from home.

Ateng was a land of balance, not bounty. Every portion was sacred, every choice intentional; neighbours shared out of a collective respect for the limitations of their home. Where the wine flowed in Nona Fahang, mountain marrow trickled in Ateng—and even then, the drink of distilled mountain water, ground herbs, and precious sediment was only allowed to the Grand Ones.

Sohmeng had been taught that high holidays were a time for prayer, for gathering together in gratitude to reenact ancient stories and reflect on the ways in which they resonated in peoples' personal lives. Celebrations were fun, of course—any break from routine was a good time, and she loved watching all of the plays and puppetry and competitions as a child. But the hmun's strict adherence to tradition made for an often solemn undertone.

By Ateng's standards, Nona Fahang's notion of worship was verging on blasphemous. Sohmeng watched it play out, trying to superimpose her childhood onto a place full of this much joy. Would she have been happier here, in this bubbling, raucous hmun that treated tradition as a living breathing thing?

Obviously, said a voice in her head. *I mean, you wouldn't have been exiled just for being born.*

"Are you hungry?" Ahn asked, peering over at one of the tables. "It looks like one of the lines shrunk."

"I could check out the food, yeah." Delicious as everything smelled, Sohmeng's didn't feel very hungry. All she had ever wanted in Ateng was to see her community really let loose, to shake off the parts of their culture that made Sohmeng feel stifled. Seeing it happen elsewhere struck an unexpectedly jealous note.

Her parents had been traders. They had known about Nona Fahang, even visited it in the past, which meant they *knew* Minhal didn't have to be a death sentence. So why had they chosen to hide her away? Why didn't they just leave Ateng and bring her to a hmun where they knew she would have been safe, where she could have lived exactly as she was?

Sohmeng took a bite of a steamed bun, thankful to have something tangible to sink her teeth into. She was deciding what food she would sneak out for Hei when Eakang came bounding over, two dark spots painted on their cheeks.

"Sohmeng!" they said excitedly. "I was looking for you!"

"Well, you found me." She willed her feet to stay planted; annoying as they were, Eakang was doing a massive favour by putting in a good word for Ahn. And if she was being honest with herself, Ahn's earlier comment was rankling at her.

"Come paint your cheeks with the other Minhals!" they said, pointing at their own face. "We saved some black paint for you, and it might clear up some confusion about the whole Par thing."

The whole Par thing. Sohmeng took a slow breath, forcing a smile. "Thanks, Eakang."

"It's no trouble, really!" They looked to Ahn, tilting their head in thought. "I'd invite you to get painted too but um . . . you don't know your birth phase, do you?"

"I'm afraid not," he replied with an apologetic smile."I'm sorry."

"Oh, no, it's okay!" Eakang patted him on the arm. "I just didn't want you to feel like I was leaving you out or anything."

"That's—that's very kind of you, Eakang."

"It's no trouble! This must all be kind of uncomfortable for you, huh?"

Ahn's shoulders seemed to drop a fraction. "It's not so bad. Just . . ."

"Complicated," Eakang finished, nodding. Ahn looked like a little kid, relieved after struggling to hold in a secret. "But we're going to make it work! Try to enjoy yourself, okay? It's a party!"

Watching this should have been reassuring. Wasn't it what Sohmeng wanted, to have Ahn find his place? To not be antagonized by the community, to have the opportunity to prove himself? She should have been glad to see how easily Eakang spoke to Ahn and invited him into their circle. She should have been thankful that *someone* here knew what to say to him to shake off that stiff posture, even if it wasn't her. That would have been the good, adult response.

Sohmeng didn't feel like an adult right now. She felt like an angry child, powerless against an oncoming tantrum.

With the light of Chisong on her head, she forced down the feeling until her chest ached. She let the Minhals paint her cheeks, listened to them chatter about their lives, watched as they invited Ahn into their conversations. Every kind word seemed to smooth him around the edges, until he transformed into a version of himself she had not seen before: charming, social, radiating warmth. Seeing him this way made Sohmeng suddenly aware of how uneasy he had been since she met him, how private and afraid.

"What are festivals like in Qiao Sidh?" one of the more inquisitive Minhals asked through Eakang's translation.

"That is a—a *big* question. We have many celebrations and holidays, and they're all a little different." He smiled, tugging at his earpiece. "The Empire is large, with many—many types of people. One of my favourites, up north in the mountains, they carve—oh, I don't know the word. It's water. Water so cold it is like stone. They make it beautiful. Make images and, and *cups* you can drink wine from."

"Can water get that cold?" the Minhal asked doubtfully. "What would happen to the rivers?"

"It depends on how fast the river is, and how deep," Ahn explained.

Before the interrogation could continue, the drums began to rise. Apparently this song was a favourite, because a bunch of them jumped up, apologizing and running off to dance.

"What about you, Sohmeng?" another Minhal asked. "Are there parties like this in Ateng?"

"Pamai!" Eakang said, giving them a stern look. "Don't bother Sohmeng about Ateng."

"You don't need to be bossy Eakang," Pamai retorted, crossing their arms and putting Sohmeng in the awful position of wanting to defend Eakang's bossiness. "You can't just hoard Sohmeng because they're in your house!"

The black circles suddenly felt very heavy on Sohmeng's cheeks. With Minhal marked on her face, she was probably going to be hearing the neutral pronoun a lot from here on out. Shame twisted in her as she wondered if it would have been easier to just keep claiming Par.

"*You* don't need to be a *jerk*, Pamai. All I'm saying is that their business is their own."

"I think *she* can decide for *herself* what to share," Ahn interjected, a firm but polite smile on his face. He took Sohmeng's hand in his, lacing their fingers together. He didn't seem to notice the way Eakang and Pamai gawked.

Sohmeng swallowed, squeezing his hand, unsure what to make of the fact that Ahnschen Qøngemzhir understood this better than anyone. "I think I'd like to go dance now."

"Dancing sounds wonderful," he agreed, rising with a poise that was, for once, actually pretty princely. It was odd to see it now, knowing Ahn as she did—but the oddness didn't stop her body from tingling when he rested a hand on her lower back and steered her away.

Leaving the Minhals behind made her feel like she could breathe again. She focused on the rhythm of the music vibrating through the soles of her feet. Was Hei feeling it now, on the other side of Nona Fahang's walls? Were the sãoni scratching in the dirt, searching for the source of the rumbling?

This dance featured partners, one masculine and one feminine, symbolizing each of the moons. In the center,

Chisong children danced in a circle, with a group of Minhals encircling them in turn.

"Shall we?" Ahn asked, looking down at Sohmeng, the reflection of the bonfire in his eyes. That's when she realized he was serious.

"No way, handsome," she laughed.

He flushed at the name, but waved it off. "I don't understand. I thought you said you wanted to dance?"

"Uh, yeah, because I was trying to bail from a weird conversation? In case you forgot, I'm kind of new here, I don't know this dance. And unless this is some elaborate prank and you're actually from Nona Fahang—in which case, I'm feeding you to Green Bites—you don't know it either."

Ahn scanned the crowd briefly, shrugging. "It doesn't look too difficult."

Sohmeng put her hands on her hips, giving him her most disbelieving look. "What, you expect me to believe that you can figure out a Chisong dance after a few minutes of watching?"

Ahn gasped in mock-offense, pretending to be wounded. "Does the lady doubt me?"

"The lady totally doubts."

"Then let me show you." He held out a hand, and the air seemed to part around it for all his eagerness.

Sohmeng laughed again, giving him a moment to squirm as she sized him up. Watching Ahn come out of his shell had been the only part of tonight she'd really enjoyed so far. After practically bullying him into joining her at all, his offering a dance was an unexpected turn of events—even if he was bluffing and about to make them look ridiculous. But if the confident grin, so different from his usual wilting apologies, was any indicator, the guy might actually have an idea of what he was doing.

She took his hand. Considering the past few phases, she figured she had earned a dance with a prince.

To her relief and delight, Ahn hadn't been lying about his capabilities. He broke the dance into simple steps for her to follow, showed her where to place her feet, glancing over at other partners for cues. While some of the other dancers seemed surprised that Ahn had joined in, no one made any move to stop the two of them.

The drums picked up, the people sang, and soon Sohmeng felt like one of them, clapping on beat and laughing when Ahn spun with her. Her voice was lost in the swell of the crowd; her body felt free of its adult burdens in the swirl of red and white. Illuminated by the fires below and the wide-eyed moons up above, Sohmeng felt, for the first time in weeks, that maybe the gods were still looking out for her.

Ahn pulled her close as the music changed. "I think they're forming bigger groups," he said, leaning down so she could hear him. A strand of his hair had come loose, black and silver glinting in the firelight. "Want to try?"

Before Sohmeng could answer, someone was already pulling them both into a small circle, shouting encouragement. She followed along clumsily, laughing when she made a mistake, cheering when she got it right. From across the circle, someone whistled at Ahn, who had picked up the footwork without any trouble. She grinned at him, allowing herself to sing along, her mouth forming words she did not understand. Together, they all swirled like the lunations of the moons, and the chaos was so controlled, so perfect, that all she could think of was—

Hei.

Hei, who walked the danger of Eiji and called it home. Hei, who showed her the magic of the sãoni, of life within the perfect system. Hei, who understood her and saw her for exactly who she was. Hei, whom she loved every wild and peaceful moment with. Hei, whom she loved.

Hei, who would not dance in this place, with these people. Who would not, *could* not, join Sohmeng in all parts of her life.

Sohmeng spun with the crowd, squeezing the hand of a stranger and wishing it came with claws and callouses. With the other hand she held tight to Ahnschen, the second unexpected thing she had come to care for in the jungle. Giddy off the energy of the party, lost in the complexity of her desires, Sohmeng humbled herself long enough to send up a prayer:

Par Go Hiwei Fua Tang Sol Jão Pel Dongi Se Won Nor Chisong Heng Li Ginhãe Mi Ker Hiun Ãofe Soon Nai Tos Jeji Minhal—

Help us, she pleaded until it ached in her heart. *Help us find our place in this together. Help us figure it out.*

She danced beneath the godseye until her feet hurt. Par and Minhal and simply Sohmeng, she dared, as always, to ask for more.

Seventeen

AS THE HOURS PASSED and the moons swelled higher in the sky, the citizens of Nona Fahang made it clear that they were intent on honouring the Chisong phase all the way through to morning. The music rose and fell, the buffet proved itself endless, and the wine flowed freely. Ahn danced with Sohmeng until he was breathless, only retreating back to the food table when Sohmeng claimed her feet might actually fall off. Even the rumble of thunder above did not stop the festivities, instead prompting some of the organizers to carry out decorative canopies for whoever might need them.

Ahn was helping assemble the musician's tent when he first saw the instrument: a fan-shaped frame of carved wood with twenty-five strings, laid flat on the lap. The sound of it being strummed made him fumble the pole he was carrying.

The musician was fiddling with it in the brief lapse between songs, laughing with her fellows in the band.

Ahn watched her, felt his fingers flutter in sympathetic yearning. Despite the thrill of dancing more freely than he had since university, he was more restless than ever.

"Isn't it pretty?" The Dulpongpa pulled Ahn from his thoughts, and he turned to see Eakang Minhal standing beside him. The moon on their left cheek was slightly smeared.

"It is," he agreed. "What is it called?"

"The jeibu," they said. "Each of the strings symbolize one of the different phases, so every song is about how they interact. You can learn a lot about peoples' phasal compatibility from music, actually! Wedding songs are really, really beautiful."

"I can imagine." Ahn smiled. Despite Sohmeng's dislike for them, Eakang had a remarkable amount in common with her. Perhaps it was just a sense of solidarity with younger siblings, but he wished she would offer them just a little more patience. "Have you seen Sohmeng? We got separated when I offered to help."

"I can look for them if you want! Last I saw, they were talking to my Damdão," Eakang said, peering back at the crowd.

Thinking of Sohmeng's expression earlier, Ahn replied with a mild: "Was she?"

"Oh. Yeah. She—she was." Eakang bit their lip. "Sorry."

"You don't need to apologize to me," Ahn said, watching the musician pluck a simple melody on the jeibu. "You have been very kind to me, and helpful. I know you want to get to know Sohmeng better, so you should know that it is important to her that you use the feminine."

Eakang nodded rapidly, fidgeting. "You're right. It's just a little different from what I'm used to, so I guess I'm still learning."

"I understand." It was true; there was so much about this place that he was struggling to learn and keep up with. "Learning new things can be challenging. But I trust that you care about Sohmeng enough to find a way."

Eakang hummed in agreement, a look of determination on their face. Ahn appreciated their compassion.

The musician plucked a chord that rang straight into Ahn's heart, and his fingers twitched once more. He felt young again, hiding near the courtesan's quarters and listening in on their recitals. He felt like a boy made a man too early, begging Master Hvu to take on a new student so he might reinvent himself as a novice, an innocent.

The strength of his longing must have made itself tangible, because Eakang caught his eye. "Do you have instruments like this back home?" they asked, looking up at him curiously.

"Not quite like this. But similar, yes." The lap harp he had first learned on had twenty-five strings, just the same as the jeibu—though of course it was played upright. "I play one of them. At least, I used to."

"Maybe you could try the jeibu!" they exclaimed.

Ahn wanted to protest, he knew how rude it was to try and get your hands on someone else's instrument, but Eakang had already approached the player. He felt himself trying to shrink as they spoke rapidly in

Fahangpa, brushing off what were undoubtedly protests from the musician. There was that common ground with Sohmeng again.

"She says it's okay!" Eakang beamed. The musician looked thoroughly beaten down, but she waved Ahn over nonetheless.

With as much of an apology as Eakang would tolerate, he sat down, crossing his legs as directed. The musician rested the wooden frame on his knees; he looked down at the earth cut through by the strings. She introduced his hands to them, demonstrating finger placement and plucking patterns. Despite the fact that he could not speak Fahangpa, the woman's instructions were clear enough: *touch here, not here. Gently. Don't you dare drop it.*

No matter the master, the first lesson was always the same. Gingerly, Ahn pulled a string, and that first note made his throat feel tight. He pulled another, and one more.

"That's Jão, Pel, Dongi . . ." Eakang listed the phases as he plucked their associated strings. Though the phases meant little to him, he thought that with each note he knew them better.

He searched for chords on the jeibu, adjusting to the way it sat on his knees, the way his back tugged against the foreign sensation of a new posture. After he'd proven he wasn't about to go on a string-breaking rampage, the musician indulged Ahn further, allowing him to explore at his own pace. Though he could hear the other musicians murmuring in Fahangpa, he didn't dare face them. Being met with judgment might make him give the jeibu back, and the thought was, absurdly, unbearable.

His fingers trailed along the strings, searching for the elementary tasks they had been given in the early days of training on the harp. The motions tumbled him into old memories: the pale coral walls of Master Hvu's living room, the breeze coming in through the window, the floral astringency of their shared pots of tea. Her voice, kind and chastising in equal measure as he disrupted their lessons to talk theory between their practice.

"But the paths of Art and Conquest are the same, Master! Didn't Janhong Sølshendtot-Qøngemtot say that 'the pen is not unlike the blade which is not unlike the cellist's bow'?"

"If I remember correctly, Jan also bled out in a field on Hvallánzhou, singing ballads to his wounds."

"It was martyrdom in the name of beauty, Master."

"Mm. Well, unless you plan on performing some sort of sacrificial glissando, which would put me in the embarrassing position of commissioning your Royal Parents for a new throw rug, I would kindly suggest you disregard the warrior poets, young Ahnschen. At least until you have your arpeggios down."

He played one then, biting back a smile. His finger snagged on one of the notes, unfamiliar with the horizontal playing, and he swore he could hear his master's quiet tut, the signal to start again.

For all she had encouraged him to separate Art and Conquest, the trials were the same, weren't they? The ongoing flirtation, the inevitable errors of amateurs, the attempt to reach understanding and improvement. His masters of Conquest, adjusting his hold on the blade;

Master Hvu, coaxing grace into his warrior's wrists, tenderness into his trembling fingers.

Break! Reset for next match.

Once more, little one. With feeling, if you please.

Adjustments were a part of the long walk towards comprehension. Ahn rested his hands on the jeibu, making to turn it vertically. He looked at the musician with a question that might have also been a plea, wanting desperately for her to see that he meant no harm.

"May I . . . ?" he asked in Dulpongpa. Despite their lack of shared language, she seemed to understand. With a cautious look, she nodded.

Ahn turned the jeibu, resting its frame on one thigh, adjusting the balance until it felt almost familiar. The grooves were all wrong, the weight distributed in nonsensical places; it was like the dream of a harp, the idea of it more than the thing itself. The musician's fists opened and closed, and he wouldn't have blamed her for yanking it right out of his hands then and there.

Then he plucked the first chord, and it no longer mattered.

A laugh escaped him, a breathless thing. He plucked another, then one more, shifting his posture to accommodate the differences in the instrument's structure. His arpeggios came more naturally now, up and down, and he played his scales with frantic longing, like a sailor too long away from the sea.

"What's going on—" There came a voice, Sohmeng's voice, and he looked up briefly to see her there, staring at him. Beside her, Eakang was grinning from ear to ear.

His mastery of Conquest earned him no favours in this place. His novice rank in Philosophy kept him tripping over his words, making errors upon errors. But in the Arts, in music, he could speak without pretense.

I can be good, he thought, meeting the eyes of the woman he owed his life. *This is how I am good.*

He played a glissando, reveling in the way the sound bubbled beneath his fingers and sang out for the fellow musicians. The texture of the strings was peculiar beneath his fingers, but everything was peculiar in Nona Fahang. There was no reason he could not make one more small adjustment.

With pleasure, with wonder, he began to pluck out a tune. A simple thing, one of the first songs he had ever learned. The mechanics began intentionally simple, an exercise in the foundations of the instrument that became more complicated as the song progressed. *The Fields of Knowing*, it was called; an old folk ballad about the ineffability of love—or art, depending on the interpretation. Ahn could feel his hands reawakening as he picked out the opening, warming back up to sensations he had long feared were lost. His eyes closed, and he fell into the story:

A man falls in love with a woman, and it is both his beginning and his end. She meets him in this tumbling fondness, this ever-churning passion, and they build a home in one another in a great wide field. In all of creation, none live in a more blessed partnership. The years pass, and the man begins to wonder how he will ever fully express the depths of his love for her.

Ahn's hands worked faster. The world around him was quiet, until another band member came in with her drum, cautiously offering him a tempo. He accepted it, gracious and grateful.

He studies the philosophy of love itself, meeting with counselors and courtesans and spiritual guides. It is impossible, he thinks, to feel something so deeply. Each morning he wakes in wonder to discover the space within him has expanded yet again to hold this ever-growing fondness. How can he comprehend it, when it changes every moment?

Though he was no seasoned vocalist, Ahn began to sing along to the ballad in Qiao Sidhur. For a moment he was surprised that no one joined in, and then he remembered where he was. Swallowing back his fears, he continued. The drum continued beside him, urging him on. He imagined a low pulse in his ear.

The man stays up late into the night with her, pondering his love aloud. She tells him to stop trying to capture the feeling with words, that perhaps there are no words for such an immense thing. He loves her enough to try and prove her wrong. Years pass, love grows, years pass, love grows. She dies.

As he buries her in their great wide field, the man thinks to himself—

"I am nearer now to knowing," Ahn sang softly, his fingers coming to a rest. "Nearer now, my love, than I have ever been."

The song ended. For a long moment, Ahn was very still, his hands absorbing the fading vibrations of the jeibu-made-harp. Time seemed to stop around him, leaving nothing but the space between breaths. Then came the rumble of thunder, the soft patter of raindrops on the tarp, and Ahn returned to himself.

The tent was packed tight with people, apparently gathered for his playing. His neck went hot at the realization that they had all heard him singing; the song had felt so personal, so private, that it was disorienting to reimagine it as a performance. Self-consciousness came over him in waves, and he wanted very suddenly for a place to hide.

Not that Sohmeng would ever have allowed it. She ran over to him with a shout, shaking him by the shoulders. "Ahn! Ahn, *what?* What in two dark moons was that?!"

"Music?" he said weakly. He handed the jeibu back to its master, thanking and apologizing in one. Her wariness seemed to have been traded out for something akin to respect, however grudging.

"Music!" Sohmeng scoffed, bopping him on the forehead with the heel of her palm. "Music, he says! Ahn, that was *beautiful!*"

He shook his head, heart fluttering at the praise. "I'm out of practice, it was hardly anything—"

Eakang jumped in then, looking around at the small crowd that had formed. "I've never heard a jeibu played like that before. It was so different—but really nice!"

Sohmeng nodded along vehemently, thumping them on the shoulder. Though she didn't seem to notice it, Ahn saw the way the gesture made Eakang light up. It lifted his own heart to know that his playing might have offered them a second chance with their new sister.

The music seemed to have reached the people around him in a way that every other attempt at reconciliation had not. For once, the gaze upon him was less hostile, more inquisitive. The jeibu player was positioning the instrument on her knee, trying to figure out how he had balanced it. A child peered at him from behind their parent's legs, and when he smiled at them, they giggled before hiding once more.

Sohmeng pulled him up from the seat, holding his hands. "Oh man, we should have gotten you an instrument sooner. Why didn't you tell me you were a musician?"

"I didn't think it mattered," Ahn confessed. It ached unexpectedly to admit.

"Éongrir Ahnschen What's-His-Phase, what am I going to do with you?" Sohmeng looked at him then with something he could not quite comprehend, a teasing fondness that made his heart flip over itself. Sometimes, when she stared at him like that, Ahn thought she just might understand him better than he understood himself.

He was still holding Sohmeng's hands—squeezing them, even. He let go, not wanting his touch to claim or impose. But perhaps his expression gave something away, because uncertainty flashed across Sohmeng's face. They pulled away from each other, and Ahn searched for something else to look at before things could go any further.

The people in the tent were talking about him, that much was clear. Even with the friendlier energy, it made Ahn anxious to be kept out of a conversation about him. He strained to catch the few Fahangpa words he could recognize: good, jeibu, festival, a few pronouns—

Tsongkar.

The word snagged his ear like a bramble. He tried to brush it off, to pull out the spines and ignore the sting, but then it came again. *Tsongkar.* Unwanted. Against his better judgment, he tried to listen to the rest, but it sounded like nonsense to him, unlike any Fahangpa he had heard before. Laughter followed, laughter that did not seem kind.

Eakang turned sharply in that direction, snapping something in Fahangpa. The voices in the crowd changed, the eyes on him grew uneasy. The child who had looked at him was quickly ushered away.

Sohmeng took his arm. "Ahn, let's go . . ."

"What are they—" He stopped, hearing the not-Fahangpa ring out once more despite Eakang's arguing. Hurt blossomed in his chest as he caught the rise and fall of the sounds, the exaggerated vowels—

Of course. They were mocking his language.

The rain broke overhead, coming down in sheets that battered Ahn's skin. If the gods of Eiji were truly looking down upon them, they had certainly sent their message. His whole body felt oversensitive, and before he could catch himself, the high of performing came crashing down in a wave of shame.

How had he ever tricked himself into thinking his trial could end with anything but death? There was no forgiveness for him here, no future, no real opportunity for reconciliation. Qiao Sidh had done too much, and there was no reason for Nona Fahang to trust him. He was going to die in this place, and he was going to deserve it. He was already so many years overdue.

Ahn felt scraped up within, dug out like blood spattered into sand—and at the thought of those sands, the crystalline pink beaches he might never see again, his feet moved of their own volition.

The crowd parted for him with haste, the tang of fear returning to their murmurings. This time, he did not try to catch their meaning. Sohmeng was calling something, following him, but he did not slow down. Not for her, not for the startled guards as he made for the walls, not for anything.

Maybe for Schenn. But Schenn hadn't said a damn word.

Ahn choked down a sob, clenching his fists as he walked; his fingers felt raw from the jeibu. He had been so sure that Schenn had guided him to this place for a reason, that he hadn't just been run into a jungle to die. But all he'd gotten were a list of ways that he was bad and wrong, and he had no idea how to make it right. He wanted to go home. He wanted to go *back*. Back to Qiao Sidh. Back to Asgørindad—no, to Kørno Wan, back to Schenn. Back to a time in his life that had never really existed, where he knew how to do something good.

Ahn thought he could use tonight to shed the parts of himself he couldn't stand, to rebuild a future. But it was impossible. He had no future. Ahn pushed through the wall of banyan, listening to nothing. Wanting everything. Grieving and raging against the wanting itself.

Eighteen

HEI AND AHN WERE ALREADY FIGHTING by the time Sohmeng reached them. The sound was muted by the roar of the rain and the celebration within Nona Fahang, but Sohmeng didn't need to hear the words to understand what was happening. The sãoni had fallen back in response to the noise of the Chisong festival; Sohmeng could see the greens and purples of their glowing throats in the trees. Lightning flashed, and she caught glimpses of suspicious reptilian eyes.

She ran over to Hei and Ahn, soaked and out of breath. The lantern she had brought with her flickered against the rain. They had moved dangerously far from Nona Fahang, far enough to get Ahn in trouble. "What are you doing? This is not the time to get in each others' faces!"

Hei's hood was up, their claws over their knuckles. They circled Ahn like Green Bites, snarling out a challenge in Sãonipa. Ahn was still, fists clenched and shaking. His expression was darker than Sohmeng had ever seen.

"I said you weren't welcome here," Hei spat in Atengpa. Their voice was shaky, their eyes wild with panic that Sohmeng suspected had little to do with Ahn. "Go back in the hmun."

"He doesn't understand you, Hei," Sohmeng said in Dulpongpa, trying to level the linguistic playing field. "Ahn—"

"I understand them fine," Ahn said coldly. "They are the one who does not listen."

Hei snapped a Sãonipa threat that he ignored. He abruptly moved to step around them, and they lunged with a hiss, pushing at his chest. To Sohmeng's dismay, he shoved their hands aside, paying no mind to the way their sharp claws tore at his clothing. In the dim lantern light, she saw three thin red lines blossom on his chest.

Sohmeng flinched—if Ahn couldn't keep his cool, there was no stopping whatever fight was threatening to break out. She couldn't breathe. The past few weeks had been spent vouching for him and Hei and the sãoni, insisting there wouldn't be a problem, all for them to explode in the middle of the Chisong festival. "Ahn, please don't—"

"Back in hmun!" Hei shouted at Ahn with another growl. The words came out in Dulpongpa this time, and their eyes flashed to Sohmeng with anxiety. She thought of the story they had told back in the winding tunnels of Sodão Dangde, the image of a child wailing as their body was pelted with rain. "Not out here. No Ahn with sãoni."

"We can talk about this," Sohmeng insisted, looking between them. The trial was so close. Why was this happening now? "We can be reasonable. I know things were tense last time you two talked, but you don't need to blow up at each other. Let's just get back to the walls, before we get in trouble."

Ahn shook his head, tugging harshly at his ear with a comment in Qiao Sidhur. Strands of his silver hair stuck to his face, and the flowing white dress he'd been leant now hung from him, limp and heavy with water. They had just been dancing together, he'd been fitting in so well. Sohmeng touched his shoulder, trying to bring back what she had seen when he was playing the jeibu. "I know people were being jerks back there, and I know that must have sucked, but it's nothing you haven't dealt with before. Now isn't the time to lose it, Ahn. We can still fix this. You and I can go to my dad's place, he won't mind . . . "

A pained chirp rang out from Hei, sending guilt stabbing into Sohmeng. She had left them alone outside the walls of Nona Fahang here, overwhelmed by the noise in the hmun, probably obsessing over the fight the two of them had last parted on. Soothing as the sãoni were to Hei, they couldn't offer the same kind of reassurances Sohmeng could.

"Or we could all stay here together," Sohmeng said. "Find someplace dry. Try to, try to talk this out—"

"Not here," Hei said again, tearful and furious. "Not with sãoni. Ahnschen not being good, no stay with sãoni. No stay with me."

"Hei, please," Sohmeng begged, reaching out to touch them with her other hand. She was so unused to hearing her voice like this, small and uncertain. She was being tugged in both directions, and neither of the people she cared about were willing to budge. "Just one night, we take a breath and calm down and stay together and—"

"I don't want to stay here!" Ahn shouted, yanking back from Sohmeng's touch with a force that made her jump. Hei squawked in protest, but he paid no mind. "Or in Nona Fahang, or, or *anywhere.*"

Sohmeng's chest hurt. "Ahn, your trial—"

"Is doomed, Sohmeng. I've ruined it, I've ruined everything and it—" His voice broke, dissolved into trembling laughter. "It's never going to be okay. Everyone here hates me, and I deserve to be hated, so I'm—I'm leaving. I can't fix it, I'm leaving."

"You can't leave," Sohmeng insisted. "Where will you go?"

"Home. I give up, I'm going home. To the camp, to Qiao Sidh."

"You don't know the way—"

"I don't care."

"Ahn, they'll kill you," she said desperately.

Ahn's response was a furious cry in Qiao Sidhur. Sohmeng could only stare as he yelled it once more, gesturing to where the scouts were supposed to be stationed in the trees. She didn't need to speak the language to know what he meant: *let them.*

Lightning slammed above them, highlighting the clearing in a shock of brightness that was there and gone. The sãoni squawked and snarled all around her, but she could not see them. Her father was just on the other side of the wall, but he could not help her. Hei was pushed beyond their limits, driven to collapse from all she had asked of them. Ahnschen, her key to negotiating with the invaders—no, her *friend*, was ready to go die in the land that had already swallowed her mother.

It was too big. It was too much. Too much to process when she just barely understood what it meant to be an adult, too much to translate between upwards of three languages.

Sohmeng gave up on making sense to anyone around her, gave up on being peacekeeper. With all the boldness of the first red shard of Ama, she closed her eyes and screamed.

It was loud. It was unreasonable. It felt *good*. She screamed wordlessly, screamed until it hurt her throat. Screamed until it felt like some of the pressure began to release from her chest.

When she opened her eyes, struggling to catch her breath, she looked up to see that the storm clouds had overtaken the eyes of the gods. Chisong turned Minhal; clairvoyant wisdom fallen into unpredictable chaos. Of course she had again been left to her own devices. But before she could open her mouth to continue, Hei's voice broke in.

It was louder even than hers. They roared ragged and raw, a feral howl to match the turbulence of the storm above. Sohmeng accepted it with relish. She opened her mouth to catch the rain, to soothe her throat, and then she kept going, wailing all her frustration to the sky.

Eventually she found her words, a stumbling stream of unfiltered Atengpa: "I hate this! I *hate* this! This is all too much and I feel so alone and I can't keep doing this! I'm supposed to be selfish but everyone's asking me for so much and I keep on failing, I'm failing both of you, and Ateng, and the gods themselves and I'm so sick of it, I'm so sick of it—"

Beside her, Ahn's voice suddenly joined in, the sharp cry of his own despair adding a new harmony to her and Hei's pain. It didn't take long for his own screams to tumble into heaving sobs, like an exhausted child. Cries in Qiao Sidhur joined her own Atengpa, curses she could not decipher and did not feel the need to understand. With the intensity that shook him, Sohmeng wondered if he had ever fallen apart like this in his life.

"This SUCKS!" Sohmeng screamed, tilting her head back to the sky.

Hei howled in agreement, stomping their feet, letting their emotions escape their entire body. Ahn joined in, shaking his fists like a madman, and Sohmeng jumped into gathering puddles, splashing and yelling until she thought she might burst into laughter at the sheer absurdity of it all.

The three of them screamed out their separate rages as one, threatening to crack the sky with all of the things they could not bear to carry alone. Eventually, their hands found their way into one another's, holding tight against the intensity. It was the sight of Ahn and Hei's fingers linked that finally brought Sohmeng to join them in crying. It was easier to do when she wasn't the only one, when she was not expected to keep it together for the sake of everyone else.

As the collective yelling subsided into tearful whimpering, Sohmeng yanked on Hei and Ahn's hands, pulling them into a group hug. Ahn accepted it with a new round of weeping, his face hidden in her hair. Hei gripped her tightly, tolerating Ahn's arm across their back as they nuzzled her, chirping Sãonipa into her shoulder.

The Qiao Sidhur Empire was still advancing down Gãepongwei. The Sky Bridge was still broken. They still had no plan for fixing these problems that were so much bigger than the three of them. As much responsibility as each of them had been given, they were all just barely out of childhood.

It felt like a good start, to behave like children. To kick and scream and, for once, abandon solutions in favour of feeling boldly and unashamed.

Eventually they collapsed together against a tree, curled up like a heap of hatchlings, seeking comfort in one another's warmth. Sohmeng closed her eyes, swallowing the rawness in her throat and softening around the space that had opened in her chest. She could not fix the world tonight, but she could breathe easier. And if the tentative tenderness of the people on either side of her was any indication, she was not the only one.

Nineteen

IN THE DREAM, they were lying together on a pile of pillows, sprawled out beneath the lilac tent they had put up on the beach. The summer storms were rolling in, breaking the humidity that had been suffocating everyone for weeks on end. Schenn was smiling, his eyes on something down by the water. It sounded like the clash of metal on metal, the wailing of someone else's children, the mindless chatter of their classmates. Ahn couldn't see it. He was busy looking at Schenn.

"Share the joke, would you?" He moved to prod Schenn's side with his foot, but his muscles felt lax, out of his control. Every time he tried to make contact, his skin slipped from Schenn's like oil off water. The boy looked at Ahn sympathetically, passing him a piece of fruit from the basket they had brought. Saka. Best to peel it first.

Ahn was about to say so when he felt a throbbing in his ear, hot and wet, like someone had punched a hole straight through the lobe. He cried out, reaching up to cup it, to catch the blood, but Schenn caught his wrist in a firm grip. The boy leaned in close to him, his dark eyes focused, serious.

"What if we didn't do it?" Schenn asked, and Ahn was startled to hear how much his friend's voice sounded like his own.

"What?" Ahn groaned. The pain in his ear was spreading, inexplicably, to his chest. A stripe burned right across. How had that happened? "Do what, Schenn? Our Six-ing?"

"What if we didn't do it?" the boy repeated.

"I don't know what you're talking about." Ahn tried to look away—the sounds from the beach were getting louder, closer. They were violent sounds now, he could tell. It scared him. Schenn was scaring him.

The boy hushed him, pressing their foreheads together. He released Ahn's wrist, instead playing with the end of Ahn's braid, rolling the strands of black and silver together as though they might catch and spark. He smiled another one of those private, tender smiles, and Ahn wished more than anything to be let in on what his friend was thinking.

"Schenn," Ahn said, his voice so young and small. "I don't know what to do. I made a mistake, and I need help fixing it, but I just want to go home. I want to forget all of this ever happened. It hurts too much and I want to go *home*—"

"Ahnschen," the boy said once more, and the sound of his name made the pain in Ahn's ear throb deeper. "What if we didn't do it?"

"Do *what?*" Ahn pleaded.

The sounds from the beach were louder now. The clash of swords, the shouting in languages he could only partially understand. His Conquest masters' voices too, barking instruction. The prayer of the priests as they pulled someone's body through the sand. His sister Ólawen, with her easy laughter and firm orders, telling their parents what they should get Ahn for his birthday.

Ahn squeezed his eyes shut, trying to block it out, but the sounds replaced themselves with images. He saw himself older, apologizing to Master Hvu as he broke yet another string. He saw himself running back to his sister's war tent, stumbling out half a plea for the Untilled and then leaving the rest in her hands; she was the real general, she was the elder, he could let it be her burden. He saw himself back in the palace, married, putting a play sword in the hand of a young child, telling the story of the years he spent on the lower continent, offering it to the holy expansion of Qiao Sidh.

He saw himself standing over a slaughtered sãoni too slow to pick up on the cues of domestication. He saw himself bring its body home as a prize. He saw himself knock a screaming human that was not a human into the dirt, hardening his heart to all its rage. He saw himself kneeling once to Sohmeng Minhal, and then leaving her to enjoy Qiao Sidh's new road. Not being good, but being *better*. The best.

He saw himself behaving as a true son of the Empire, perhaps one day its father. Accepted, beloved. Making the easy choices, the ones that freed him from all shame and complication.

"What if we didn't do it, Ahnschen?"

In the dream, Ahn opened his eyes. He took Schenn's face in his hands, cradled the curve of his jaw with fondness and longing. His ear no longer throbbed but rang clear as silver: a reminder through the realms of the first time he made the mistake of choosing what he'd been promised was easy. "I could live with that."

He woke to the sound of shouting.

Ahn opened his eyes with some difficulty, his skull sore from the previous night's crying. He wanted to rub away the salty grit that had gathered in his eyelashes, but he found his arms occupied, wrapped around his companions. He didn't even remember falling asleep.

Sohmeng was curled up between him and Hei, groaning groggily at all the noise. Hei was quicker to pull themself up, squinting at the canopy. Dawn was just breaking, the warmth of the sun slowly steaming the air.

The sãoni that had hidden from the chill of the rain had inched closer overnight, snuggled in heaps. A few of them were growling unhappily at having been disturbed from their slumber. Ahn wiggled his trapped arm from beneath Sohmeng, let go of the hold he'd had on Hei's waist with a flush in his cheeks. They did not seem overly bothered by the intimacy, focused instead on the commotion above.

The voices grew louder, and Ahn caught sight of scouts running across the extended arms of the banyan trees. They had moved far from Nona Fahang; he hadn't realized the upper branches were so sprawling.

"Weren't we done with screaming?" groaned Sohmeng.

Nearby, Mama rumbled along in what sounded like agreement.

Hei clicked, low and cautious, standing to get a better look. Their makeup was smeared, tear-streaked, and Ahn felt a sense of vertigo from all that had happened since last night. He wondered if Hei and Sohmeng's throats felt as raw as his own.

The scouts were shouting in Fahangpa, beyond his understanding. One word sounded familiar though. Ahn frowned, trying to feel out the differences on his tongue. "Bas . . . Basong . . . ?"

Sohmeng grasped it before he could. She jumped up so suddenly that Hei squawked in alarm. "We need to get back to the hmun."

"Why?" Ahn asked. The sãoni that had stirred were echoing Hei's sound, nudging their snoozing neighbours with their noses. "What are the scouts saying?"

"*Batsongkar*," Sohmeng said. "*Ba.* 'More than one.' It's not you, Ahn. It's Qiao Sidh. They're here."

Once the word was given form, Ahn could hear nothing else. *Batsongkar, batsongkar*! It came down from the scouts like a hailstorm, chilling Ahn despite the jungle's heat. A curse escaped him in Qiao Sidhur, panic gripping his heart in a vice.

Share the joke, would you?

A sharp sound from Hei drew his attention out of the uncanny and back to the present. He shook off the unease that had claimed him. The knucklebone pulsed persistently in his ear. "Let's go. There might still be time to stop whatever's about to happen."

The three of them took off toward Nona Fahang, trailed by two of the sãoni that had been curious enough to follow along. Ahn wasn't sure when he had become so accustomed to their presence, when they had stopped looking at him like he was a meal. One of the sãoni squawked something at him as it trotted along; a marking on its head identified it as one of the adolescents that had hissed at him during the first battle with Green Bites. It had grown so much in the past weeks.

When they made it to the walls, scouts were waiting for them on the ground. One of them grabbed Ahn roughly by the arm. The man's cheeks still had paint left over from last night's festival.

"Tsongkar!" he barked in Dulpongpa. "Where did you go last night? Did you do this?"

"Don't be ridiculous!" Sohmeng snapped back, trying to step in. "He was with us all night, we don't even know what's going on."

"And he didn't sneak off?" the scout demanded. Ahn kept his mouth shut even as the man's fingers dug into his arm. Despite the aggression, he could feel the way that hand was shaking. "Didn't call his friends here while you were asleep?"

What if we didn't do it?

Behind them came a warning growl from Hei, echoed by the two sãoni. The scouts stepped back, raising their spears, but the animals made no move to attack. Whether it was their weeks of exposure to humans or Hei's clicking that kept them back, Ahn couldn't say. Perhaps both.

"How many are there?" Ahn asked, forcing his voice to remain even. "And how close are they?"

"The sãoni—"

"Won't hurt you, just answer the question!" Sohmeng's voice was bold as ever, but Ahn could hear the fear beneath. It stirred an unfamiliar anger in him, to learn how it sounded when she was afraid.

The scout hesitated, eyes on Hei and the sãoni. ". . . a small party. Ten or so, coming from the northwest. We sent our own to try and hold them back, but it isn't—" Another shout from above. The man shook his head. "I'm sorry. The Grand Ones said you need to get inside right now. You first, tsongkar."

"Would you *stop* calling him that?" Sohmeng snapped. "He's trying to help you!"

"He can help by following orders and resisting the urge to crawl back to his own."

What if we didn't do it?

The sound of their arguing dissolved around him, melting into a near-meditative silence. Meditation had been a key component of his Conquest training: survival was simply a matter of the speed and confidence with which one made choices, and a sense of inner calm was needed to choose correctly. It had never been Ahn's strong suit. A day ago, he wouldn't have been able to slow his panic long enough to think clearly, but something had broken in him last night, opened him to a part of himself he could not access before. A part of him that had broken earth every summer in Haojost. That had lived and died in a series of confident choices. That tried so hard to reach him through the bilateral realm, if only Ahn could find the courage to listen.

Ahn took a slow, deep breath. With the world around him at a peaceful distance, he weighed his options. Ahead of him was a guarantee that he could return home: all he had to do was wait for his soldiers to enter Nona Fahang. With centuries of warfare behind them, he knew it wouldn't take much for even a small force to destroy the walls. Once they found Ahn, he'd be saved and returned to his sister. He would push the conversation toward peaceful negotiations, then head home without ever having to sit through a trial. Get back to school and put this behind him. But also—

What if we didn't do it, Ahnschen?

—that wasn't enough, was it? That wasn't right. There was no such thing as peaceful conquest, there never had been, and going home with his tail between his legs did nothing but perpetuate the lie. It was easy to bemoan his powerlessness against the culture he'd been raised in, but it was also untrue.

Ahn had power. Despite the fact that he had done nothing to earn it, he had been born with power over others—instead of denying it, it was his responsibility to use it for good. He needed to stop the encounter before it happened. Which meant giving up his own comfort for the sake of other peoples' survival.

"Who's in charge, here?" Sohmeng was yelling now,

standing between Ahn and the scout. Cautiously, Ahn took a single step back.

"I need your help, Hei," he said quietly.

They clicked uncertainly.

"I can stop this. But I need a sãoni."

They snarled in response, and Ahn made his own sharp noise back, challenging them. Sohmeng was still fighting with the scout, but that distraction wouldn't last forever.

"I want to be good, Hei," Ahn said. "I want to make this right, and I know I can do it." The pulsing in his ear grew with every word. Good. He needed Schenn now more than ever. "I need to go stop this, but I cannot get there fast enough on foot. Leave me there alone if you want, but please. Help me. Help me be good. For you, for Sohmeng. For Eiji."

Ahn turned to face them, holding out his hands in supplication. Hei stared him down, their black-rimmed eyes hard in judgment, the green piercing straight through him and weighing the sum of his heart.

Almost imperceptibly, they nodded. They reached for the sãoni to their left, clicking low.

"Fine!" Sohmeng shouted at the scout. "Fine, we're coming, you don't have to be such a—"

"Sohmeng," Ahn called. She turned to him, cheeks still red from shouting, and he smiled in spite of himself. "I'm very sorry about this."

"What?" She yanked at her bangs, aggravated. "What are you talking about?"

"Go inside," he said, taking another step toward Hei.

"And trust me, if you can."

"Trust you?" Sohmeng stopped, looking at him suspiciously. "Ahn. Whatever you're about to do, please—"

One of the scouts copped on that something was wrong. They made a move to grab Ahn, alarmed, but Ahn was too fast. He raised his hand, shouting his command in Qiao Sidhur: "UP."

The sãoni jumped up on its hind legs, the full height of it sending the scouts barreling back in alarm. With a loud snarl from Hei, it dropped back down, and Hei leapt on its back, offering an arm to Ahn. He took it gladly, swinging up behind them, and they barreled off into the jungle, Sohmeng's screaming fading behind them.

The second sãoni stayed close, following Hei's lead as the first charged along. Ahn held tightly onto Hei, ignoring the yelling of the scouts, the inevitable panic at his seeming desertion. "Northwest," he said. "Do you know how to—"

Hei scoffed, tugging on the sãoni's head spines with a trill. The creature adjusted its course smooth as any steed, and Ahn smiled. His work with Lilin didn't even compare.

"What you do now, Ahnschen?" they asked with a sniff. Vaguely, Ahn caught the scent of smoke pushing through the sweet decay of the jungle. They were close now.

"I'm going to end this," he said, and believed it.

"What, with smart Ahn words?"

Leave it to Hei to make that seem implausible. A fair enough assessment, given the past few weeks. "Or a sword."

"Your sword in Nona Fahang." Hei pulled on the sãoni's

spines with another sound, urging it on toward the smoke.

"I'm sure I'll find another," he murmured. The Empire had no small supply. "When we find them, keep the sãoni back. They don't need to get involved with this battle, and neither do—"

The battle found them first. One moment an expanse of jungle—the next, a patch of scorched trees, broken up by the clamour of war. Ahn shouted in alarm and Hei yanked back, pulling the sãoni to a halt. Energy surged once more through his earpiece, forceful and familiar as the hours he'd spent sparring with Schenn. He leapt from the sãoni and into the fray.

The Fahangpa were sorely out of their depth, but holding their own nonetheless. Their experience with the banyan trees put them at a height advantage, but Qiao Sidhur silver and steel cut deep. Bracing himself, Ahnschen charged forward, surprising an armoured soldier with a kick to the back. They stumbled fast enough for him to disarm them with a strike to their arm that made his bones howl. He grabbed their sword, knocking its owner to the ground.

"Enough of this!" he yelled, but no one heard him over the fighting and the roars of the sãoni. Hei was keeping the animals back, but he couldn't risk the Qiao Sidhur turning on them.

Ahead of him, a Fahangpa fighter collapsed, bleeding from the thigh. Ahnschen would recognize that face anywhere—the furious sneer, the twisted scar.

"No!" he shouted, jumping in to block the soldier who

lifted their blade to Lita Soon. Ahnschen caught the killing blow, throwing it back with a series of brutal parries. Years of training returned to him in a flurry of muscle memory, and he quickly morphed defense into offense.

"Stop!" he barked in Qiao Sidhur, sending the soldier to the ground. The man pulled off his helmet to get a better look, eyes widening in recognition. "I order you to *stop.*"

The next soldier that charged Ahnschen was given the same treatment, a series of easy strikes that pushed them back. This time, their realization came sooner.

"The prince!" the soldier cried. "Éongrir Ahnschen! The *prince!*"

The words rose in Qiao Sidhur until they rose above the cacophony of violence. His name, his title, echoing until the battle came to an abrupt, bewildering halt. *Éongrir Ahnschen-Eløndham Qøngemzhir*, over and over again.

"Tsongkar . . . ?" murmured Lita Soon, looking up at him in disbelief. The wound in his leg looked vicious, pulsing blood onto the jungle floor. This was twice now that the Empire had marked him.

Éongrir Ahnschen would have no more of it. With the eyes of his soldiers on him, he straightened his back, held out his blade. "Enough of this," he demanded, the words smooth on his tongue as elderflower wine. "It is done. You are done. This land is not yours to claim."

One of the soldiers stumbled to him, removing her helmet and taking a respectful knee. The carvings on her chestplate marked her as their captain. "We are here on the orders of Éongrir Ólawen-Eløndhol Qøngemding. My prince, we thought you were dead."

The rest of the Qiao Sidhur party followed their captain in kneeling. The Fahangpa took the opportunity to gather their own, falling back from the battle. Ahnschen could hear scouts retreating through the branches to report what they had seen.

"You were mistaken," he said simply. "I am very much alive, and I order you to leave this place, and these people, unharmed. Put out your fires and go."

The captain hesitated, not meeting his eye. "We would be glad to escort you back to the General. But her orders for the Untilled were—"

Ahnschen thrust his blade into the dirt, hearing a voice that sounded not like his at all. Schenn had always been the brasher of the two of them. "Am I not your prince?" he asked. "Or has Ólawen become Empress in the weeks I've been gone? Last I remember, our authority was quite equal."

The captain winced, lowering herself further to the ground. "I mean no disrespect, Eleventh Beloved."

"Then you will listen to me very clearly: you will lead your soldiers back to camp, and you will not touch another village in this land without my say. Is that understood?"

A murmur of assent rippled through the clearing. Ahnschen felt a rush of relief bordering on nausea. They were listening to him. They would leave. It had been so long since his words had any power that it made him dizzy to exercise it now.

"My prince," the captain said, pressing her forehead to the earth. "I humble myself before you for my disrespect.

When we return to the base camp, I will gladly submit myself to—"

"I will not be returning with you."

There. He had said it. The words were out, and there was no taking them back. Much as the selfish part of him wanted to return to Ólawen, weep into her arms, and then figure out how to manage a retreat plan from Eiji, he had unfinished business with Nona Fahang. He had promised to stay for a trial. Breaking that promise, whatever the reason, would go no way toward establishing the mutual trust needed for a future alliance. Toward being good.

He took another slow breath, feeling his earpiece positively vibrating with satisfaction. Feeling the ghost of Schenn's fingers, playing with the bottom of his braid.

"My *prince*," the captain said once more, her voice strained. "The General—"

"Will have to be patient." Ahnschen pulled his sword from the ground, promptly bringing it through the bottom end of his braid. With the tie cut free, it fell loose past his shoulders, silver and black melded together. An Imperial failure, by this standard at least. He dropped the proof of his survival at the captain's feet, hoping it would be enough. "For now, I am staying behind. Tell my sister that I'm coming for her. I will find her at the basecamp, when the moons next go dark."

The timing was tight, but not impossible. And if the moons' fortune truly favoured the people of Gãepongwei, then perhaps Sohmeng's namesake would serve them all well.

Ahnschen swallowed, willing himself not to lose his nerve. “And pass along my orders to leave the villages untouched. If General Ólawen violates them, tell her I will bring my concerns to the Emperor and Empress.”

It was the first genuine military decision he had ever made, the first time properly using his sixth ranking, and it was for an order to retreat.

The captain didn’t look happy to be the messenger of this news, but she agreed. With his severed braid in hand, she led her soldiers out from the clearing, dousing fires on their way.

As the parties retreated, Ahn looked for Hei. They were at the edge of the clearing, soothing the sãoni with low murmurs and head strokes. To his relief, they all seemed unharmed—and not at all eager to eat any of the remaining humans. Perhaps his socialization strategies had worked better than he thought. When he met Hei’s eye, they offered him a grudging nod, and what might have been a hint of a smile.

“Tsongkar,” came Lita Soon’s ragged voice. Ahn’s stomach dropped as he turned to face the Fahangpa scouts that had remained to treat their wounded. The people who looked at him were wary, wide-eyed, and Ahn realized then that no one could vouch for his integrity. The whole conversation had been in Qiao Sidhur. As far as they were concerned, he could have just told the soldiers to come back in larger numbers.

This was the risk he had taken to do the right thing. Now he had to live with it. With a deep breath, he took up the posture of the captain he had sent away, dropping to one knee.

"I know you do not have reason to trust me, but this is the truth—I have ordered the soldiers to leave Nona Fahang alone," he said in Dulpongpa, the language clunky on his tongue after its brief return to Qiao Sidhur. "Instead of going with them, I will await my trial to answer for my crimes. I accept whatever punishment you see fit for my disobedience."

He offered his wrists to be bound once more, feeling the way they had begun to tremble as the adrenaline caught up with him. The scouts murmured something in Fahangpa before two of them pulled him gently to standing. Ahn looked at them with confusion.

"Just get up, Ahn," muttered Lita Soon, tying off a cloth around the wound on his thigh. Even with the amount of pain he must have been in, the man still managed to spare Ahn a half-hearted glare. "Before I bleed to death."

Twenty

"—RUNNING BACK TO HIS PEOPLE!"

"What do you *mean* with one of the sãoni?!"

"And that other one, the strange one, probably a spy—"

"Never trusted the tsongkar, never trusted him a bit."

Sohmeng felt like she was plummeting down the side of Fochão Dangde all over again, flailing against the inevitable impact. No matter how she ground her feet into the earth, she couldn't shake the sensation of falling, couldn't make sense of what was happening.

After Ahn and Hei had taken off on the sãoni, Sohmeng had been dragged straight to the Grand Ones to answer for their desertion. Despite her fury at Ahn's horrible decision-making, she didn't believe he had betrayed them to Qiao Sidh—certainly not with Hei's support, backed by two sãoni. There had to be a good reason for why they had left. She just had no idea what it was.

The moons had shifted overnight; Chisong had become Heng. The same people she had danced with, the strangers whose hands she had held, now stared at her with distrust. She crossed her arms, hiding the ring that glinted silver on her finger.

Sohmeng insisted that her companions weren't traitors or Qiao Sidhur spies. No, she hadn't known about any of this. No, Ahn hadn't somehow *brought* the Qiao Sidhur to Nona Fahang. But she had no proof, no evidence beyond her own feelings, which were not enough for even the sensitive Grandfather Heng.

The leaders of Nona Fahang were urgently trying to form a plan of defense against the oncoming invaders, consulting with survivors of the northern attacks. Anxiety spread, and soon the perimeter of the Grand Ones' gazebo was surrounded by members of the hmun, speaking all at once at a volume that made Sohmeng's head spin.

Nona Fahang was not prepared for war. *Gãepongwei* was not prepared for war—and why should it be? The hmun network had lived for thousands of years by a simple standard: *each to itself, but all in harmony.* There was no precedent when it came to planning for an invasion.

Sohmeng swallowed, entirely out of good ideas. At this point, she doubted she had any bad ideas left in her either.

Nearby, Eakang's voice rose above them all as they faced down Grand One Minhal. They were crying, pounding their heart, abandoning all decorum as they demanded to be allowed to fight with the scouts who were currently facing the Qiao Sidhur. Given the fact that they were fourteen, it made sense that Grand One Minhal was refusing. Tonão Sol was standing back, holding Jaea Won's shoulders as she cried for her child to stop.

Is that what I used to look like? Sohmeng wondered, trying to place Eakang's expression on her own face.

As chaos grew around her, Sohmeng wished suddenly that she was home. It would be so much easier to be back in the caves, to drop Ahn and Hei in front of Grandmother Mi, tell them to shut up and listen to a story. It would cost nothing but a little pride to make Viunwei's day and ask him, the older and wiser sibling, what she should do now. How much safer the world had been, when her questions were the most dangerous thing in it.

A small group of scouts ran across the highest points on the walls, yelling something in Fahangpa. She was about to ask her father for a translation when another sound broke through—the unmistakable roar of a sãoni. The deep and furious snarl of the alpha. Mama.

Sohmeng froze, staring at the walls. Burning godseye, this was *not* the time for a lizard rampage. With no one paying enough attention to stop her, she ran for the exit.

Before she got there, the scouts emerged, bloodied but upright. At the center of them was Ahn, not bound and blindfolded but half-carrying an injured Lita Soon. Sohmeng rushed over, barely containing her panic.

"What happened?" she snapped. The man's white clothing was stained Ama-red with blood. "Ahn, what was that?"

"I apologize for leaving," he said grimly, adjusting his hold on Lita Soon.

"No, not that!" But oh, did she have words for him about

that later. She swallowed her fury, focusing on the topic at hand. "That sound, that was Mama. Where's Hei, Ahn? What happened?"

"Ah." Ahn's jaw set, and he spoke with a calm that struck Sohmeng as dangerous. "The scouts at the entrance wanted to bring Hei into the hmun. Mama and I found that unacceptable."

Sohmeng paled. "Godless night. Tell me she didn't eat anyone."

"It didn't come to that," Ahn said. "She calmed down when they let Hei be."

Lita Soon laughed weakly, flopping his head on Ahn's shoulder with a woozy grin. "And after you threatened them with that new sword, you animal."

"You WHAT?" Sohmeng shrieked.

She stared at him in horror, pressing her palms to her forehead. *So much for a trial,* she thought. *He's dead. He's so dead. The gods blessed him with a gorgeous face to make up for his empty head. Listen for the sound of wind between his ears!*

One more step was all that Lita Soon could take, and the man's legs gave out beneath him. Ahn held him up, addressing the scouts: "He's losing too much blood. Bring him to your healers, quickly."

The scouts complied, apparently unbothered by the authoritative tone in Ahn's voice. One of them even gave him a pat on the shoulder that looked ridiculously like an act of camaraderie. Considering the way he had fled into the jungle—and apparently raised a sword to their fellows—Sohmeng had no idea what to make of that. She looked Ahn over, trying to figure out what had changed, where this feminine self-assurance had come from.

Also, was his hair shorter?

Before she could ask, Ahn was walking toward the Grand Ones' gazebo. His back was straight, his head held high; despite the blood and soil that clung to his skin, he was the very picture of grace.

"Ahn, level with me, what's the plan here?" she demanded, jogging to try and keep up with his long strides. "What are you doing, what were you *thinking*? Because I sure have no idea!"

"I could not stand by and let them invade," Ahn said, tugging on his earpiece.

"You could have explained yourself!" Sohmeng was shouting. She could hear her voice, but it sounded like it was coming from outside of her. There was that feeling of falling again. "You could have—you could have told *me* at least! How am I supposed to protect you like this?"

Ahn stopped in front of the gazebo, turning to face her. He took her hands in his own. "You have done enough to protect me, Sohmeng Minhal," he said. "Now I must face the Grand Ones myself. I need to take responsibility for what I've done."

He leaned in close, nudging their foreheads together. Her breath caught, her heart stopped—the motion was so unexpectedly *sãoni*-like that she nearly bit him, nearly snarled out her frustration the way she would with Hei. When had the two of them learned to communicate this way?

"Last night—" she began, searching desperately for understanding. But the Grand Ones wanted answers even more than she, and Ahn did not see fit to keep them waiting.

The crowd fell silent as Ahn entered the circle. A group of scouts were relaying messages between the Grand Ones, speaking too quickly and quietly for Sohmeng to have any chance of following. The terror of earlier had been rendered down into something different, a collective tension strung tighter than jeibu strings. At Ahn's approach, Grandfather Heng gestured for Tonão Sol.

"Ahnschen," the old man said. "You have returned to us."

Before Tonão was finished speaking the words in Dulpongpa, Ahn had gotten down on one knee. It was the mirror image of their first day in Nona Fahang, though this time Ahn spoke for himself: "I apologize for leaving, and breaking your terms."

One of the scouts jumped forward, recounting the story of Ahn's actions against the Qiao Sidhur invaders: the sãoni bursting through the clearing, Ahn's swift rescue of Lita Soon and methodical control of the soldiers. Apparently, Hei had persuaded one of the young sãoni to carry both Lita Soon and Ahn back together, before the man could lose too much blood.

"Bring the sãoni scraps from the feast," Grandfather Heng said, a smile pushing up the moons tattooed on his cheeks. "Nona Fahang has seen heroism this auspicious morning, and not just from Ahnschen."

Sohmeng's heart lurched in hope as she felt the lightening of the atmosphere. But Ahn said nothing, shaking his head slightly at the praise. Sohmeng would have called it modesty, if it were not for the way he clenched his jaw.

"After Ahn saved Lita, he said something to the batsongkar," the scout continued. "In his, his language—he said something and they kneeled, just as he does now. They kneeled and they left."

"Will they be coming back?" Grandfather Heng asked. This time his voice was not so playful.

"Not today," Ahn replied. "I ordered them not to invade Nona Fahang, to halt their campaign altogether. There was no time to negotiate further—Lita Soon was injured, and it wasn't right to leave you without explaining myself. I told them I would meet the general at her camp come Minhal."

Minhal. Half a cycle from now. Fifty days and fifty nights. Assuming he made it through the trial, Ahn had bought them more than enough time to get to his sister.

"Minhal," Grandfather Heng echoed. "An interesting choice."

"Watch your tone, Heng," Grand One Minhal shot back with a wicked grin. Laughter broke out among a few of the Grand Ones, the sound setting the people even further at ease.

But where Sohmeng's shoulders relaxed with every passing moment, Ahn's seemed to rise further to his ears.

"I am sorry," the man said suddenly, looking up from the ground to meet the eyes of Grandfather Heng. He was trembling, not with fear but anguish, his voice strained as he spoke. "I am sorry that it has come to this. I am sorry that I—that I *participated.* I caused harm in Kongkempei, and I caused harm here in Nona Fahang, and I cannot take it back. Lives have been taken by my people, under my watch. Needless death." Ahn dropped to both knees then, leaning down to press his forehead to the earth. The display troubled Sohmeng to look at, made her want to pull him up to standing, but she didn't move. "It is not my place to ask your forgiveness. Instead, I would ask your permission for me to try and atone. To end this campaign. I ask you to sentence me early, and to spare my life so I might use it in service of Gãepongwei." His fingers curled slightly in the dirt, but his voice held true. "If you find these terms unacceptable, I understand. Should my death be a truer payment for my crimes, I would consider it an honour."

Back in Ateng, exile was the harshest punishment one could receive. There was nothing more shameful than being hãokar, cast out from home, but it was not necessarily a death sentence. Especially not before Fochão Dangde had been swarmed by sãoni. Sohmeng could not imagine what Ahn's home was like, if this was how they handled justice.

Grandfather Heng seemed to feel much the same. "My boy," he said, "I think we all have had enough unnecessary death. Grandmother Ginhãe, the passing of judgment is usually your domain. Might I, this once, impose?"

The old woman nodded her assent. "With my blessing. I would say the gods have made their wishes clear."

"In that case," said Grandfather Heng, "I spare you from exile and execution—"

The gathered crowd responded immediately, the cicada-buzz of hundreds of voices competing with each other. In the wake of it all, Ahn remained still, prostrated on the soil. Unable to take it anymore, Sohmeng pulled him to standing, brushing the dirt from his face as the leaders of Nona Fahang worked to hush the crowd long enough for Grandfather Heng to finish his thought.

At last, the old man cleared his throat, continuing: "I grant you the rights offered to traders. These should be sufficient as you work towards atonement for your crimes. In Nona Fahang, you are neither citizen nor criminal—you are our guest. Respect our customs for your time here, and we will offer you hospitality and support in exchange. Do my fellow Grand Ones find this acceptable?"

One by one, each of the Grand Ones raised a hand in agreement. Sohmeng looked at their faces, watching the motion of the phases reflected in their tattooed cheeks. Breathless, she clung to Ahn, hardly daring to believe it as the reply came unanimously. As the representative of the current phase, Grandfather Heng's word was final, but the approval of the rest of the elders would offer Ahn the sort of acceptance Sohmeng had never even known for herself.

Satisfied, Grandfather Heng rose to standing. "Then it is done. On behalf of gods and Grand Ones, we welcome you to Nona Fahang, Ahnschen."

Ahn tugged his earpiece, bowing low in gratitude,

stumbling over a response that Sohmeng did not let him finish. Before his nose could touch the dirt again, she yanked him into a tight hug, crying out in delight, in relief. After weeks of uncertainty, it was done. They could move forward now—they could go to the Qiao Sidhur camp and actually start *fixing* things.

"We need to tell Hei!" she said, laughing. "Ahn, you did it, you did it!"

"We did it," Ahn repeated. He looked a little dazed. A moment later, that expression settled into a frown. "But . . ."

"What?" Sohmeng asked, thumping his shoulder with her fist. "What could you *possibly* have to complain about right now?"

Arms still around Sohmeng, Ahn faced Grandfather Heng once more. His voice was steady as it had been with the scouts. Confident, as though Ama's influence had soaked him to the bone. "I would like to discuss the terms of my atonement."

Grandfather Heng raised his eyebrows, but nodded in assent.

"I have fifty days until I meet with my sister, General Éongrir Ólawen-Eløndhol Qøngemding," Ahn said. How disorienting, to hear elements of Ahn's name superimposed on another's. On their common enemy. "I have done what I can to buy us time, but I can make no promises on what will be honoured. For now, I can train your scouts, and determine strategies for keeping back the Empire. War is not unfamiliar to me."

"Your expertise would be appreciated," replied Grandfather Heng.

"A request, Grandfather Heng—" Ahn bowed his head. "While I work to prepare Nona Fahang to face any threat from Qiao Sidh, I humbly ask that you lend your time and resources to Ateng. It is my belief that the safety of Gãepongwei depends on cooperation between each hmun. If you stand together, you will be better prepared for whatever might come next."

Sohmeng covered her mouth, feeling her heart jerk in her chest. She heard her father's voice break as he relayed the request to the Grand Ones in Fahangpa.

"We have a strong vantage point in the mountains," she said, overcome with new determination. "If it came down to it, Fochão and Sodão Dangde could serve as a stronghold for other people, provided they brought resources of their own."

"All of the hmun should be alerted," Ahn continued. "But I think it would be wise to start with your neighbours, if only as a show of goodwill."

"I can't speak for my Grand Ones," Sohmeng said, voice stacking on top of Ahn's, hands trembling with eagerness. "But if you can help us, Ateng has so much to offer. It's, it's *beautiful*, Grandfather Heng. It's alive, and it's important, and it's worth saving, worth it as much as any other hmun—"

Grandfather Heng raised a hand, gently silencing her. Where the voices of the gathered crowd had been loud before, now they were still and quiet, listening intently as the Grand Ones spoke among themselves. Half of it seemed comprised of subtle looks and gestures, a shared mode of communication inspired by the gods alone. Private, powerful. As the moments passed, Sohmeng heard nothing but the ragged breathing of her father, translating through his own longing.

She was not the only one who had been waiting for this. Not by a long shot.

It was Grandfather Jeji, representative of stories and cycles' end, who spoke. He was a frail man, one of the oldest of the Grand Ones, and his voice was brittle as river reeds. "It was the wisdom of the ancients that encouraged us to split into our separate hmun, living as distant cousins. With respect, but without interference. It was a strategy to keep safe and humble, and it has served us well. But the world is changing once again—and if we learned anything from our ancestors, it is that survival depends on how we might change with it."

Grandfather Heng nodded, looking to the other Grand Ones as he continued to speak. "For now at least, I agree that it would be wise to work together with the rest of the hmun network. Sohmeng, Ahnschen—we leave you to our scouts and community leaders. Develop your plan together. We will do what we can for Ateng, and for Gãepongwei. Their watchful eyes upon you."

"Their watchful eyes upon you," echoed the Grand Ones.

"Their watchful eyes upon you," Sohmeng responded in turn. Her father was rushing to her; she opened her arms to him with a grin, and the way he embraced her was what made her believe, more than anything, that this was actually happening.

Ahn stepped back to give them room. Despite his instrumental role in what was coming next, it seemed he was not rushing to take credit. From the corner of her eye, Sohmeng saw him silently mouth "their watchful eyes upon you", practicing the shape of the blessing on his tongue.

Twenty-One

WITH HIS FREEDOM GRANTED, Ahn felt as though he was meeting Nona Fahang for the first time. It was easier to meet the eyes of individuals, to imagine them as neighbours. He was not so afraid of asking questions, and warmed with pride every time his offers to help were accepted. Many of the refugees from Kongkempei and Hosaisi were reluctant to speak to him, which he could not blame them for; he did his best to keep a healthy distance, and lead with humility when he was addressed. He would be grateful if they chose to forgive him, but he knew that wasn't something he could control. That wasn't the point.

As the phases shifted once more, the high banyan trees felt no longer like prison walls, but marvels of natural architecture. He watched the growers work, in awe of their ability to guide shapes which would not emerge for months, or even years.

Jaea Won, who Ahn had conceptualized as one of

Sohmeng's stepmothers, was pantomiming the growing process for him when Sohmeng emerged from her father's house. Despite the task ahead of them, she seemed calm, determined.

"Are you ready?" Ahn asked, taking the pack she had in her arms.

"As I can be," Sohmeng said, tugging at her bangs. "Not much left to do but have the conversation."

Ahn offered his hand. Even though Sohmeng rolled her eyes, he didn't miss the small, grateful squeeze when she took it.

Outside the hmun, the sãoni colony was lounging in the afternoon night. There were more of them gathered today, which Ahn supposed was on account of mating season winding down. At the center was Mama, enjoying a sunspot as Hei scratched between her head spines.

"Hey doofus," Sohmeng called, and Hei looked up with a friendly chirp. "Hope you didn't eat with the sãoni already. We brought stuff that's way better."

At the sound of squeaking hatchlings, Ahn quickly returned the pack to Sohmeng and braced himself for impact. The creatures leapt onto him in an instant, wiggling excitedly as they chewed on his clothing.

"Calm now," he cooed, pulling one of them off his head before its claws took out an eye by mistake.

Hei came over, rubbing cheeks with Sohmeng. "What food?"

"Stuff from my dad's place," she said, pulling the pack away before Hei could get into it. "Pim packed up enough for all three of us, even made extra sweet buns."

"*Sweet buns.*" Hei waved them over to the small fire smouldering in the clearing. "Come, we eat here. Sweet buns now."

Ahn laughed, trying to keep one of the hatchlings from crawling down his pants. He doubted he would get much eating done with the little creatures attached to him. He walked over to Mama, nearly juggling the hatchlings, and deposited them carefully at her feet. Her friendly rumble and nose-nudge felt like a warm welcome.

The three of them sat together, unsupervised and untroubled. They ate skewers of blackened vegetables, squeezing citrus juice over them and laughing as the hatchlings hissed at the sour rinds. The meatballs were a source of chaos; Hei nearly choked laughing when Ahn frantically stuffed three into his mouth before they could be snatched up by any tiny jaws. For a while, they simply enjoyed a meal together, savouring the budding comfort that had grown between them after the night of the storm.

Ahn wished it could stay like this, easy and playful. But with several of the past weeks' problems now resolved, it was time to face what troubles were still to come.

Midway through the sweet buns, Sohmeng took the plunge. She'd pulled out her dice to fidget with; Ahn watched the faded blue stones pass between her fingers. "Hei, I want to talk to you about fixing the Sky Bridge."

"Grand Ones said yes, yes?" Hei asked, looking between them. The other day, they had seemed genuinely happy for Sohmeng and Ahn when the two of them had breathlessly recounted the events of the trial.

"They did," Sohmeng said. "But it's going to take some work. And . . . I'm sorry, Hei, but I need to ask you for help one more time. You might not like it, but it would mean a lot if you would hear me out, okay?"

They clicked slowly, fixing her with a wary expression as they leaned back against Mama's strong mid-leg. Ahn swallowed. If anyone could sell this idea to Hei, it was Sohmeng. But it didn't make the task any less intimidating.

"Ahn and I have been working with my father for the past two days to finalize the details of our plan for the Sky Bridge. We think we've covered everything, but there are a few problems we need to work around." With a deep breath, Sohmeng explained everything to Hei in a mixture of Dulpongpa and Atengpa. Kind as the gesture was, Ahn wasn't sure it was necessary—they had gone through this plan so many times that Ahn thought he might start practicing it in his sleep:

Gather a small party, journey to the mountains, string up the portion of the Sky Bridge between the Third Finger and Sodão Dangde, make the crossing to the First Finger, and—with the help of the residents of Ateng—repair the Sky Bridge. A simple plan, in theory. But reality was a different matter, one which required both ingenuity and a generous portion of luck.

The first problem they faced sat at the foot of Fochão Dangde—the territorial sãoni colony that had originally destroyed the Bridge, and later attacked Sohmeng's father.

Though they were kept from climbing too high by the sãoni warriors in Fochão Dangde, nothing was there to stop them from staking their claim on the jungle below. Careful mapping revealed an alternate route, one which could bring them to Sodão Dangde without ever setting foot within enemy lines. However, the terrain was not easy on humans, and would take nearly twice as long to navigate.

If they arrived at Sodão Dangde unharmed, the next step would be splitting the party into two groups: one to climb the Third Finger and shoot the arrow that would reconnect the Bridge, another to play the role of the batengmun in Sodão Dangde and catch it. This was where the second problem came in: the Third Finger was treacherous to scale, even more so with the amount of rope they were planning on bringing to assist with the Sky Bridge.

Then there came the final problem they faced. There was only half a cycle before Ahn was supposed to meet his sister miles and miles away. Between preparing for the journey, reaching and scaling the mountains, and repairing the Bridge itself, Minhal was likely to arrive far faster than anyone was prepared for.

All three of these problems came down to timing. The good news was, there was a possible solution. The bad news was—

"Bringing the sãoni with us would make everything run a lot more smoothly," Sohmeng said. "They move *fast*, Hei. With the colony on our side, we would actually have a chance of fixing the Sky Bridge without Ahn missing his deadline. We might even have time to warn a few other hmun about Qiao Sidh on the way up."

Ahn nodded along, feeding small pieces of his sweet bun to the hatchlings. Hei was quiet, fidgeting with their sãoni claws as they leaned against Mama. Their expression was unreadable as ever.

"I know you don't like the idea," Sohmeng said, inching closer to them. "You've already said that you don't want humans using sãoni, that you'd rather everyone just leave them alone, but that's not, it's . . . " She trailed off, looking to Ahn for help.

"Qiao Sidh has put down their first colony at the top of the migration route," he said. Sohmeng was translating rapidly into Atengpa, making sure Hei didn't misunderstand him. It was a sensitive topic, after all. "If the sãoni continue on that route, they will walk right into the Empire. Hei, I . . . I killed one of them myself. You saw it." Hei's eyes flashed to him, a look that told him how clearly they remembered what he had done. He bit back the urge to try and justify himself, or overapologize. "I am only one man—there are *thousands* more coming. The sãoni are fearsome, but they would not stand a chance."

"It's why so many fled south in the first place, right?" asked Sohmeng. "It's what caused this whole problem, all of the new territory conflicts. I know you don't want the sãoni to get wrapped up in human problems, but it's already happening." Ahn watched the corner of Hei's mouth quirk, but Sohmeng did not give them a chance to argue. "It isn't fair that their way of life has to change, but if we want them to survive, we have to intervene. We all want the same thing, Hei. We want everyone to be safe. Humans and sãoni and everything in between."

"If the sãoni help Ateng, it could go a long way to building some trust between species,"Ahn added, smiling hopefully to Sohmeng. She nodded enthusiastically in agreement, but when she looked at Hei, her expression was sincere.

"But we won't do it without you," she said. Even though it wasn't directed at him, Ahn couldn't help but warm at the fierce kindness in her voice. "We haven't even brought it up with the Grand Ones yet, or the scouts. We wanted to talk to you first and tell you that even though having the sãoni would make this so much easier, even though I really don't want us to be separated . . . we won't do it without your go-ahead. If you want to say no, the answer is no. We'll find another way."

With everything out in the open, Ahn and Sohmeng were quiet. She had told him that this would happen, reminded him that Hei often needed to take their time before replying verbally to a difficult conversation.

Hei thumped their head back against Mama's belly, sighing loudly. They did not seem overly upset, or angry—if anything, they sounded exasperated.

"You two," Hei muttered, wrinkling their nose. "Big ideas, so smart. Not thinking that I already thinking these . . . these . . . " With an irritable growl, they sat up, speaking to Sohmeng in Atengpa. It sounded like a question.

"Oh," Sohmeng said, glancing to Ahn. She put her dice

away. "They um, do you mind if I just translate for them? Just to make it easier to understand?"

"Of course," Ahn replied quickly. This was an unexpected start. "Whatever is easier."

Just like that, Hei took off in rapid Atengpa, speaking with an eloquence that Ahn had never seen before. Their body language had the same feral grace as ever, and their expression maintained its typical shift between intense eye-contact and avoiding looking at people altogether. But without the Sãonipa peppered through the conversation, they were different, and Ahn realized with a low sense of shame that he had been misjudging them based on how they preferred to communicate.

"Do you two really think that I have not considered these things?" Hei asked, shaking their head. "I have lived with the colony for years longer than either of you. Sohmeng, I *told* you about the invaders, the Qiao Sidhur, when we first met. I told you about the danger they put the sãoni in. I know the migration route is a mess, and I am not sure why you think I believe things can go on as they have been."

Sohmeng sputtered something in defensive Atengpa, but Hei cut her off with a sharp Sãonipa sound before Ahn could catch its translation.

"You and Ahnschen do your thinking out loud. Thinking about Nona Fahang, thinking about Ateng, thinking about sãoni and each other and everything. All of it out loud, with your voices, to anyone who listens. I do my thinking *here.*" Hei tapped their temple, looking at them seriously. "I do my thinking with myself, and I share when I have something to say. So listen to what I am saying right now: while you have been dealing with Nona Fahang, I have been with the sãoni. I have been waiting for mating season to end, and watching Mama very closely, and trying to figure out how we can keep the family from getting killed. There is not *one* solution that makes me happy. But just being unhappy is not a solution either."

Ahn tugged at his earpiece, feeling an old heaviness in his chest. He understood the danger of inaction.

"So . . . " Sohmeng began, raising her eyebrows hopefully.

"So you are right," Hei conceded. "I *don't* like your idea. I don't like strangers near the sãoni, and I don't like strangers near me either. I don't like that the sãoni will need to change because of human foolishness. I don't like your solution, but it is the only one that makes sense. Sãoni and humans need to find a way to work together."

Ahn thought he might collapse in relief. Despite Sohmeng's reassurances to Hei that they could "find another way" if necessary, he'd honestly had no idea how they ever expected to fix the Bridge in time for next Minhal without the sãoni's help. Sohmeng leapt onto Hei, kissing their face with such force that Mama let out a confused rumble.

"Thank you!" Sohmeng said, squeezing them. "Hei, thank you, I knew you'd understand, I—"

Hei squawked loudly, wrestling Sohmeng to the ground. "Wait, I wasn't finished!"

The conversation rapidly devolved into play-fighting,

with Hei shouting as Sohmeng goaded them in Atengpa. Ahn averted his eyes with a small smile, petting one of the hatchlings as he felt something complicated churn in his heart.

"Okay, okay sorry," Sohmeng said, blowing her bangs out of her face and grinning sheepishly. "What were you saying?"

"Only that you have both forgotten something very important." Hei gestured to the creatures around them. "These are *sãoni.*"

"Well, yeah?" said Sohmeng. "They certainly aren't pygmy hogs."

Hei glared at them with the withering disbelief of an underpaid master. Ahn couldn't help but feel like a student who had forgotten to bring their book to class. "You think it is that easy? You ask the sãoni to go, and they go? Why would they ever listen to humans?"

"They listen to you," Ahn offered.

"They *understand* me," Hei shot back. "Sometimes. And that is not the same as listening."

"Okay, so maybe sãoni aren't always the easiest to work with," Sohmeng said. "But the colony has come a long way since we arrived at Nona Fahang. They're more tolerant of humans, especially when they can get a treat out of it. Maybe we could keep using food as encouragement to follow some small instructions!"

As if on cue, one of the hatchlings hopped up on its hind legs, peeping at Ahn for a piece of his sweet bun. He handed it over, feeling hopeful. "The hatchlings are attached to me, and very quick to learn. Even some of the older members of the colony seem open to training. If we take some time to prepare, maybe we could strengthen these skills."

"And with your cooperation, it could be so much easier!" added Sohmeng, gesturing energetically. "We could mix your understanding of Sãonipa with Ahn's training experience. We could make something completely new, something that's perfect for the sãoni. With your help—"

Hei growled, closing their eyes and waving their hands for quiet. Mama nuzzled against them, chirping. Ahn did not know what it meant, but it seemed to calm them down.

"I am not the alpha," they said eventually, stroking Mama's nose. "My word is not final, no matter how many tricks we make up. But I will do what I can, okay? Now no more talking, please. More sweet buns, but no more talking."

Sohmeng nodded, clicking what Ahn believed to be an affirmative. After a moment, he cleared his throat, trying to mimic the noise. The look on Hei's face told him that he was nowhere near close—but they were smiling. If he could earn one or two more of those smiles, they might come out okay.

Twenty-Two

FOLLOWING THE APPROVAL of the Grand Ones, preparations for the excursion to Sodão Dangde started immediately. It was decided that leaving under Ginhãe was the most auspicious choice, and so the date that had originally been set for Ahn's trial became the day that they would try to fix what he had broken. It felt good, promising, but it was also coming in less than two phases' time. Half of Heng, all of Li, perhaps a day more for buffer—all godly fortune aside, it amounted to no more than seven days. Seven days to achieve what Ateng had not been able to do in two years.

With Ahn's meeting with his sister looming, there was no choice but to pull it off. Failing Ateng now meant potentially failing all of Gãepongwei.

Thankfully, all of Nona Fahang was coming together to help. Everywhere Sohmeng looked, people of all phases and specializations were figuring out how their individual skills might serve their distant cousins in Ateng.

Many of them wound up braiding rope. Once the crossing to the First Finger was complete, repairs to the Sky Bridge would take far less time if they had the materials already. Most of Sohmeng's mornings were spent on this task, working side by side with her father's neighbours. Tonão's weaving hobby came in handy; she was amazed by how quickly his fingers moved.

It was hard not to think of the last batengmun. Thirteen children left alone, trying to do the work this entire hmun was now attempting together. Soon she would bear witness to their bodies once more. This time, she would give them the closure they deserved.

This is how I honour them, she told herself. *This is how we finish their Tengmunji.*

At first, Sohmeng was uncertain about using the fibers from a different plant than what was used in Ateng. But after being reassured of its sturdiness, she began to see beauty in the symbolism: the pain of Ateng being healed with the care of Eiji. It felt like a promise that Gãepongwei really could come together.

"There is a hmun called Sorwei Chapal that spans across the Ãotul," Tonão said one afternoon, bouncing Kuei on his knee. "They use this plant to build the bridges for their own crossing. Perhaps you will meet them, when all of this is done."

"Maybe you'll come with me," Sohmeng suggested. "Get back on the trade route."

Her father simply smiled, but the sadness in the look stopped Sohmeng before she pushed the issue. It was obvious how much he wanted to be a part of the journey to Sodão Dangde—he would light up every time they discussed their plans. Until the sãoni were brought up. Then, all she could do was pretend not to notice the way his hands would tremble, the way tangles would form in his previously smooth work.

Tonão Sol was not the only person who had reservations about the colony's part in their plan. No matter how much Sohmeng saw the sãoni as family, she couldn't deny the fact that they were predators, and working with them came with its own risk.

So when she wasn't up to her elbows in rope, Sohmeng was spending hours on end with Ahn and Hei, trying their best to make the creatures a little more human-friendly. Though Hei claimed they couldn't control the sãoni, it made a world of difference when they participated in the exercises. Ahn knew what strategies encouraged the sãoni to follow instruction, but Hei's ability to *speak* with them made the instructions clear. Together, they built a shared language.

After a couple days, they identified which members of the colony would make the best mounts: Mama for the sake of authority, Singing Violet for her calm demeanor, and the two impressionable adolescents that had followed Hei and Ahn into battle. Much to Ahn's horror, Sohmeng had taken to calling them Qøngem and Sølshend.

"To defeat the Empire, you must *think* like the Empire," she declared smugly, ignoring the high-pitched whine from her friend.

The plan also placed Hei firmly atop Green Bites. The end of mating season had mellowed the troublesome lizard out, but he had never really lost his—well, *bite.* Even as the other sãoni adapted to having more humans in their space, he was inclined to stalk, hiss at, and generally menace anyone he decided was in his way.

While Sohmeng and Ahn worked on socializing the sãoni, it was Hei's job to keep their brother in check. The snarling in the background did little to calm anyone's nerves, nor did the afternoon where Green Bites decided to drag Hei around by the leg in a show of dominance. Mama's tolerance of the new humans, provided they were introduced to her first, was one of the only things that reassured Sohmeng that it was possible to include new riders.

"This is crazy," Sohmeng groaned one night, her face smooshed on Hei's lower back. "What were we thinking? Do we even think?"

Hei offered a single dispassionate click before promptly falling asleep on the banana leaf mat Pimchuang Ker had given them. This whole process was exhausting for Sohmeng, but it was doing even more of a number on Hei; they were stretching the limits of their comfort with humans on a daily basis as they socialized the colony.

Sohmeng did what she could to make it easier: no one who disrespected Hei's space was allowed through the walls. Any questions were directed to Sohmeng and Ahn, with no expectation of a response from Hei unless they decided to give one. It seemed to help; every now and then Hei would briefly engage with someone new, especially if Mama had taken a shine to them. When the training days were over, Sohmeng always made time to cuddle Hei somewhere quiet and decompress.

Ahn, on the other hand, rarely had cuddle time to spare. When he wasn't helping with the sãoni, he spent his days working on strategic planning and endless combat drills. While Sohmeng rarely attended the defense meetings, she did have the chance to stop by one afternoon to watch Ahn train a group of volunteers.

He was in his element, moving with efficiency and grace. The students who had joined him seemed to be picking up on his instruction, which must have meant he was a good teacher, too. Sohmeng wasn't sure, really. She was busy looking at the muscles on his back.

"I have no idea how you do this," she said after Ahn had cheerfully called a brief recess, much to the relief of his students. "I'm exhausted just looking at you."

"Don't say that too loudly," Ahn replied with a little grin, tightening his high ponytail. His cheeks were flushed as he spoke; a bead of sweat rolled down his temple. "We're just getting started."

Sohmeng passed him the damp cloth she'd forgotten she was holding. "I'll send up a prayer."

"It's not so bad!" Ahn insisted. "It's nice, really. Like being back at school—except I suppose I'm the master, now." He looked over at his students, satisfaction flickering in his eyes as two of them reviewed their drills privately. When he made faces like that, Sohmeng sometimes forgot he was only two years older than her. "I just wish there was time to train more of them. My hope is that if I can do a good enough job with this group, they can pass it on to the rest. I don't want Nona Fahang unprepared if my sister . . ."

Sohmeng winced. "Do you think she'll wait for you?"

"Ólawen has always been the sibling I am closest to. But she's also very . . . strong-willed. She doesn't appreciate demands being made of her." Ahn rubbed the cloth over the back of his neck, biting his lip. "So, I don't know. I hope so."

The doubt in his eyes sent a pang of uncertainty through Sohmeng—it was a lot easier not to give into panic when everyone held strong. She nudged him with her elbow, forcing a grin. "Hey. You got *Lita Soon* swooning over you. If you can make that happen, you can do anything."

"That's not funny," Ahn said with a groan. "He isn't *swooning*!"

"*Oh tsongkar!*" Sohmeng sighed, holding her hand to her forehead. "With your dreamy sword and your dedication to personal redemption! We were sworn enemies, but now my heart—!"

"Sohmeng!" Ahn was laughing even as he tried to shush her. Thank both the gods that he was such a good sport about her teasing—him and Hei both, really. "I need to get back to training before everyone cools down too much. Let me know how our options for sãoni riders are looking later, okay?"

"Will do."

Sohmeng had determined that they needed no more

than five additional riders to assist in repairing the Sky Bridge. The sãoni themselves reduced the number of bodies needed to carry supplies, and left plenty of people to defend Nona Fahang should the worst happen.

One of the riders had already been confirmed as Polha Hiwei. She knew Eiji well, and had been welcomed by Mama with the happiest rumble Sohmeng had heard so far. The next best choice came from an unexpected place.

"Well hello there," crooned Eakang, pressing their forehead to Singing Violet's. The sãoni clicked happily, pushing back. "Aren't you just the sweetest thing?"

Singing Violet had been the first sãoni Sohmeng had ever ridden alone. She had been there after Sohmeng found the batengmun, a companion through all of Hei and Green Bites' power struggles. When the other sãoni had first been so scary to her, Singing Violet had been gentle and patient.

It seemed the sãoni's generous heart extended beyond Sohmeng alone. She took a deep breath, reminding herself that this was a good thing.

Beside her, Hei clicked quietly, their arms crossed as they watched Eakang fearlessly play with Singing Violet. They offered two noises in Sãonipa: *You. Alpha.*

"I know," Sohmeng murmured in Atengpa. Mama was unlikely to tolerate a new person guiding her, and with Hei stuck to Green Bites, Sohmeng was the next best candidate. It made sense. Someone else was always going to have to ride Singing Violet; the sãoni had been chosen as a mount specifically because of her unmatched tolerance for new people. But why did it have to be *Eakang*?

Eakang Minhal had been born into the life Sohmeng had always wanted. They had a community that called them by their name without any fear, that cherished their bold differences and never asked them to hide. The years Sohmeng had lost with her father had fallen straight into their lap, and they didn't even know how lucky they were. She doubted that Eakang had ever gone a moment in their life without the padding of unconditional love and acceptance. It was easy to hate them.

But hating them wouldn't undo the years Sohmeng had spent feeling alone. It certainly wouldn't fix the Sky Bridge. Much as the angriest, most childish parts of Sohmeng wanted to be spiteful and difficult, she recognized how little there was to be gained from it. How much there was still to lose.

With Hei by her side, the two of them ran through the interview with Eakang. She watched them master the directions Ahn and Hei had cobbled together, adjusted their hold as they attempted to ride Singing Violet for the first time. They asked a lot of questions, as per usual, but the questions were thoughtful, and framed respectfully enough that they even got a few answers from Hei. When the process was done, Sohmeng did not hesitate to suggest their name to the Grand Ones. It was only when Sohmeng released some of her grudge that she realized how heavily it had been weighing on her.

Of course, Sohmeng's newfound sense of inner peace

didn't change the panic that went through the household when Eakang's role in the excursion was announced.

Pimchuang Ker positively exploded, shouting at both Sohmeng and Eakang in Fahangpa while Jaea Won tried to calm her down. For once, Sohmeng was thankful for the language barrier.

"Child!" Pimchuang Ker shouted at Sohmeng, pointing to Eakang. "Child, a *child!*"

"Pim, please," Tonão said softly, but he did not move from his seat, his face in his hands.

Eventually, the arrival of Polha Hiwei and Grand One Minhal settled the issue. In Nona Fahang, Tengmunji was designed based on each individual's life path. With Eakang set to become a scout, this excursion was the perfect opportunity to earn their adulthood, with Polha Hiwei present as judge. Eventually, this reasoning settled some of the tension, and Eakang was given permission to spend their days training with the sãoni.

To Sohmeng's surprise, their company was much less grating in this context. Once the other two members of the party were selected, Pangae Ãofe and Mochaka Tang, she even found herself warming up to the idea of Eakang being on the journey. It would be kind of nice, she thought, to introduce them to Grandmother Mi and Viunwei.

But they were no replacement for her father.

As the first day of Ginhãe drew closer, Tonão Sol drew further into himself. He was quieter than usual, his anxiety palpable every time he entered a room. Sohmeng could never tell if he wanted her to spend time with him or stay away, and she didn't know how to broach the question without hurting him. No matter how many adult roles she was stepping into, being with her father made her feel like a child all over again.

One night, as she was preparing to go back outside the walls after dinner, he approached her. "I'd like to meet Hei," he said.

Sohmeng could only blink at him, taken aback. "Um . . . ?"

"They're your partner, aren't they?" Tonão asked quickly, clearing his throat. "Well, I'm your father. No matter how long I've been away. It's only right that I know who my daughter is involved with."

"I mean, sure?" Sohmeng laughed a little. There was no need for him to be so insistent; she had wanted to introduce the two of them for a long time, to merge her separate lives. "But Dad, I've already told you. Hei isn't really, they aren't super comfortable being around lots of people. I've asked them to come meet you in Nona Fahang, but—"

Tonão cut her off, his voice oddly stilted: "That isn't necessary. I can—I can go to them. Outside the walls. I can meet them there."

His determination made Sohmeng ache, if only because it could not completely hide the fear in his eyes. "Dad, the sãoni . . ."

"I want to meet them too." His words poured out in a rush, as though he was racing against his own doubt.

"I know your interviews and training are done for the day, and you're likely very tired, so I understand if you'd rather not. It's alright if you don't, it isn't—" The man paused, pinching the bridge of his nose and taking a deep breath. Sohmeng tried not to let her gaze linger on the old scars up his arm. "Forgive me. Let me try this again: if you have the energy, I would very much like you to introduce me to your partner and their . . . family."

Sohmeng bit her cheek, fought the urge to try and protect him. Tonão Sol was her father, a grown man capable of making his own hard decisions. "Of course, Dad."

As the two of them went hand-in-hand through the banyan wall, Sohmeng felt like she was back on the floor of Eiji for the very first time. Her father's palm was clammy against hers, his step slightly uneven as they navigated through the trees. The world below the safety of Ateng had changed them both.

"Hei?" she called, helping her father through the final steps. She heard them chirp a hello, and the sound made her nervous all over again. She wanted so badly for them to like each other. "I have someone for you to meet."

"Aren't we done with interviews?" Hei grumbled in Atengpa. They had gotten used to keeping their complaints in a private language. "Mama and I need a break."

"Not an interview this time." With a deep breath, Sohmeng turned to face them, fighting the urge to bounce with excitement. "Hei, this is my dad. He wanted to meet you, to say hello."

Hei's eyes widened, their shoulders hunching in surprise. Sohmeng laughed a little; she loved their nervous lemur face. Behind them, Mama let out a friendly rumble, crawling over to greet Sohmeng.

"Hello to you too," she said, stepping forward to receive her customary nose press.

"*No*—"

Sohmeng felt her father before she saw him, felt the grip on her hand tighten almost painfully as he yanked her close. Mama growled in alarm, and Tonão stumbled backwards, his face gone white.

"Dad!" She did her best to keep him from losing balance and knocking them both over. "Dad, it's okay—that's just, it's just Mama. She's the colony's alpha, she's friendly! She's just curious, she's curious, it's a good thing—"

Another uncertain rumble from Mama prompted the other sãoni to echo the noise, and Tonão gripped her tighter. He seemed like he was trying to say something, but he couldn't take his eyes off the colony.

"Dad," Sohmeng said, her own anxiety rising as the situation escalated. "Dad, please talk to me. It's okay, it's safe here." She knew her father was scared of the sãoni, but she had never seen him like this before. He was her dad, the grown-up—what was she supposed to do?

Hei's voice was a balm in the chaos, chirping Sãonipa reassurances from a human throat. They were stroking Mama's cheeks, settling the alpha back down. When mother and child were both satisfied, Hei turned their attention properly to Tonão. Wary, curious.

What a thing it was, to be given Hei's full focus. As they slinked over, Sohmeng saw them as her father must have seen them: their animalistic movements, the wildness in their green eyes. Tonão seemed unsure of where to look, trembling so hard that Sohmeng felt it down to her bones.

A loud chirp from Hei pulled the man's eyes fully from the sãoni and onto the small human before him. His brow furrowed as he swallowed, stumbling through his speech. "I'm sorry, this isn't—this isn't how I wanted to . . ." A chirp from a sãoni made him flinch violently, losing what words he had found.

Hei clicked quietly, tilting their head.

"Hei," Tonão tried again, but as he met their gaze, a new pain flashed in his eyes. "Heipua Minhal. Burning godseye, you look—I knew, I knew your grandmother, I am so, so *sorry*—"

This was too much. This was a mistake. Sohmeng was getting ready to pull him back in through the banyan, introductions be damned, when Hei stepped in. The brief look they spared her halted her in place before they turned back to Tonão, regarding the man and his terror and shame with inhuman silence.

They offered him their hands.

Sohmeng's breath caught. Hei stood, palms open, waiting for Tonão to make first contact. It took the man a moment, but he found his way, and their fingers met so delicately that Sohmeng thought the world might crack then and there.

Tonão did not try speaking after that, simply allowing

Hei to guide him away from the wall. Each step was slow, punctuated by reassuring chirps from Hei. When the man realized he was being taken to Mama, he dissolved into a stuttering uncertainty that Hei met with patience. They patted his arms, trilling quietly until they could coax another step from him. One step, then another. Each an act of bravery and trust. Sohmeng could only watch, not daring to interrupt.

One step, then another. It felt like a lifetime before Tonão Sol found the courage to place his palm on the sãoni's nose. Mama huffed, pressing back to meet his touch. She'd always had a soft spot for lost children.

"Nice to meet you, Sohmeng's father," Hei said, guiding his hand between Mama's head spines.

"The pleasure is mine, Hei," the man replied tenderly. "Thank you for looking after my daughter."

Though they didn't say much after that, Sohmeng thought she felt something pass between them, something that did not need to be spoken aloud. Together, they scratched Mama's head, eventually inviting Sohmeng to join in. The moons rose high, ushering in the final day of Li.

The next morning, they had their final volunteer.

Part Three:
Ateng

Twenty-Three

"DOING ALRIGHT THERE, AHNSCHEN?"

Ahn looked over to see Sohmeng flapping a hand at him from Mama's back. Her voice rang boisterous and clear; her spirits had been high since leaving Nona Fahang, and the energy was contagious. Even her father seemed to be relaxing after a tense start adjusting to the sãoni.

"Ask Sølshend," Ahn replied with a smile. "She's the one doing the hard work here."

"Well, she can ride on your back on the way home. It's only fair you take turns."

Ahn laughed, patting the sãoni on the nose. The creature chirped for a treat, which he popped into her mouth. Soon the sound was being echoed by the rest of the colony—snacking on the go was one of the best ways to keep them happy and moving.

Knowing this, the party had brought along an absurd supply of rations for their reluctant mounts. The sãoni were willful, greedy; getting them to listen at all often felt like training a palace kitten to be a hunting dog. But with a lot of persuasion and no small amount of grumbling, Mama seemed willing to follow Hei's route. The breakneck pace the alpha had initially set seemed almost retaliatory, but had slowed as the afternoon progressed, much to the relief of the human party.

The group of riders was small but capable: Sohmeng and Tonão were taking the lead with Mama, Ahn was close by on Sølshend, Polha Hiwei and Mochaka Tang on Qøngem, and Eakang and Pangae Ãofe on Singing Violet. Hei's troubles with Green Bites had been at a minimum so far, mostly thanks to their constant redirection.

"How long do you think we'll ride for?" asked Eakang, leaning over to feed Singing Violet a treat of her own.

"At the rate they're snacking, the sãoni probably won't stop to do much hunting," Sohmeng said. "My guess is that they'll slow down just before nightfall, when their bodies start to cool, and then we can make camp."

"Wait until you see how they glow at night," Ahn said to Eakang, smiling at the way their face lit up. He was glad they had been allowed to come; it was important for young adults to start doing what they loved early. And Sohmeng seemed to be getting less prickly with them too.

"That's also when we'll tie off the food, I assume?" asked Polha Hiwei.

"High." Everyone looked at Hei, surprised to hear them speak. Their shoulders hunched at the attention, but they kept their gaze ahead. "Food high in the trees—no sneaking sãoni eat it."

Mochaka laughed at that, adjusting his hold on Polha. "These things are massive. How could they possibly sneak up on anyone?"

Ahn cleared his throat, pulling one of the hatchlings from his newly-returned chestplate. "You'd be surprised."

The hatchlings had grown in the past few weeks: each had been no longer than his forearm when they first hatched, but now their bodies were bigger, tails thicker and legs stronger. When they cuddled up in his arms, Ahn delighted in holding their fat little heads in his palm. It felt nice, to be wanted with no complications. There was no telling how Ólawen would receive him now that he was changed, but the hatchlings loved him for exactly who he was.

The sãoni's antics were also a solid distraction from the daunting responsibility he'd been assigned. As the best archer among them, Ahn had been chosen to shoot the arrow that would reconnect the Sky Bridge. It was a tremendous honour—but also a lot of pressure.

On the third day of their journey, the mountains appeared: colossal pillars of karst, blanketed in the frilled greenery of hanging, clinging flora. They looked nothing like the mountain ranges of northern Qiao Sidh, which sloped like jagged arrowheads and were topped with the porcelain white of snow.

"There it is."

Tonão Sol pointed ahead, but Ahn recognized the sight from Sohmeng's description alone: five mountains, clustered together like a hand. Fochão Dangde, the three fingers, Sodão Dangde; the mountain range that made up Ateng. The hmun above.

It was technically a straight shot from where the party was located, but they had to travel the long way around to avoid hitting any enemy sãoni. As always, the easy route proved to be the deadly one. They spent all of Ginhãe Three and Four circling the mountains, feeding their mounts while Hei growled directions in Sãonipa to keep everyone on track. When they made their camp for the night on the bank of the Ãotul River near Sodão Dangde, it was with the knowledge that tomorrow would begin the climb.

The sãoni found their preferred heaps, throats glowing green and purple, and the humans followed suit. Polha Hiwei set up her bedroll with Pangae and Mochaka, who were all adapting to spending more time on the ground rather than the banyan trees of home; Eakang stayed close to Tonão Sol, chattering all the while. Ahn was nudging the coals in the fire when he felt a foot poke his back. To his surprise, the owner of said foot was Hei. They clicked at him, nodding in the direction of the river.

Ahn frowned a little. “Sorry . . . ?”

They rolled their eyes with a hiss, yanking on his arm. Unsure of what else to do, he followed.

They brought him to the river in silence, relaxing with every step away from the rest of the riders. Their charcoal makeup couldn’t hide the exhaustion on their face. As far as Ahn had seen, Hei was the first to rise each morning and the last to bed, constantly keeping an eye on the sãoni.

“Thank you,” he blurted out. “I know this has been hard

for you. Thank you for the work you've put into all this."

Something like a smile twitched at the corner of their mouth. The two of them wove around the heaps of sãoni, Hei occasionally pausing to pat a head or two, before they came to the spot by the river where Mama was resting. The hatchlings had curled up beneath her chin, snuggled in the warmth of her purple stripes.

Sohmeng was there too, scratching between a sleepy Green Bites' head spines. When she saw them approach, she grinned like a maniac. "Are you seeing this?" she stage-whispered, pointing emphatically at the sãoni. "It's a miracle. I have done miracles today."

Ahn covered his mouth with the back of his hand, trying to stifle a laugh. He didn't want to startle Green Bites in the midst of such an accomplishment.

The sãoni rolled over with a rumble, belly to the sky as Singing Violet slinked over to join him for the night. The moment he was distracted, Hei grabbed Sohmeng and pulled her into a heap of their own. "Me now. My turn."

Sohmeng laughed, giving their head a brief scratch before shoving them back. "Treats first!"

"Sohmeng," they whined.

"Treats."

With a grumble, they stumbled over to the bag they had hung up, pulling out an armful of saka fruit. Ahn couldn't help the laugh that escaped him. It felt like an entire lifetime had passed since he'd last seen one of those. Hei smiled wryly, making quick use of their sãoni claw to peel one and pass it to him.

"Thank you," he said.

Hei shrugged. "Your favourite."

"Hei!" Sohmeng cackled at the joke, swatting them gleefully on the arm. With the saka fruit successfully delivered, they flopped back against her. "Wow, okay, Hei was funny. Miracles all around! What have you got for us, Ahnschen? Can you turn that sword into a harp and play us a tune?"

Ahn took a seat, slicing his saka into pieces with a knife. "If only."

"You should really hear him, Hei," Sohmeng said. "Next time we're near a jeibu, I'm making him play you something."

"Do they have jeibus in Ateng?" Ahn asked.

"Nope. We have lots of flutes though, and some drums." Sohmeng took one of Hei's saka slices. "We play them in the parts of the caves that have the best acoustics. You can get some really neat echoes if you know what you're doing."

Despite the fact that they were currently in the shadow of the mountain range, Ahn still felt like they were talking about some far-off place. In his mind, Ateng had become more of a symbol than a physical location. He wondered how his perception would change once they repaired the Bridge and made the crossing, how he might begin to see Sohmeng differently within the context of her home.

"Are you excited to go back?" he asked, thinking of his own homesickness.

Sohmeng's brow quirked. "To Ateng?"

Ahn nodded. "It's been some time since you've seen your family, hasn't it? I know you've said before that you left on difficult terms, but I'm sure they'll be happy to know you're . . ."

"Not splattered on the ground?" she finished, blowing her bangs out of her eyes. "Yeah. I hope so. Home has always been kind of hard but . . . well, I miss my grandmother. And my idiot brother, I guess." The brief smile on her face told him how much she was underselling the point. "Plus I get to bring my dad back to them. Minhal or not, no one can call me unlucky ever again."

Hei hummed, reaching up to give Sohmeng another bite of saka. Despite himself, Ahn felt a bubble of curiosity rise up. Even though they lived with the sãoni, Hei spoke the same hmunpa as Sohmeng; it wasn't hard to draw conclusions.

"What about you, Hei?" Ahn asked. Their eyes landed on him with surprise, and an unexpected openness. "Are you ready to—"

"HA," Sohmeng laughed suddenly, loud enough to make Ahn jump. "Obviously! Of course Hei's excited to rest with the sãoni for a while. Guiding Mama around like they're the freaking alpha, no wonder they look so pooped. I don't know anyone who deserves a splash in the river more than my little lizard." She leaned over, patting their cheeks until they squawked in annoyance.

"I was just saying so earlier. They've been working very hard." Ahn knew a topic change when he saw one.

It wasn't his place to ask about Hei's life if they didn't want to share.

Ahn had been thinking a lot about the time he would be spending with Hei and Sohmeng now that he was staying in Eiji. In the past weeks, they both had become important to him. Every day he felt like he was learning something new, and every new thing he learned only made him more curious. Sohmeng challenged him to be brave, Hei challenged him to be good. Warrior's traits, by all accounts, but reimagined into something benevolent.

It had been so long since he'd allowed himself to connect to other people. Now that it was finally happening, the complexity of his feelings was frightening. He didn't want to act impulsively or cross any boundaries. He didn't want to interfere with their relationship.

But he wanted to be accepted. He wanted to belong. He wanted to dance with Sohmeng again, to rest his hands on her soft waist and listen to her laugh. When she tussled and cuddled and shared old jokes with Hei—he wanted that, too. He wanted them all to fall asleep together again.

The thought filled him with guilt, made him lonely despite being so close to them.

"Hey." Hei's voice pulled him abruptly from his thoughts just in time to catch the peeled saka fruit they tossed his way. "Worrying, Ahnschen."

Ahn swallowed, startled, caught in the act.

"What? Worrying? Why is he worrying?" Sohmeng turned to look at him. "Ahn, what's up?"

"I—I'm sorry." He shifted uncomfortably. It was getting

late—the two of them probably wanted some private time. "I just was thinking that maybe I should get to bed. Give you both some space."

"We invited you over though?" Sohmeng wiggled over to him, ignoring Hei's squawk as they toppled over. "Why are you being weird?"

Ahn flushed, looking between the two of them. "I don't want to impose."

Sohmeng snorted. "Ahn, buddy, it's not mating season. We have the power to show *some* restraint." Hei smiled a little, resting their head on her lap. She played with their hair as she spoke. "Besides, what kind of relationship doesn't let you hang out with other people?"

The question hit him in the chest. Ahn thought of the private worlds his masters had constructed for the pairs of students participating in their Six-ings. While friends were allowed, and flirtations tolerated, Conquest partners were expected to be everything to one another. It was a way to secure their bond across the bilateral realms.

Ahn loved Schenn. He loved what they'd had in life, and missed it every day. But now he wondered—could things have gone differently if they'd been allowed to talk about it with other people?

"I was—" He stopped. His voice sounded overly loud to his ears. "I was discouraged from being involved with others. During my last . . . serious relationship." It felt like tattling, like breaking a rule his parents had set down. Ahn's body tensed, awaiting trouble that did not come.

"Not by my partner, but by the—the rules." It was a gross oversimplification. It was about all he could say without being overtaken by panic. "Maybe I don't understand the culture here."

Hei was frowning as Sohmeng translated. He avoided their eye, afraid of revealing more than he could handle. Afraid of exposing himself.

"I mean here, it's sort of expected that having close relationships with other people is important? Phase-mates aren't anything like spouses, but they're still a big deal." Sohmeng scratched at Hei's head as she explained. She was always so generous in what she shared about her home, and eager to learn more about his. "And even with spouses, it's not just two people alone together—sometimes they need a damwei to have kids, or they're both into a third person. I've heard of a family with four spouses before, but then juggling everyone's phasal compatibility gets messy."

"Ah," Ahn said. "In Qiao Sidh, we take one spouse. Other relationships matter, but that relationship is meant to involve no more than two."

This was one thing that made the Six-ing participants unique—their partnership could be conceptualized as a different but equally ranked sort of marriage. When the living partner was married later in life, their spouse would also marry the spirit in the bilateral realm.

"Sounds restrictive," Sohmeng said. After receiving their translation, Hei clicked in agreement.

"Maybe it is." Ahn pulled gently on his earpiece, wishing for Schenn's perspective. The boy had felt more present recently, but Ahn still didn't feel like it was a two-way connection.

"My brother got really bent out of shape when the Grand Ones suggested a different match from the person he was dating." Sohmeng sucked her teeth. "He probably could have worked something out with the matchmakers instead of just dumping his boyfriend. But I guess love made him an idiot."

"It does that," Ahn replied.

Sohmeng squinted at him as if something had occurred to her. "Hey, question. You said you've been in love before, yeah? How did that feel for you?"

Again, Ahn was taken aback. He tucked a stray strand of hair behind his ear. It was more difficult to keep tidy since he'd cut it.

"I suppose it feels like . . ." He wished he knew how to translate the word *magnetism*. The image of two pieces of metal yearning for each other through the seeming pull of spirit alone was the best metaphor he had. An internal compass. "It's this sort of tug towards another person, a curiosity that I can't fully explain. Everything the person does makes me want to connect with them more." Hearing it aloud, it sounded like embarrassing poetry. But it was how he felt. "It's not founded in any logical reasoning, but it seems like the truest thing in the world. Attraction feels like . . . faith. A sense of faith in someone I might not know very well, and a desire to prove that faith right together."

The face Sohmeng was making at him now was far more suspicious than the one she'd made when he'd first explained being zhørmozhør. Hei, on the other hand, nodded along, looking at Ahn with understanding. That was a first.

"Alright," Sohmeng eventually said. "Sounds weird and inconvenient, but alright."

Ahn laughed. "It is! Very weird, very inconvenient. But it's also . . . I don't know. There's nothing like it." Once more, Hei clicked in acknowledgement, reaching up to feed Sohmeng another slice of saka. The difference in their responses seemed odd to him, considering their relationship. "Have you ever felt that?"

"I don't think so," Sohmeng said, playing with Hei's hair. "I mean, I love this doofus, right? But I didn't just feel drawn to them like it was some story. I loved them because I liked how they acted, what they said. It wasn't faith, it was proof. And I knew I was attracted to them because—" She gestured at them like it was obvious, grinning. Ahn bit back a smile at the way Hei puffed out their chest in response. "Is that weird, do you think?"

Ahn shook his head; he had met aromantic people before. "Not at all. I think everyone's experience is a little different." Cautiously, he looked to Hei. "What about you?"

Hei cocked an eyebrow, pointing to themself with their claw.

"Yeah Hei," Sohmeng teased, messing up their hair. "How do you know that you like me? Tell us about your special lizard senses!"

To Ahn's surprise, Hei laughed, grabbing Sohmeng's arm and biting. He so rarely heard that sound from them, hardly ever saw them take a moment to unwind. Perhaps that was his fault; his arrival in Eiji had been a source of so much stress for them that they likely hadn't gotten a chance to calm down in months. Silently, he made up his mind to fix that.

After another brief wrestle, Hei actually answered Sohmeng's question. "Even though you made me very frustrated, I did not want to be away from you. I couldn't explain it." They rubbed their nose shyly, glancing at Sohmeng. "And you are very beautiful."

Sohmeng beamed through her translation, looking incredibly satisfied. "Guess I just need to keep being hot and annoying! Gets me all the good ones."

Ahn laughed along with them, trying not to linger too long on the words *good ones*, plural. "You're very spirited."

"That another thing I share with your old boyfriend?" The teasing smile she wore quickly faded when she met Ahn's eye. He tried to arrange his expression back into something more casual, but the damage was done. "Shoot—Ahn, I'm sorry. I shouldn't have said that."

Hei chirped at Sohmeng, who quickly mumbled what Ahn assumed was an explanation. His chest tightened; he wanted to keep relaxing with them, enjoying the feeling of speaking openly, like he was any other nineteen-year-old camping with his friends. But these things were so heavy, so complex. Could he balance being honest with being happy?

"It's okay." Ahn took a deep breath. He could tell the story at his pace. He could offer a little at a time, if he needed to. "The two of us—we loved each other. I still love him. I just . . . made some mistakes. I don't know if I know how to make them right."

"That's tough," Sohmeng said. Her voice was sympathetic.

"It is," Ahn agreed. Before he could stop himself, his hand was at his earpiece.

"Was that his?" Ahn felt panic strike him before Sohmeng continued, "It's a really unique piece of jewelry."

"It—it's one of a kind. It was the last gift he gave me."

It was enough of the truth to satisfy him, enough to keep a conversation moving in a direction that felt safe. But Ahn didn't miss the way Hei's eyes lingered on the bone, and he didn't think he imagined the understanding in their eyes. They peeled another saka and passed it his way.

"Relationships are *hard*," Sohmeng blurted out. "Did you know my dumb brother's breakup is actually the reason I fell off that cliff?"

She launched into the drama with enthusiasm, even including what Ahn assumed were poor imitations of the people involved. He laughed along, settling down, breathing through the shakiness in his hands. It was a relief to have spoken about Schenn, even if he could not yet tell the full story. Up until now, he hadn't felt safe enough with anyone even to mention the boy. It meant something, that he'd managed it tonight.

Ahn was doing what he could to make things right with the people of Gãepongwei, the land of Eiji. Fixing his Empire's mistake was the right thing to do, the only thing that would allow him to sleep unburdened. But it was also something he wanted to offer his friends.

They're my friends, he thought, and it felt wonderful to believe. To trust.

The three of them passed the hours tucked together in the shadow of the mountain, sharing stories and pointing out constellations. Ahn even managed to recognize a seeking star twinkling in the scattered sand of the heavens. A beacon, a guide. A piece of his old home, reborn in a new patch of sky.

Twenty-Four

ON THE OPENING MORNING of Third Mi, Sohmeng woke with the sun. Despite the late night she'd had with Ahn and Hei, she was full of potential energy for what was to come. It had been over a cycle since she landed in Eiji—one hundred and twenty-five days, to be precise. Shorter than a traditional Tengmunji by far, and yet she had lived a small lifetime on the jungle floor, learning new languages and forming new relationships, navigating culture clashes between humans and sãoni alike. Her life had come apart and together again into something new, with all the challenge and triumph of Ama and Chehang.

Today, she would return to Ateng. She would climb Sodão Dangde, light the batengmun's lantern, and then, once all of Fochão Dangde could see that hopeful flame, she would begin repairs on the Sky Bridge.

The new beginning opened with a temporary good-bye. While Sohmeng would be leading the party up Sodão

Dangde, Ahn and Hei were responsible for ascending the Third Finger with all of the rope that Nona Fahang had been able to produce. Once both groups were ready, Ahn would shoot the arrow that would unfurl the Third Finger's portion of the bridge so Sohmeng's group could reconnect it to Sodão Dangde. Bridging the gap in the same tradition Ateng had upheld for years.

"I'll meet you up there, okay?" Sohmeng pressed her forehead against Hei's, not caring if she got smeared with charcoal.

"At the top of the world," Hei murmured. "Are you ready?"

Sohmeng laughed a little. "You'd think waiting nearly five years would make me more ready than ever. But I don't know. I just want it to work."

She kneaded at Hei's arms, taking a deep breath. Realistically they would see each other come nightfall, but Sohmeng's plans had gone wrong enough times for her to be cautious. Still, it filled her with warmth to know that Hei would be there, playing the role of the adults receiving the batengmun. Their time together had been Sohmeng's Tengmunji; it only made sense that they would help her with this final step.

She bonked their foreheads together. "Don't feed Ahn to Green Bites the second I'm gone, alright?"

"I wouldn't do that. We need him to shoot the arrow." The spark of mischief in Hei's eyes made Sohmeng glow like wovenstone. Their parting kiss was hungry and lingering; it made Sohmeng even more determined to fix the bridge and get back to them soon.

After a final nuzzle, Sohmeng went to find Ahn, who was loading the last of the supplies onto Sølshend's back. He was speaking with the sãoni in quiet Qiao Sidhur, stroking the creature's back encouragingly. The happy rumbles made Sohmeng release a breath she didn't know she had been holding.

"Need any help?" she asked.

Ahn tightened one of the rounds of rope, looking over his work. "I think that's the last of it, actually. But I appreciate the offer."

For a moment they were both quiet, Sohmeng watching Ahn, Ahn watching the sãoni. After all that time trapped together in Nona Fahang, she wasn't sure how to say goodbye to him. They'd barely figured out how to say hello before all this mess began.

"Ahn—" Sohmeng sighed heavily, giving up on words. All of this sentimentality was getting exhausting. She stepped up on her toes and yanked Ahn down in the same way she had when they first met, rubbing their cheeks together. "Thanks for everything, okay? Be safe."

Ahn returned the gesture with a little smile. She wasn't sure what was more unexpected, the lack of stammering or the faint scratch of stubble on his face. Hei's skin was always smooth. "Same to you, Sohmeng."

With the future of her home at stake, Sohmeng's racing thoughts found a hundred good reasons to delay, a thousand different conversations to make them wait just a little longer. They had put so much into this moment, and she feared the possibility of something going catastrophically wrong. She steadied herself, searching for the feminine boldness that kept Par so close to her heart; avoiding the risk of failure only ever came at the expense of the opportunity for success. It was time to be brave.

So the day began.

The two teams reviewed the plan one last time over a light breakfast, with Tonão Sol looking over everyone's practiced knotwork for securing the bridge. With the group's confidence built up, they turned to the sãoni.

By the blessings of the moons, Mama was incredibly mellow about Hei and Sohmeng directing the colony. The alpha had come to treat the new humans like a group of adopted hatchlings; it didn't bother her when they played and explored with the rest of the colony. Hei suggested that starting the excursion in her formerly hard-won territory was playing a part in her calm demeanor, but they could make no promises about when she might cut their games short and start migrating. Once the bridge was reconnected, Hei would come straight back down to try and keep her still for as long as possible.

Following the alpha's laid back lead, the sãoni they had trained as mounts were happy to set out on a new adventure. Except, of course, for Green Bites. Splitting the party meant parting him from Singing Violet, which Hei managed in a feat of strength and stubbornness that earned them a bite on the thigh for their trouble. The snarl Mama directed at her children just about scared the humans out of their skin, but it also made the difficult sãoni back down. He even offered Hei a begrudging nudge as they bandaged up the shallow wound.

Sohmeng couldn't dream of wrangling the sãoni with such ease, but with Hei split from the group, the humans looked to her as their new leader.

"Okay," she said, holding tight to the belt she'd attached to Singing Violet. "Who's ready for the scariest ride of their life?"

Sodão Dangde hadn't gotten any less vertical since Sohmeng's last sãoni ride up the mountain face, and the terrified sounds of her companions was a walk down memory lane. Frantic praying, nauseous moaning, the occasional shriek—all perfectly reasonable, though Sohmeng hoped they at least took a second to enjoy the view.

Between encouraging shouts for them to *hold on tight* and *wait until you're off the sãoni to pee your pants,* Sohmeng guided Singing Violet with Sãonipa directions. The rest of the sãoni followed her lead, cheerfully scrabbling up the rocks while their riders held onto their rope belts and each other for dear life. Her father clung to her so tightly Sohmeng thought she might burst, but his shaky laughter gave away the sense of wonder that he had passed down to her.

Everyone was grateful to reach the plateau. As a merciful and compassionate leader, Sohmeng allowed them a moment to kiss the ground and throw up as necessary. While they prepared for the next stage of the climb, Sohmeng gave each of the sãoni their treats as reward for a job well done.

"Couldn't have done it without you," she murmured to Singing Violet, kissing her on the nose.

Once everyone unloaded the supplies from the sãoni, Sohmeng sent the creatures on their way. There was no need for them to wait when the party would be crossing to Fochão Dangde instead of coming back down. Sohmeng stood at the edge of the cave, facing the same stretch of sky where she had first told Hei she was Minhal half a cycle ago. This time, the journey to the caves' entrance would not feel so lonely.

That didn't mean it came without challenges. Even with the sãoni's boost up the most treacherous leg of the mountain, there was still a lot of walking to be done. Six people needed a lot more check-ins than two, especially when four had never been up so high and one was trying to climb on a wooden leg. Sturdy as Tonão's prosthetic was, it had not been designed with long hikes in mind. But years as one of Ateng's traders made him familiar with the route, and he had come prepared with a cane to balance his weight and some medicine to manage the pain.

"I've had worse," he assured Sohmeng as he worked his way over a rocky patch. "It's worth it, for where we're going. And I have Polha to help me cross when we get there."

Spirits were high as everyone made their way to the trader's entrance. Sohmeng thumbed the flowering vines affectionately. The slot in the mountain had felt like such a secret when Hei first brought her here, but now it was simply another door, being used as though they were just another group of traders come home from a long journey. Sohmeng supposed that was true of her father, at least.

The man grunted with effort as he worked his way through the tight rocks, supported by the other scouts. Despite the fact that half of the party were essentially strangers to her, Sohmeng was grateful they had come. Tonão's longing to return home was obvious, but she could also see the life he had made for himself in Nona Fahang. She understood the need to have one home meet another.

It happened all at once, bold sunlight yielding to Ateng's persistent darkness. Wovenstone glowed in welcome, and Sohmeng felt herself glow right back with pride to hear the others murmur in awe. Maybe it wasn't a banyan fortress, but these mountains, these caves, they were her home.

"Give your eyes a moment to adjust," Tonão said, but Sohmeng was already heading toward the winding system she had walked through once before. "Sohmeng, where are you going?"

"Just getting a head start," she called back, peeking around one of the walls.

"Not sure where to," he replied. "That's not the right way."

Sohmeng frowned, resting her hand on the cool wall. That couldn't be true. She remembered Hei standing right here, remembered the thick vein of wovenstone behind the shadowed silhouette of their body. She didn't think she could ever forget the image of them slipping into the blackness. But then she remembered Hei's words as well: *too narrow, too unstable. Easy to get lost in.*

"My bad," Sohmeng said, splaying her fingers against the boulder that protected the privacy of Hei's childhood. Some secrets did not have to be shared. "Glad you're here with us, Dad. I'd have brought us right into a dead end."

The trader's route Tonão took them up was easier by far. The stairs had been carved with care through wide-walled passages, and there was no need to do the same sort of intensive climbing as last time. Still, the unforgiving stone began to take its toll on Tonão, who was sweating as he chewed on one of the painkilling leaves. Sohmeng stayed by his side, looking for ways to distract him.

"How did you know you wanted to be a trader?" she asked him in Atengpa. The language was like cool water on her tongue, the relief of speaking it amplified by its familiar echo off the walls.

"It wasn't an obvious decision," the man admitted, wiping his forehead. "I was a timid kid, scared of absolutely everything. During my Tengmunji I made up my mind to spend time with people who were braver than me, so I might have a chance at being a brave adult. Naturally, I gravitated right to Lahni—who was delighted to have a shy boy to do her bidding! Especially with no elders around to make her give me a break." His laughter made Sohmeng smile, biting her lip. That sounded like her mother. "Falling in love with her was easy, but I always assumed she was far out of my league. Imagine my surprise when we returned to the hmun and the Grand Ones suggested us as a match.

Imagine my surprise when they said it had been *her* idea—supported by her assertion that there was no one in the hmun who made her feel more secure than quiet, scared Tonão Sol."

"Not so quiet and scared anymore?" Sohmeng asked.

"That's what they told me," he said. "When Lahni was put on the trader's path, I requested to join her—mostly because I wasn't sure what else I wanted to do. But the moment my feet touched the ground, I fell in love with Eiji. Perhaps even more than she did. So we never stopped. Even after you and your brother were born, we relied on the good graces of our parents and neighbours to look after you while we were on rotation visiting the nearby hmun."

As he told the story, Sohmeng's smile faltered at the reminder that her parents had always known about Nona Fahang. About another life that could have existed for her. Sohmeng bit her cheek; she'd started this conversation to take her father's attention off of the pain, not make things hurt more.

"What's wrong, little trouble?" The question made Sohmeng cringe. She had never been good at hiding her feelings.

"It's just . . . why didn't we all go to Nona Fahang when I was born?" she asked, swallowing the lump in her throat. "Why did you have me hide instead?"

For a moment, all she heard was the sound of her father's laboured breathing, the knock of his cane on the stone stairway. "Your mother and I were scared," he finally said. "We had planned you for Hiwei, but you came so early, and—and we didn't know what to do. The thought of exile was impossible—what about Viunwei, or Grandmother Mi? Lahni's mother died before you were born, but you remember your Grandfather Tos. Would we leave him behind too, without his family? The situation was much bigger than any one of us." He paused to rub at his sore thigh, the pain on his face illuminated by wovenstone. "You're right—if anyone could have survived exile, it was me and your mother. We probably could have gotten you to Nona Fahang. But we were scared, and when Grandmother Mi offered us an easy solution, we jumped for it. Fear made a child of me, and I listened to my mother. I know . . . I know we should have considered the effect it would have on you. It's why I was so against it when Lahni told you the truth."

"But I'm glad I know!" Sohmeng insisted, surprised by her own vehemence. "Everyone has the right to know who they are. Without that, how are they supposed to figure out who they want to be? There's no way to know where you're going if you don't know where you started."

"Wise words." Tonão smiled, ruffling her hair before continuing the long ascent. "Where, ah . . . where do you suppose you'd like to go?"

Sohmeng hesitated. There were so many answers to that question.

"Par?" he asked. "Minhal?"

Sohmeng sighed, tugging at her bangs. People always made that sound like it was such a simple question. Especially when they were comfortable with their own birth phase. "I feel like both, I guess? Maybe that doesn't make sense, but I feel like both of them at once."

Tonão caught her eye, nodding with unexpected understanding. Maybe even approval. "You know, in a hmun to the west, farther west than I've ever travelled, they treat the two phases as one. They call it Parminhal."

Parminhal. Sohmeng felt her stomach flip. There was no way to describe the sensation of *home* that came with imagining those two distinct phases merged into something new. Perhaps something of her own.

With every step, Sohmeng felt herself changing, and the space around her seemed to reflect it. The staircase levelled out, the walls slowly widened, and the wovenstone grew brighter, guiding the party with celebratory light. Every corner was overflowing with different kinds of mushrooms, bouquets of bounty that had grown in the years left undisturbed.

When the echoes of their footfalls changed, Tonão halted the party.

"We're just about at the main hall," he said. "Sohmeng, Eakang, both of you wait here."

"*What?*" To Sohmeng's horror, they had both shouted in unison.

Before they could protest, Tonão halted them with an uncharacteristically firm look. "Sohmeng, you have already told us about the batengmun. Their bodies need to be moved, arranged with dignity before the rest of the hmun arrives. This is not something you or Eakang should have to do."

"I've already seen them—" she began.

"And for that I am sorry." Tonão took her cheek, looking at her with a pained sort of affection that reminded her of Viunwei. "Please let me be your father about this."

Sohmeng swallowed, thinking of the first time she had seen her friends' bodies curled up around the cold fire pit. In truth, she *didn't* want to do that again—maybe demanding to be treated like an adult was an old habit she needed to break. Maybe it would be nice to be a kid for a minute. "Okay. Sorry."

Once the adults left, Sohmeng and Eakang were stuck alone together. Sohmeng had been speaking with her father in their shared hmunpa for a lot of the journey so far, savouring their time together back in Ateng. Now she sat in awkward silence, tracing patterns on the floor while Eakang gawked at the glowing walls.

"It's, uh—it's called wovenstone," Sohmeng said, trying to fill the space between them. "It grows everywhere in this mountain range. Gives us light and stuff."

Eakang perked up. "Do you make anything out of it? Or does it just stay on the walls?"

"We don't just hack it off for any reason, but we do use it. The Grand Ones grind it up into a powder they put in mountain marrow, which is this drink that only they can have. It's supposed to help them get closer to the gods, but I think it smells kind of foul. Oh, I also have wovenstone dice—" She took them out of her pocket, jostling them in her palm. "They were a gift from my Grandmother Mi, when she took her Grand One's vows. They're the nicest thing I own."

"Your craftspeople probably can't make too much new stuff, huh?" Eakang asked, peering at the dice. Taking pity on their twitching fingers, she passed the little stones over, trying to manage the anxiety of sharing something so important to her. "Resources are scarce when there are only two mountains."

"Yeah." Sohmeng watched them turn the dice in their hands, careful and curious. She hadn't expected Eakang to understand value this way, having come from such a land of plenty. Maybe her father had taught them. Or maybe they were less oblivious than she thought.

" . . . thanks for letting me come with you, Sohmeng."

"Uh, yeah. I mean, you were pretty good with the sãoni, so . . . " Sohmeng rubbed at her arm, not sure what to do with the sincerity of their gratitude. "And like, I guess it makes sense because my dad's pretty much your damdão. So that means you should probably meet my brother and grandmother and stuff, because I met your moms and Kuei." Burning godseye, this was all coming out so clumsily. Why was it so hard to be nice to this kid?

"I'm really excited!" they said, handing back the dice.

"See how excited you are when you actually meet Viunwei." Sohmeng couldn't help smiling as she said it. It had been so long since she'd seen her brother that she found herself missing him more often than she cared to admit.

Eakang laughed a little, but their expression betrayed a nervousness Sohmeng hadn't seen before. "Um, Sohmeng?"

"Yeah?"

"Should I not tell anyone that I'm Minhal?"

The question took Sohmeng aback. For a second all she could do was stare at them, trying to shape a response on her tongue. The guilt on Eakang's face made her wonder just how hard they'd been straining to try and find words they understood in her and her father's Atengpa. Apparently they'd caught at least one.

"Maybe—maybe you're the wrong person to ask this," they quickly backtracked, looking at the floor. "I don't want to be rude, I know it's a hard subject, but I just . . . I'm not sure what to do."

How strange it was, seeing this dilemma on another person. Young, uncertain, eager to be wanted and cared for by a new community. "Do you want to tell them you're Minhal?"

"I don't know what else I'd do," Eakang admitted. "I don't know how to be anything else."

"Then say you're Minhal." Sohmeng shrugged. "If anyone gives you trouble, I've got your back. Phase-mates are supposed to stick together, right?"

Eakang lurched forward to try and hug her—which Sohmeng promptly shut down with a forearm. It was like training hatchlings with this one. Even still, they beamed at her, and the look was enough to make Sohmeng straighten up a little. There was no harm in performing extra self-assurance. Both of them needed it right now.

Soon, Polha Hiwei called for them. It had not been terribly long since Sohmeng last entered the main hall of Sodão Dangde, but the novelty hit her again all the same. The shape of the houses, the smell of the air—and now her father, reborn from the ground below.

The adults had moved the batengmun somewhere private and cleaned up the remains of their final darkened hearth. All that was left was a peculiar stain, and a sense of loss that Sohmeng was not sure would ever fully go away. Pangae and Mochaka were setting up a cooking fire while Tonão prepared fresh ingredients for dinner. Long as their journey had been, it was far from over. They would need to eat something before facing the next challenge.

Sohmeng smiled to hear her father humming as he worked with the delicacies of the mountain: overgrown armour bugs, sweet edible moss, meaty fungi from the high walls. Silently, she helped him with the ingredients, basking in the miraculous normalcy of it all. One more sit down, one more meal, and she would return this feeling to all of Ateng.

"It's good to have you home, Dad," she said, leaning her head on his shoulder.

"It's good to be home, little trouble."

Loss had changed everyone, and time had forced them to grow. Sohmeng couldn't unbreak the Sky Bridge, but she could rebuild it stronger. She could love Ateng both for what it once was and what it could become moving forward. With a fresh fire and laughter warming the long-quiet halls of Sodão Dangde, Sohmeng believed, for the first time since she was very young, that her home could be something wonderful.

Twenty-Five

BREATHE. MIND YOUR FEET.

Ahn exhaled slowly, repositioning himself. The gap between the Third Finger and Sodão Dangde was wide—not impossibly so, but enough that he had to make each practice shot count. It would be harder when the entire party was staring at him; better to perfect it in advance. This was his fourth attempt.

Don't make your body fight to center itself.

The wind whistled in his ears, tickling his scalp with cool air. Ahn's brow creased at the sensation. Between the wind conditions and the distance, he couldn't decide if he wanted to open his stance or square it. He'd consult Schenn, but Ahn had always been the better archer of the two.

Doubt invites failure. Make a choice and stand by it.

He swallowed, exhaled deeply to slow his heartbeat. To invite elegance into his skill, shape mastery from acquired grace. He had done this so many times before.

The blade was his most recent paramour, but his early days of Conquest had begun with the bow and the critical eye of his masters. This was not so different.

Your grip, Ahn—don't torque the bow. Hand to your jaw, tip of the nose to the string. You know this. What, you nervous now that your sister's watching?

His fingers twitched, releasing the arrow in a spark of tension that set it off course. The arrow struck low on Sodão Dangde, its thin rope line fluttering like a kite string.

"Relax," he muttered to himself in Qiao Sidhur. Disapproval burned in his gut like bad wine.

Ahn crouched, tugging firmly on the rope. The arrow released easily from the mountainside, which he took as further indication of the poor quality of his shot. He knew he was just being harsh on himself; all he really needed to do was land the arrow accurately at the mouth of the cave. Then it was up to the rest of the party to do the long labour of pulling the weight of the attached bridge across the chasm and securing it inside.

The process was completely foreign to Ahn. All of the bridges he'd ever seen in Qiao Sidh were made of stone or wood, meant for crossing broad rivers. No matter how many times Tonão Sol had described it to him, it was still challenging to visualize. It was easy to imagine all the ways his small mistakes might lead to colossal failure. He pulled up the line, fishing the arrow from the open sky. His first two practice shots had landed well. There was no reason he couldn't do it again. It would be fine, it had to be—

"Ahnschen."

Ahn jumped at the sound of his name, quickly looking over his shoulder. "Sorry, what?"

Hei was crouched behind him, staring. They clicked at him, frowning.

"Have—have you been calling me?" he asked, cheeks burning. Practicing was just supposed to pass the time, he didn't realize how caught up in it he'd gotten. "I'm sorry, I was lost in my thoughts, I didn't—"

"Stop." Hei sighed, scooting over to help him pull up the loose line. "Stop with thinking, and stop with arrow. Watching you is . . . makes me . . ." They wiggled their fingers with a frazzled growl, and Ahn laughed despite himself.

He hadn't realized how much pressure had built in his chest until he felt it begin to loosen. Hei was probably right—he wasn't doing anyone any favours by getting all wound up. They reeled in the rope together until Ahn had the arrow back in his hand. Another chance.

Looking over the side of the mountain, Ahn shivered to see the scope of Gãepongwei. He had never been up so high before, and while the experience had been initially disorienting—especially on the back of a rambunctious sãoni—he found that he was adjusting to the altitude with unexpected ease. Hei appeared to be handling it calmly as well, their awe given away only by the dart of their eyes across the landscape, as if they were committing it to memory.

"It's beautiful here, isn't it?" Ahn asked, sitting back

against the side of the mountain. Enormous birds soared by, the melody of their calls splitting the vast sky.

"Beautiful," Hei agreed. They sat beside him with a wince, poking at the bandage around their thigh. Green Bites really took a snap at them. Newfound comfort with the colony aside, it had been a relief to send the sãoni back down the mountain.

"Is your leg bothering you?" he asked.

"Small bite." They shrugged at him, rolling their eyes. "Family."

Ahn laughed a little, thinking of his own siblings. Their poison fans and their riding accidents. "I know the feeling."

Up close, Ahn could see a few small scars on what was visible of Hei's skin. Old wounds grown over, gone shiny with years to heal, bite marks from past power struggles in the colony. It was incredible that they were so fearless with the sãoni—though he supposed this was how they had learned to be. His eyes landed on their bicep: another imprint of Green Bites' teeth and the dark line of where his own hot blade had once cut through. The claw scratch they had left on his chest that night in the rain was nothing compared to the scar he had marked them with.

Ahn leaned his head back against the mossy rock, feeling the tug of the old slash across his chest. The poets all agreed that love was the concession to be marked by another, but he did not think that had to be taken so literally anymore.

"I see up high with my grandmother." Hei cleaned

under their nails with one of their sãoni claws. "When I was being small."

Ahn hesitated, unsure of what to say. Rarely did they offer any personal information. "Um . . . sãoni grandmother, or human?"

Hei's mouth twitched in a smile. "Human. She is dead now."

"Oh. I'm, I'm sorry to hear that."

"Long time dead," Hei said, turning their claw over in their palm. "Long time since I see up high. Looks big."

Their voice was slightly stilted, but Ahn couldn't say if it was the Dulpongpa or something else. Emboldened by their unexpected openness, he asked, "Do you think you'll come see it again, after the bridge is fixed?"

"No. What I care for is below. Eiji."

"What about Sohmeng?"

Hei paused, considering. Ahn was growing accustomed to their long silences; he only hoped that the question had not been too forward. The two of them were so rarely alone together, he still was unsure of what they felt safe sharing.

"I do not think Sohmeng stays in Ateng," Hei finally said, eyes meeting the mountain across the great divide. "Also I do not think Sohmeng stays always with me in Eiji. Sohmeng go where Sohmeng go. Both. All."

Ahn was amazed by the ease with which they said this. It was clear how much the two of them cared about each other. It was unthinkable to imagine them apart. "Doesn't that trouble you?"

"No trouble, Ahnschen," they said, amused. "Just com . . . compri . . . ?" They growled in irritation, looking at him expectantly.

"Compromise?" he offered.

"Compromise." Hei nodded, giving him a little Sãonipa chirp of gratitude. "Her choice is hers, but I not worry. Sohmeng loves me. I love Sohmeng. We compromise, make life for us. Maybe hard, but good."

Ahn's time in Gãepongwei had introduced him to the ever-moving, ever-changing nature of Eiji. He supposed it was only natural for Hei to have inherited some of the land's mutability. Still, it was not something he had expected from them. He hadn't *known* what to expect, what with how little the two of them had spoken. Though it shamed him to acknowledge, he had to admit the part his own bias had played in that.

Hei's emotions ran deep, though they were not always easy for him to understand. He had accepted their private nature with little trouble, but he had not stopped to consider the breadth of their inner life. They weren't just driven by feelings and instinct—they were thoughtful, intelligent. Brilliant, even.

Be good, Ahn, he thought to himself, frustrated by his carelessness. Arrogance. *Be better. Be better than this.*

Beside him, Hei hugged their arms, a small tremor going through them. Ahn started, worried that he had upset them somehow, but then realized that they were shivering.

"Oh—you're cold, aren't you?" He sat up, suddenly aware of the temperature difference on the mountain. It hadn't bothered him much; he had grown up with snowy winters. But for Hei, even this slight change must have felt extreme. He looked around for a coat he knew he did not have, trying to figure out how to help. "There has to be something . . ."

With a little grunt, Hei inched closer to him. They stared at the space ahead, not saying a word as their sides pressed together.

Ahn bit his lip, trying not to smile. He didn't want them to think he was making fun. After a long moment, he gingerly placed his arm around them. Hei tensed at first, but as their skin warmed with the heat of his own, they clicked quietly, their body slowly relaxing.

For a while, neither of them spoke, adjusting to one another. Ahn had no idea what Hei was thinking and did not dare to ask. For his part, it simply felt nice to hold someone.

Hei was the first to break the quiet, and with words Ahn truly did not expect: "You like Sohmeng."

"Yes." His throat felt very dry. "She's my—my friend."

Hei hummed a single laugh, shaking their head. "No, Ahnschen. Yes friend, but you have other like—big heart like. How you say last night. *Faith*. You have faith with Sohmeng, want Sohmeng to feel same."

Cuddled close as they were, he wondered if Hei could feel the way his heart was pounding. This was not how he wanted this to go—if he'd had it his way, neither of them ever would have found out at all. But there was no use backtracking and trying to hide it. "Yes. I suppose I do."

"Why you do not tell her?"

Were it not for the previous night's conversation, the question might have sent him into a far greater panic. Instead, all he could do was be honest. "I don't know."

Hei's fingers took hold of his earpiece. Ahn froze, unable to breathe. They must have seen the fear on his face, but they didn't let go. "Him?"

"I, I don't—"

"His?" they repeated, examining the knucklebone. Ahn could only nod. After a moment, they let go. Their voice was unexpectedly gentle. "Hard losing people."

It was not the response he'd braced for. He rested his hand on his chest, trying to ground himself. Trying not to run too quickly from the feeling. "It is."

"No lose Sohmeng, Ahnschen," they said. "Not with me here."

The matter-of-factness of their voice made him smile in spite of everything. Their devotion was something to behold. "May I ask how you knew? That I like Sohmeng, I mean?"

Hei snorted, making a ridiculous face at him. It was comically maudlin, entirely unlike anything they had ever—oh *no*, it was an impression. An impression of him, however exaggerated, and how he must have been looking at Sohmeng.

Well. It was official. Though he would carry no honour into the bilateral realm, it was time for Ahn to die.

"Sohmeng knows, too," he said, feeling dazed. Hei clicked an affirmative, sounding quite pleased with his embarrassment. While he knew his anxieties were mostly a matter of culture clash, he felt the need to check in. "And you're . . . you're alright with this? That I like Sohmeng."

Hei shrugged, chirping quietly. "I like Sohmeng. Good taste, Ahnschen. But—" They finally met his eye, looking at him with their old intensity. It was almost comforting to see such a familiar look in such a strange circumstance. "You talk to her. No more hiding. Choice together."

Ahn nodded quickly. "Of course. I—yes, of course."

"Sohmeng says yes? You are new mate? You be *good.*" Hei poked him hard in the chest, their words deadly serious. "Be good with Sohmeng. Be good with Sohmeng's human family. Be good with sãoni. Or you leave colony. Maybe alive, maybe not."

Ahn caught their hand in his own. They let out a low growl, but did not pull away, instead looking at him with wary curiosity. "If Sohmeng will have me, I promise I will be good to her and those she loves. Including you."

Hei's shoulders crept up slightly, their eyes darting over his face. Had their cheeks gone a little pink beneath their charcoal? "Good to me."

He nodded, squeezing their hand. "Whatever you want it to mean, I will be sure to be good to you."

Hei made a few Sãonipa noises, glancing away from him as they processed his words. Ahn stayed quiet, wanting to give them space to respond.

" . . . warm is good," Hei finally muttered. "Good to me is warm."

They tucked their body back against his, snuggling

under his arm. This time, Ahn let himself smile, holding them as close as they asked. "I can do that."

For a long time, they simply sat together, watching the colour of the sky change with the sun's long journey to the west. Ahn loved his long conversations with Sohmeng, the way they would trip over each other's sentences when they both got excited, but he found a sense of peace up on the mountain with Hei. Together, they sank into an easy sort of quiet, without demand or expectation. Now and then, Hei would point at something—the shape of a cloud, or a colourful bird—and Ahn would ask a brief question or two. They opened up more saka fruit, tossing the discarded skin over the side of the cliff.

At one point, Ahn realized he had started humming. He stopped, not wanting to disturb Hei, but they urged him to continue. The humming turned to singing, and the morning passed with ease into afternoon.

Then, fire.

Above the entryway to Sodão Dangde, the batengmun's lantern glowed to life. Ahn stood quickly, smiling to see Sohmeng and the others cheering across the way. Ateng's lanterns were not a part of Ahn's own traditions, but he couldn't help the pride that flooded him to see the flame restored. It was a promise, Sohmeng had told him. A promise that everyone was alright.

With a whistle from Tonão, Ahn picked up his bow. He had checked the line with Hei twice over, and examined their stretch of the Sky Bridge as best they could, looking for any damage that had come with age. They had it piled in a massive roll beside them, ready to be pulled across the way. With a final tap to Schenn for luck, Ahn set his eyes on Sodão Dangde.

He focused on the placement of his feet, his knees, his hips; drew his attention to his back, his arms, his breath. His knuckles were solid against his jaw, the string of the bow tickling his nose. This time, he heard no voices in his ear, not from memories of his sister or his own internal doubts. Nothing even from Schenn beyond.

Inhale. Exhale.

Behind him, a sound: Hei, clicking once in Sãonipa. Not a question, not even a reassurance—an acknowledgment. A witness. *I see you.* Without a single thought of how he might sound, Ahn returned the noise.

Inhale. Exhale. Feel the wind, feel your breath, guide your eyes with the arrow. Focus on feet, knees, hips, back, shoulders, arms, hands, fingertips, relax, release—

The arrow flew in a long and perfect arch, the line trailing behind it like a comet. A seeking star given flight, come down to grace them with its findings. Ahn watched it wordlessly, his heart serene despite all that was at stake.

It struck perfectly at the mouth of the cave, soundless from where Ahn stood. Sodão Dangde exploded into cheering, everyone jumping in place and hollering their praise across the chasm. Ahn lowered the bow, a sob of relief escaping him as he stared at the line. A connection made, long overdue. A second chance.

Twenty-Six

ALL THAT REMAINED was a single step.

Well, no, that was a bit of an exaggeration—after the first step came another, then another, until the entire party made it across the full expanse of the Sky Bridge. Not to mention the rebuilding that came after that. But as Sohmeng ran her palms over the taut railings of the rope bridge before her, she couldn't shake the feeling that her entire life had led up to this breath, this heartbeat. This single step.

It had taken the work of every single person to raise and secure the bridge to Sodão Dangde. Sohmeng's muscles were burning from effort, her stomach in excitable knots from anticipation. The ties were checked and rechecked until Tonão was satisfied, the bridge itself examined as best as it could be from a distance. It was not frayed from lack of use; the people of Ateng had long since mastered their craft.

Sohmeng's eyes followed the path ahead of her, the

thin barrier across the open sky. Behind her was Sodão Dangde, a home turned crypt turned home once more. Ahead of her was Hei and Ahn and whatever came next, whatever lasting change they could bring to Gãepongwei.

Her father's voice, no longer the stuff of memory: "You ready, little tengmun?"

She glanced back over her shoulder at him, grinning bright as Chehangma. "Been ready my whole life."

Maybe that was an exaggeration too, but the Sky Bridge didn't mind. It caught Sohmeng's foot with practiced ease, the pressure of the rope welcoming against her arch.

Sohmeng had crossed the Sky Bridge seven times in her life, the First Par tradition timed to mark every other birthday. The burst of adrenaline was an old friend, and she gripped the railings with giddy fingers, feeling the trembling vibration in her heart each time she dared look down. She thought of Jinho Tang, swaying peacefully on the side of Fochão Dangde like he'd been plucked out of a nest himself. Crossing didn't exactly bring her peace, but it certainly brought joy, along with newfound satisfaction with having secured the bridge herself. As a child, she'd always trusted that the adults had known what they were doing when the hmun's life was put into their hands. This time, she had to put that trust in herself. With every step, she found it easier.

The party paced themselves at Tonão's recommended distance, and Sohmeng felt little strain on the bridge as a result. Not that it calmed the rest of them—Nona Fahang's idea of height was measured in treetops alone. Sohmeng tried very hard not to snicker at the sounds coming from behind her. Even in Ateng, there were plenty of people who dreaded facing the mountains' full height.

"How many—oh, I'm going to be sick—how many times do we do this?" moaned Pangae, who did in fact sound on the verge of retching.

"Three!" called Tonão. "Then a fourth time once the section between the First Finger and Fochão Dangde is repaired."

Sohmeng wished her father could be closer, but his wooden leg was not designed for crossing rope suspension bridges. Polha Hiwei carried him on her back in the way Ateng carried elderly Grand Ones at the crossing. It was unthinkable to deny someone the full sight of the gods based on mobility alone. Sohmeng was grateful for the woman's strong back, her steady disposition. In a life where she had been born on time, the two of them would have been phase-mates—the thought made it easier for her to trust the woman with her father's safety.

Sohmeng peered at Eiji until it made her head start to go fuzzy, then raised her eyes back to the First Finger. Each step brought Ahn and Hei further into focus, and she had to resist the urge to run to meet them. In a moment of mischief, she released the railings, spreading her arms like a bird as she glided across the sky.

Reckless as ever, she thought to herself. *But at least there aren't any rings for you to grab this time.*

She ignored what might have been a shout behind her, focusing on what lay ahead. Ahn had one hand to his heart, the other to his ear—she could practically feel the force of his freakout. Hei, on the other hand, stepped forward, spreading their arms to match hers. To catch her a second time.

She called their name in Sãonipa, relishing in the smile that spread across their face, until she finally stepped from rope to stone and crashed into their arms.

"You're beautiful," Hei said breathlessly, pressing their forehead into hers. "You're perfect. I love you."

The wind sang cool against her skin as Sohmeng sank into the warmth of Hei's body. She only had a moment to indulge in being held before she turned her attention back to her community on the bridge. That was what Tengmunji was about, after all.

With the help of Ahn and Hei, they guided everyone to the Third Finger. They couldn't pause for too long if they wanted to maximize what was left of the daylight, but Tonão encouraged the scouts to take a moment to rest before the next two crossings. Thankfully, the gaps between each of the Fingers were slightly shorter than those that led to each of the habitable mountains.

Ahn passed out rounds of rope for each of the scouts to carry. If Sohmeng wasn't mistaken, she even saw Ahn and Hei say goodbye to each other—a nudge of cheeks, a squeeze on the shoulder. Now *that* was a development. Before she could get properly nosy, Ahn had turned his attention to Pangae, whose hysterics had returned at the remembrance that he would be crossing with additional weight on his back. Ahn crouched beside him, offering reassurances until the scout was breathing easier. It was hard to believe that just a few phases back, Ahn had been nothing to Nona Fahang but a prisoner, the tsongkar.

The thought was interrupted by the sound of her father's voice. He was standing by the bridge, talking to Hei. "Are you sure you'll be alright going back down Sodão Dangde alone?"

They clicked once in affirmation. "I know the mountains."

"Without the sãoni, the rest of the walk to Eiji can be a little precarious," Tonão said, reaching into his bag. "Take extra food, in case it takes more time than you think."

Hei tilted their head, glancing between the man and the offering. Slowly, they repeated themself: "I know the mountains."

Tonão's brow was furrowed in a look Sohmeng knew, strangely enough, from her brother. A parental sense of anxiety, a need to nurture regardless of necessity. After a moment, the man sighed, laughing softly as he pressed the food into Hei's hands. "I trust you do, Hei. But for my sake, would you please take the food?"

Confused though they looked, Hei conceded. Sohmeng bit back a grin at the exchange, the sweet novelty of watching two people she loved behave exactly as themselves with each other.

Hei caught her eye then, chirping a little *help!* Tonão didn't speak lizard, but he had a sense of when to make a graceful exit. He smiled as he passed Sohmeng, leaving her to her goodbyes.

"He gave me food," Hei muttered, holding out the evidence.

Sohmeng smiled, flattening out Hei's hair where it insisted on sticking up. They were overdue for a trim. "Did you say thank you?" Hei's eyes widened in such alarm that Sohmeng couldn't help but laugh. "It's fine, Hei. Save it for next time."

"Next time," they echoed, nodding. For a moment they were quiet, watching the rest of the party prepare. Sohmeng squeezed their shoulders, readying herself for the coming days when she would not be able to touch Hei, or even know what was happening with them.

"I'm so sick of saying goodbye to you," she said, sighing in frustration. "After this, no more splitting up. I'm not myself when I'm not with you and the sãoni. Humans are great and all, but they're kind of exhausting, huh?"

Hei laughed at that, louder than she'd heard in a long time. With a final grin, tender and feral, they kissed her, pressing cheeks even as they stepped away.

"Stay safe," Sohmeng demanded, but they simply waved a hand at her. As if it was so easy.

Hei hesitated for only a moment before stepping onto the Sky Bridge. Sohmeng heard their sharp inhale, and realized that this was the first time they had ever set foot on Ateng's sacred architecture. Every crossing before had been made in Esteona Nor's basket, peeking out through whatever tiny hole offered them a sliver of sky. Hei made the journey with fearless wonder, even crouching to try and get a better look at Eiji from this new angle. They looked back at Sohmeng only once, eyes full of childlike wonder, before continuing on.

You've always deserved this, Sohmeng thought, the truth of it burning straight through her heart. *You, me, every other Minhal. When I'm done with this place, no one will dare speak the word hãokar ever again.*

She carried the thought across each section of the Sky Bridge until it became a promise. The world was constantly changing, for better and for worse, and no matter how high Ateng held itself up in the mountains, it could change as well. She could not move the mountain, but she could work with the people inside to make no night feel truly godless.

When they finally reached the First Finger, the party was met with sound. At first, Sohmeng couldn't tell what it was; she rubbed her ears as she walked the perimeter of the mountain, peering at the sky for the source of the noise that was both a rumble and a buzz, its faintness growing louder until—

—she faced Fochão Dangde, and the crowd that had gathered at the cave. They had been called by the rekindled lantern upon Sodão Dangde. They were cheering.

Tonão Sol grasped her shoulder for support, his entire body shaking as he looked upon his neighbours. Sohmeng squeezed his hand, took a deep breath, and howled. Her lead was all it took for her party to join in—Eakang hollered greetings in Fahangpa, Polha and the scouts sang trader's songs across the sky, Ahn whistled so loud and bright Sohmeng thought it could pierce the clouds. Fochão Dangde positively *roared.*

Eventually, they got ahold of themselves. Tonão passed

Ahn a folded note marked with the trader's written code to explain their situation. Sohmeng had helped him compose the message back in Nona Fahang, trying all the while to remember what each individual symbol meant. Even with the progress they'd made, there was still so much for her to learn.

With a whistle of warning and a whispered prayer in Qiao Sidhur, Ahn let the arrow loose. It landed just on the edge of the cliff, out of the way of the crowd. Sohmeng had never been more grateful for his good aim; if he could keep it up, the bridge would be rebuilt all the easier.

It would take time, of course. But she couldn't worry about that now. Not when they had made it this far.

A sound. A familiar sound—her name. Sohmeng stepped forward, trying desperately to get a better look at the crowd. She couldn't see faces, but she saw someone pushing forward. Loud, skinny, just a little too tall. Dressed in the colours of Ateng's leadership, and behaving most inappropriately.

She burst out laughing, cupping her hands around her mouth. "VIUNWEI!" she shouted. "VIUNWEI SOON!"

Faintly, she heard it back—*Sohmeng!*

"Viunwei!" she yelled again, waving her arms. She grabbed her father, shaking his shoulder. "Dad, it's him! It's Viunwei—look at how tall he is! Say hi!"

For a while, it went on like this. Shouting and cheering, barely intelligible words between distant cousins. Soon Ateng let loose an arrow of their own, the response scrawled down on what precious little parchment remained from their trading stores. After the scramble to retrieve it, Tonão shared it with the party, a new determination in his eyes.

"They're ready," he said. "The leaders are making everyone wait inside so they can get the weavers out. We're starting tonight, for as long as we have the sun. We begin where we left off tomorrow at daybreak."

Sohmeng's eyes fell to the horizon, where Chehangma seemed to glow twice as bright, even on its way to splitting back into the moons. She couldn't help the swell of pride that grew in response. What a sight they had given the godseye today.

Watch closely, she thought. *We're going to fix the world.*

Tonão Sol passed Ahn the arrow, its line secured in place. Ahn positioned himself in silence, and the world seemed to stop with his breathing. Sohmeng came to his side, following the trajectory with her eyes, willing the gap to be bridged. She rested her fingers on his arm, feather-light.

"Their watchful eyes upon you, Ahnschen," she said. He smiled at the contact, the string of the bow brushing his lips.

"Upon us all, Sohmeng Minhal," he murmured.

With a tender strum of his fingers, the arrow released. Soared. Landed true.

THE SÃONI CYCLE

WILL CONCLUDE IN 2023

Acknowledgements

Writing acknowledgements in May 2021 for a book I began in October 2019 is complicated. My heart is full, but my memory's shot; I'm a different person than I was when this began. Where *Two Dark Moons* was written in a time of bounty, surrounded by support and energy, creating *Three Seeking Stars* was often a lonely experience. My NaNoWriMo goal was met the same day my estranged stepfather passed away; the first draft was finished during a week sick in bed with what was likely COVID. So much of this process was marked by grief—but I am still able to look at this book, in its final form, and feel joy. For that, I have these people to thank:

Dad, whose support has allowed Shale to thrive, and whose shouts of "Team Hei!!" were so funny that they ended up in the book (Hei approves of Ahn, Dad. I hope you do too!). Mom, whose care for her LGBTQ+ students makes me less scared for the future, and who has brought the *Sãoni Cycle* to so many young readers. Grandma Ronnie, who found me the lizard earrings I didn't know I needed. My siblings, who routinely show such care for my work—special thanks to Ryan for gassing me up every time I get ready to Give Up On Writing Forever, and Natalie who sends impeccable memes. My cousin Cass, who might have accidentally named the third book after themself. Lots to think about.

Carisa Van de Wetering, who gives so freely of her generous heart. Cortni Fernandez, whom I cherish. Natalie Lythe, who bites. Claudie Arsenault, whose championing of this series makes me glow. Brandon Crilly, a fellow reptile parent and believer in this book. Haley Rose, who designed the cover of my dreams yet again! The entire *Augur Magazine* staff, who make me a better writer, editor, and person. Big shout out to Amy Wang, whose enthusiasm never fails to get me rowdy.

All the readers who have asked for more, especially the young adults. I'm so grateful my words reach you, and I am humbled by your care for this story. Shale's patrons over at Patreon—your donations kept us afloat for this past year. Thank you. I also need to thank everyone involved in the making of *Haikyuu!!* The volleyball boys gave me energy and joy when nothing else did.

I have so much love in my life to be thankful for. Irene, who is the funniest person on the planet, proof that the triangle is the strongest shape, and a font of sleepover secret-telling magic. You're the best night shift I could ask for; let's keep learning from and with each other for years and years to come. Sienna, whose thoughtful eye and dedicated heart makes this whole thing possible. Again and again my love, you make it all possible. What a gift, to share these words and worlds with you. You turn my ideas into living creatures, and I'm so thankful to hold your hand and watch them *run.*

And finally, Jevick. Our bad baby, our chunky beardie, our little sãoni, the best thing to come out of 2020. You can't read this because you're a lizard, but I'm so glad you're here.

One more book to go—thanks for sticking around.

With love and a bite,
Avi Silver
May 2021
Hamilton

Glossary

GÃEPONGWEI

Ama—the small red moon, feminine; ruler of reason and material matters

batengmun—initiates; singular would be "tengmun"

Chehang—the big white moon, masculine; ruler of emotion and spiritual matters

Chehangma—the sun, conceptualized as the combined eyes of the moons Ama and Chehang

damwei—the third party required to make a baby, either a surrogate or sperm donor; affectionately referred to as "damdão"

Fochão Dangde—the mountain that Ateng's people are currently trapped in; "Brother Mountain"

Gãepongwei—a name for the interconnected hmun network; recently coined

hãokar—the exiled; literally "without family"

hmun—term for a village/community in Gãepongwei

Hosaisi—a hmun far north, one of the first to be contacted by Qiao Sidh

kejangar—"hospitality" in Dulpongpa, the trade language of Eiji; an important organizing principle for the hmun

Kongkempei—a hmun far north, destroyed by Qiao Sidh

Nona Fahang—a hmun surrounded by thick walls formed of living banyan trees; currently hosting refugees of the Qiao Sidhur invasion

Sodão Dangde—the final resting place of Ateng's batengmun; "Sister Mountain"

Sorwei Chapal—a hmun located on top of the Ãotul river, known for its masterful knotwork

Tengmunji—initiation into adulthood

tsongkar—a Fahangpa word for intruder, invader; "one who did not ask"

QIAO SIDH

Asgørindad—the university where Ahnschen studied Philosophy after his Six-ing

Gurinn—the last region of the upper continent to fall to the Qiao Sidhur Empire

Haojost—the small town Schenn grew up in before attending Kørno Wan

Hvallánzhou—one of Qiao Sidh's capitals, where the Winter Palace resides

Jin Fóll—walled city overtaken in The Thousand Hour Siege

Kørno Wan—the academy where young and privileged Qiao Sidhur train in the Path of Conquest

Six-ing—a necessary requirement to achieve sixth ranking in the Path of Conquest; a fight to the death

zhørmozhør—asexual; rarely used outside of a lecture hall

THE NINE PATHS OF MASTERY

Alléndou—Fertility

Hvundpar—Health

Idhren—Discernment

Ødselo—Spirit

Siengung—Philosophy

Søngjudh—Aesthetic

Sølshend—Arts

Qøngem—Conquest

Zhøllong—Advancement

PATREON | THE SHALE PROJECT

A massive thank you to everybody who supports us on Patreon! You make this work possible; we love you to the moons and back.

Charlotte Ashley

Nick Calow

Carisa Catherine

Spenser Chicoine

Emily Colgan

Rebecca Diem

Laurence Dion

Maria Dominguez

Stephanie Elnomany

Cheryl Hamilton

Minh

Natalie Lythe

Nicholas Mackenzie

Cass Meehan

Susan Meehan

Amy Raboin

David Senft

Joy Silvey

WWW.PATREON.COM/WELCOMETOSHALE

About the Author

Avi Silver is an author (*Two Dark Moons*, 2019), editor (*Augur Magazine*), and poet. Find their short fiction in *Common Bonds: An Aromantic Speculative Anthology*, and their poetry appearing or forthcoming in *Strange Horizons* and *Uncanny Magazine*. For more information, visit mxavisilver.com. For lizard pictures, follow them on Twitter @thescreambean.

About the Project

The Shale Project is a multimedia storytelling initiative roughly in the shape of a planet. It's about three things: top-notch worldbuilding, daring and exploratory fiction, and the philosophy that art is medicine.
You can discover what else it has to offer at www.welcometoshale.com

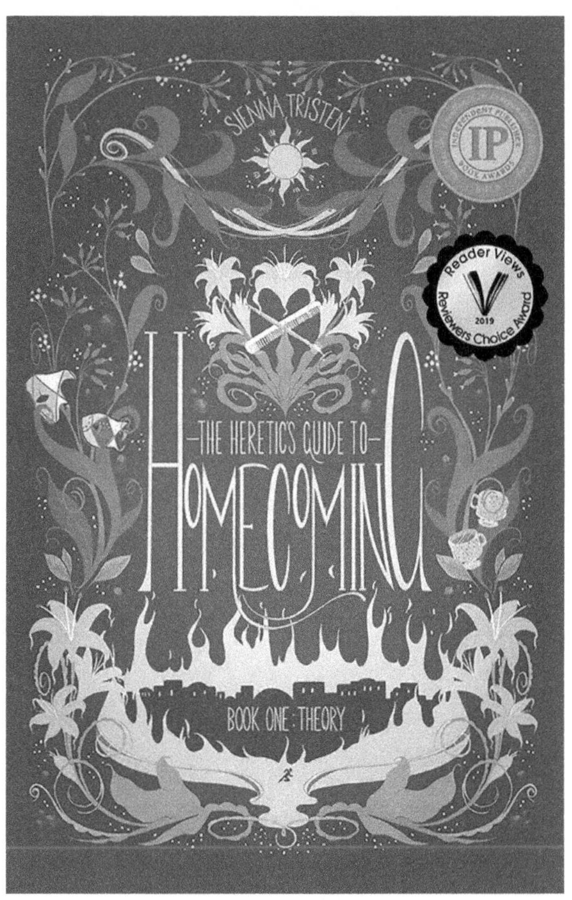

The Heretic's Guide to Homecoming
Book One: Theory

Sienna Tristen

"Compelling and complicated in all the right ways."
—Reader Views

". . . fans of detailed fantasy worldbuilding will revel in this voluminous story."
—Publisher's Weekly